THE
NIGHT
OF THE
FLOOD

ZOË SOMERVILLE

HEAD
of ZEUS

First published in the UK in 2020 by Head of Zeus Ltd
This paperback edition first published in 2021 by Head of Zeus Ltd

9 7 5 3 1 2 4 6 8

A catalogue record for this book is available from
the British Library.

ISBN (PB): 9781838934620
ISBN (E): 9781838934637

Typeset by Divaddict Publishing Solutions Ltd

Printed and bound in Great Britain by
CPI Group (UK) Ltd, Croydon CR0 4YY

Head of Zeus Ltd
First Floor East
5–8 Hardwick Street
London EC1R 4RG

WWW.HEADOFZEUS.COM

To Will

1954

A year after the flood

It's over a year since the flood. Verity sits in the window seat of a train to London. Now she sees that some things loop and circle and come back again and again, like the tide. What keeps returning is the image of his body. Behind her eyes, when she dozes, or at night when she sleeps, or even, like now, fully awake, gazing through the rain-spattered train window – this is what she sees, half memory, half nightmare.

In the ruined aftershock of the flooded marsh, she is running, hurtling towards the pine trees. At the far edge of her vision, a flash of white. She falls and trips and her mouth is filled with saltwater, choked with marram grass. Sinking into the bog, she is submerged. When she rises, spitting, retching, the white flash is transformed. It is an arm dangling down from a tree, the skin mottled and pale. Outlined against the setting sun over the salt-wrecked marsh, a white arm reaching from a black tree. It does not make sense.

Then in the flare of a bright light – a torch – the rest of the body is illuminated, hanging, up-ended, ghoulishly white. The legs are twisted up, the face in shock, like a puppet thrown from the sky.

The train whistles and Verity starts. Through the smeared glass, a shaft of sun breaks through the cloud, illuminating the window and blinding her temporarily.

PART 1

LOW TIDE

May 1952
Nine months before the flood

Temperatures above average for the time of year
Fog expected on the coast
Waxing crescent moon

1.

Verity was jittery. As she walked towards the woods on her way to see Arthur, the barley sheaves scratched her bare legs. She was glad to get out of the gloomy house where no one spoke of anything that mattered. Pollen caught in her nose, making her sneeze. It had been a day like this then too, the day her mother died. The same sudden heat and sunlight. The same grass-green and dazzling white sprung up on all sides. The same tang of manure from the fields. Everything erupting, spilling over with life. It had been the wrong kind of day to die. Too much life. In a burst of impatience, she took long strides to the last field, stopping short at the sight of the pines that divided the land and marsh from the sea. Mother must also have walked this way that day. It was the route Verity had later run down, desperate to see for herself. As she had then, she stood still on this spot, transfixed by the way the trees curled along the coastline in a long spine of darkness. There had been a sudden feeling of plunging, of vertigo. Her brother had been forced to hold her back.

They hadn't let her see the body but in her mind she saw it as a beached fish, silver-coloured, curled and semi-translucent, shining in the pale spring morning. An aberration.

*

A shadow unfurled across the field. Arthur emerged from the gloom of the woods. Usually he would wait by the hollow tree but here he was, blinking in the sun like a woodland creature, unused to light. From her vantage point on the slight slope down from the farmhouse, she could see him clearly, his form cut out by the cool sun and looking away from her towards the sea. Warmth trickled into her blood at the familiar sight of him. And yet, as she watched him, his mouth looked set, hard and fixed. He didn't look the same. Was it some new hardness that had been instilled in him by National Service? She remembered her letters, or the lack of them. She had no good excuse – except that when she'd lifted her pen to write she didn't have the words to describe her motherless state. And with his absence she'd begun to wonder what they were to each other. Arthur was all tied up with her childhood and now that world had been shattered. He might be tired of her now. He might have met a girl... Her whole body withdrew and the heat evaporated from her skin. She felt like turning, running back and carrying on running, as far away as she could.

But she was being a coward. It must be something in her – some coldness, or distance. Since the funeral she'd hardly seen him. In her grief she hadn't noticed, but now it felt as if he was no longer part of the family. She bit her thumbnail. It was Arthur, her beloved Arthur. She'd known him since he was a skinny eight-year-old evacuee, brought home by her mother. Still, she didn't move. Then there was a whisper in the barley – a snap, a vibration in the sheaves – a ferret or a fox – and he looked up and saw her.

Quickly, she began to walk towards him, closing the gap across the last field. He stood still, his hand shielding his eyes. As she reached him, she took in his wavy brown hair that wouldn't lie flat, the dark eyes and the thick eyebrows she liked to touch. The months apart vibrated between them.

She said, 'There's something different about you but I can't think what it is,' and reached up and ruffled his hair. It wasn't what she'd planned to say to him.

He frowned. 'You too,' he said, and took her hand.

In the woods, something sour mingled with the sweet pine sap, making the air smell sickly. An animal rustled in the ferns underfoot and scooted off. A light breeze shook the pine needles and she shivered.

They found their place by the hollowed-out tree. As they talked, she took out the Thermos she'd brought and poured the tea, spilling it over his mac, though he didn't seem to mind. They ate some raisin cake washed down with weak tea.

'I brought beer,' he said, and poured some into their empty teacups. Dozy and laughing, they lay on their backs. Above them, the tops of the trees swayed in the breeze. He picked up her hand and kissed it. She wriggled and laughed but didn't pull away. Their faces were close now. He leaned over her and kissed her mouth, biting at the bottom lip. She felt his tongue probing between her teeth and allowed him to prise them open.

'I've missed you,' he said, and she murmured, unable to speak. His breath was malty and sweet with beer and cake. His hand crept down her dress to her legs and her skin rippled under his fingers. But it was too soon. She withdrew, pulled her mouth from his. Her heart beat hard in her chest. Aware of him watching her, she clambered on top of him like she used to do when they were children, tickling him and pinning him down. But he took her wrists and looked up at her without laughing, and she climbed off, confused.

She yawned and stretched, and moved an inch or two away from him on the coat.

'Come on then, spill the beans. I've been dying to hear what you've been up to. Your letters say absolutely nothing. It's been dull as ditchwater round here. No doubt Peter will bore you rigid about the farm. He's desperate for Father to get a new-fangled milking parlour and stop doing any by hand so we can sell more to the dairy, but Father doesn't want to. Says we can't afford it. Peter doesn't understand why not. They talk about money all the time. Back and forth, back and forth. It's constant. But I just can't be bothered with it any more, Arty.' She looked at him, sighed. 'I've been too busy with the books. Thank God it'll be over soon.'

'But when the exams are over, you can have the summer, can't you? There's no hurry, is there?' he said, circling her ankle bone with tickling fingers.

'Yes, I suppose I can,' she said, and smiled at him, taking his hand off her ankle and holding it.

The summer, then. It was theirs to take.

They lay on their backs on the rug and she wondered if he would try to kiss her again but he didn't. Her body relaxed and she closed her eyes. She felt his bulk next to her, his hand resting near her thigh, and she imagined what it would be like for him to be on top of her as she'd read about in novels.

Strange to think of their first innocent kiss in the midst

of war. There had been the noise of German bombers overhead, but empty of bombs. The girl and the boy in the pine wood knew the Luftwaffe would have dropped the remaining ones on Norwich if they had any left after London or Coventry. They had grown used to the bombless planes, heading back to Germany, so they weren't afraid. Sometimes she waved at them, though she felt a prickle of fear. And sometimes, looking up at the black lines flying past on their way to Nazi Germany and Soviet Russia, she imagined with a delicious shiver the terrifying dark woods and endless snowy wastes of unknown, dangerous lands.

They met by the hollowed-out tree, where the sand met the pines, past the beach huts, beyond Pinewoods caravan site and the brackish lake, Abraham's Bosun. The two of them – eleven and thirteen in her memory – were crouched, heads together. They were inspecting each other's hands. A trickle of blood was crawling down Verity's left hand from where Arthur had cut her.

'Your turn now,' she said, and took the penknife from him. He kneeled, eyes open, fixed on the knife, and she held the penknife aloft. It caught the light from the morning sun. Her right arm, holding the knife, trembled a little but she stilled it. This was all her idea and she was exultant at it coming to pass. They had decided the words together.

'Here in this sacred wood on the 24th April 1945, we hereby...' She was pleased with the *hereby*, that was one of hers. It made it sound official and important. '... hereby make a pact of undying friendship and unity in all things. Unto death do us part.'

'Until,' Arthur said. His eyes were still fixed on her hand and the knife.

'Yes, until,' she said, slightly annoyed at the interruption. 'And with this mark I do unite us.'

She glanced at him, but his eyes seemed to say yes so she looked down at his hand held out. It was darker than hers, and bigger now with a hardness that was new. He had only recently found out that his father was missing. Missing presumed dead, they said. He'd not said anything about it. With a sudden, quick movement she cut into the flesh below his left thumb. It was tougher than she thought it would be. The skin didn't yield much and she realised belatedly that there was muscle there. She thought she might have to cut it again and blanched at the idea but there was no need for more. Blood was already beading up along the cut. Quickly, it became a line and the line lengthened, grew and began to drip down on the sandy floor. The two of them knelt, suspended, both watching the red blood mingle with the dusty sand and dirt of the woodland ground.

'We have to mix it,' he said.

'Yes,' she said, and they put their bloody left hands together. Her blood was browning, drying, but the fresh blood on his hand was still bright. She gasped as the cuts on their hands met. The pain was sharp and sickening but ebbed as soon as it came, leaving just a throb. She licked her thumb. It tasted metallic and sweet.

'I think we should kiss now,' she said. She tried to keep her voice calm and serious, like his was, but her heart was pumping hard. She was thrilled and shocked at herself.

Arthur looked up at her with a pained expression. She had made a mistake. Slowly, he said, 'I don't know.'

'We don't have to,' she said, her throat hot with the shame of it and her eyes instantly pricking with tears.

'No, it's just I didn't think. I've never...' He seemed to be squirming with embarrassment.

'Me neither, silly,' she said.

The excitement rose again. She leaned towards him and put her lips against his, which were surprisingly fleshy and wet.

A crackle in the undergrowth and they both flinched and spun round. Nothing but the tail of an animal. They collapsed in a laughing heap.

'Come on,' she said, pulling him up. 'I'll race you back.'

A twig snapped. Next to her, Arthur tensed. She had a sudden sensation that they were being watched.

They were. Opening her eyes, she caught a brief glimpse of a fox staring at them. Its eyes were gold, rimmed with black, its coat a deep, tawny red and across its white muzzle a black mouth that seemed to smile. Then it was gone.

It was late. She stood up, brushing crumbs from her skirt. Without looking at him, she said, 'It's getting on, Arty, I really ought to go. There's a tea. Nothing too formal. But Father wanted to mark...'

'How have you been holding up?' he asked.

She shook her head. 'It was a year ago, actually. It was a year today.' It came out apologetic as if it was embarrassing to mention. She wanted to be open with him as she'd always been but something was clamming up her mouth. It had been the same on the day of the funeral. He'd tried to comfort her – he'd put his hand on the small of her back, followed her into the pantry and kissed her clumsily. She'd stiffened, unable to accept the affection. He was going back to his posting that night but she couldn't bring herself to touch him.

'I'm sorry, I—' he started but she waved it away.

'You never did tell me about what you've been doing all this time,' she said, brightly, realising too late that he'd said hardly anything, while she'd chattered inconsequentially in her nervous, overwrought state. The distance between them remained.

Out of the woods, Verity arched her back, tilting her face to the sun. She heard the low buzz of aircraft and ducked. Laughing at herself, she straightened and looked up. It was a silver plane, low in the sky, not one she recognised.

The plane drew its black course through the blue, cloudless sky, south-west, away from the sea. She watched it go, imagining the pilot inside peering down at the dark-haired girl in the long skirt standing in the field of barley. She twirled round, her skirt flung out wide and her arms stretched out. When it had gone, she swayed and blinked at the waving sheaves and remembered she needed to hurry home. Mrs Timms, their housekeeper, was baking a special cake, supposedly to fortify her for the imminent school exams, but really in honour of their mother. It was bound to be as bland as all the others but she saved their sugar rations and put some effort in, which was much more than anyone else did now Mother was gone. Mrs Timms was the only one left now from the old staff. It was wrong that Arthur hadn't been invited to the tea, but it was just too awkward. If she was being completely honest, it was a relief for him not to be there, to avoid any evasions about their relationship. And to avoid a repeat of the way he'd hovered on the edge of the funeral tea a year ago, not family but more than a friend. She had made her choice. It was more important to persuade her father to allow her to take the Oxford entrance than to make a point about Arthur. In the woods, sharing wet, hoppy mouths, and pushing each other over like they used to do when they were younger, she was both there and not there. It had felt like they were children and yet they weren't children any more.

She could hear Peter's voice. *Arthur? Are you joking?* Behind the patronising tone would be something else too. She couldn't bear her brother's confusion, or worse, revulsion, at what he would consider wrong. But she and Arthur were not brother and sister any more; they had long ceased to be that. If only she knew what they were now. She didn't want to decide. He was just her *Arthur* and had always been there. She conjured a picture of her coming home to him one holiday from Oxford and telling him she'd found a lover. It gave her a kind of exquisite pain to imagine the expression on his face. They would make ferocious goodbye-love. Though what that actually entailed she had no idea.

The farmhouse stood on a headland, or what passed for one here. It was on slightly raised land, above the farmland below. She could see it now, dark even in the sunshine, through the poplar trees that lined the field from the eastern approach. It was a lonely house, stuck out here on its own, away from the town, separated by fields and marsh. The days of nannies and parties and visitors arriving in motor cars along Leafy Lane were all gone. She couldn't identify the exact moment it had ended but it had not been with her mother's death. The rot had set in before that.

The farm had been her mother's dowry on her marriage. Her mother had been used to life on a much larger scale of course. The Felford estate had once owned great tracts of land in Norfolk, though it had all been sold off now. Although Verity had barely been aware of it, there had long been the murmurs of money worries, as far back as she could remember: her father absent for long periods and the farm run mostly by land girls long after the war. When the parties stopped, the house echoed with emptiness. The only visitor was the man from the dairy coming to collect the milk churns. Her mother had stayed more and more in her room. An awkward adolescent, Verity used to creep sometimes into the darkened room to lie next to her mother's tiny, sleeping form. More than anything, she'd yearned for her to wake up and put her arms around her, to tell her it would all be all right. But her mother never woke, and Verity had tiptoed back out again.

Verity stood now trying to remember when the end had begun as if, in pinpointing the moment of decline, she could understand why it had happened. But however hard she tried, she could not, in the end, remember.

She reached the kitchen door and her fingers automatically felt along the groove etched into the brick at the top of her hip. It marked the high tide from the 1930 flood.

'Home!' she called, letting herself into the kitchen at the side of the house. No sign of anyone. It was cold in the dim, echoing room, but the kettle still hissed on the range: the tea must be made already. No one was in the dining room but she poked her head around the drawing room door and saw that Mrs Timms had laid it all out there on the occasional table, by the window. Father was in his chair with a pipe and Peter was tucking into a bun with his feet up on the table. They had held the funeral tea in this room, with the doors open to the garden and its verdant green spilling in. No one had mentioned the manner of her mother's death, but people didn't, did they? Everyone knew she'd drowned but no one said how or why.

'You're late,' said Peter, his mouth full. 'Where've you been? You look like you've sat in a hedge.'

'That's because I have,' she said, amused by the ease of lying. Or rather, the use of little truths to hide the larger lies.

Her father blew out a plume of smoke. 'Whatever gallivanting you've been up to, the least you could do is be here for Mrs Timms. After all she does for you.'

Verity bit her lip. 'Shall I get the tea then?'

Outside, the light glittered like broken glass but the drawing room faced east and none penetrated inside at this time of day.

'I saw a plane,' she said, to break the silence. They had an unspoken agreement not to mention the significance of the day and it occurred to Verity again that Mrs Timms was very clever in planning the tea for this particular afternoon. It was not usual to have a good-luck tea, and certainly not on the anniversary of a death. But they were all deliberately averting their gaze, determined to keep her mother and her shocking death submerged. 'Not like the RAF, not one of ours.'

'Americans,' said Peter, who had helped himself to another bun. No amount of gorging ever made any difference to him. He remained gangly whatever he ate. It was so unfair.

He had inherited their father's height but their mother's slenderness, whereas she had only received the height. Too tall and ungainly for a woman, her father said once.

'What?' her father said. 'Haven't we had enough of them? Not got enough to do meddling in Korea?'

'I heard they're taking over the RAF base at Holkham. Rumours all round the town.'

'How do you know this, Peter?' she asked, passing him a cup of tea.

He tapped the side of his nose and grinned at her.

'Bloody all we need. An invasion. Already had one in the war.' Their father puffed a jet of smoke from the side of his mouth, as if he could blow it into the invaders' faces.

'Mother threw a party for them once, I seem to remember,' said Peter.

Her father paid no attention, as if he hadn't heard. 'I suppose they think we're overrun with spies, after those bloody Reds shipped to Russia last year. He was an Old Boy at your school for God's sake – Maclean. Humiliating.'

'He was there years before me, Father...' began Peter. 'Look, about the milk parlour. Everyone's going over to mechanisation. I know we've got the bucket milkers but we could get so much more milk out of the cows if we had a new system. And we could buy more cows. I really think now would be a good time.'

'Sad state of affairs. School seems to produce a lot of effeminates and traitors these days. It was a fine school in my day. I can't fathom it – an Old Greshamian publicly exposed like that.'

'You mean people like Benjamin Britten, Father?' Verity said facetiously. He looked at her blankly.

'Leave it, Ver. Father, please. The cows.' Peter's neck was flushed at the collar.

'Peter,' she said, warning. She saw how their father's face had drooped – dismayed, even angered by her brother's insistence. They were in danger of blowing up at each other.

Mrs Timms bustled in and cut up the cake. They all stopped talking, glad of the interruption. 'Don't stop on account of me,' she said, but they always did.

No one mentioned the memory of that terrible tea Mrs Timms had made for everyone nearly a year before, another one of stored-up rations scraped together. There had been a coffee cake, made with Camp, and rock cakes, which suited their name; tiny sandwiches with edges that had dried up and lots of sherry that Father had found from somewhere. Conversation had steered determinedly away from the reason for the gathering in the first place. That had been the rule since Mother died. They were used to the atmosphere of silent grief for what was lost.

The drawing room was filled with relics from her mother's past – clocks that had stopped ticking, heavy, dark tables and a grand piano that no one played. On top of it stood a series of photographs in gilt frames memorialising her mother's family. The central picture was of the old hall itself with her mother as a young girl in an Edwardian-style white dress, flanked by her two older brothers. All the people in the photograph were now dead, both brothers lost in the war.

Verity watched as her father topped up his tea with something from a decanter and his heavy-lidded eyes grew heavier, his face sagged and his long body collapsed in his chair. Finally, she heard the raspy sound of his snoring. She sighed, impatient. The exams were starting next week. She had her first one – Classics – on Tuesday and she should be cramming rather than sipping tea.

'I met one, you know,' said Peter into the deathly quiet of the drawing room.

'Met one what?'

'An American. Jolly sort.'

That piqued her attention. She did not want to give Peter the satisfaction of too much interest but she *was* curious. Since the war, there was so much talk of the Americans and yet one hardly ever saw one. Most of the local boys would loathe them. English boys hated Americans. Everyone knew that. But it didn't entirely surprise her that Peter would be chummy with the newcomers. Since that sticky fix at his school a few years ago, he often took up with unusual chaps. The incident had all been covered up and the next thing Verity knew was that Peter had failed his final year. Nothing was ever said, but it made her wonder.

'Met him at the Shipwright's in town.' Mother would have been horrified to know that her beloved son was hanging around at a pub in the East End of Wells. 'Flies B-45s, he told me. It's their new bomber. Amusing fellow, likes horses apparently. I said he can ride here and we'll take him shooting in the season. He seems rather keen on getting involved in local life.'

She yawned and stretched. 'They might not be here by the shooting season.'

'They will. He told me. They're going to be stationed here for a few years. All very hush-hush. And they're having a party, a big bash up at the Hall in June. We're invited.' He said it as if this was a great honour.

'Not that hush-hush then, is it?' she teased, but in truth, she was rather pleased by the arrival of the Americans. She imagined that any chum of Peter's would be a bore, harping on about blood sports, playing bloody golf, but God she was sick of the farm, Wells, the whole of Norfolk, stuck out here, away from the real world. Oxford – if she even got in – was still ages away and it would be fun to have something to distract her while waiting for the results of the exams. If nothing else, they could surely cadge some cigarettes and nylons off them. Maybe even chocolate. She smiled to herself, tasting the rich, creamy sweetness on her tongue. She couldn't wait to tell Arthur. They could laugh about the newcomers, put on accents, parade around pretending to be film stars. But she stopped abruptly in her daydreams, remembering the grip of his hands on her that day. It made her feel afraid of what he wanted from her.

Silence settled on the room. A shaft of light fell on the photograph of her mother.

'You know what day it is, don't you?'

Peter had his mouth full. 'I know,' he said when he finally swallowed.

After the tea, she walked to the churchyard and laid a clutch of bluebells she'd found at the end of the garden. There was a small clump of cuckooflowers, narcissi and bluebells already placed next to the headstone. Her brother had been. Her mother had liked irises and always had a vase of them on her dressing table but Verity hated them: the sickly honey-sweet smell reminded her of her mother and now they would always make her think of death.

A throbbing sound overhead. Another plane, like the one before. It shone in the afternoon sun and even from here

nervous. There had been an awful incident early on during the evacuation. He'd never been in the sea before. It often came back to him, that panicked feeling of putting his foot down, and finding there was nothing there. It turned out there was a shelf and a sudden drop so you could quickly get out of your depth. Peter saved him. He hadn't wanted to admit he couldn't swim. He never wanted to go back in after that. They'd tried to teach him and he learned the basics but he could never love it. It was yet another thing that the Frosts had, that he didn't. He and Peter never spoke of it but it was there between them, a bond of indebtedness.

He kicked at a tuft of dune grass. It couldn't be the end. He'd swapped one set of stifling rules for another, from the military to the rural. It wasn't possible that the pointless ritual and play-fighting of National Service could be as close as he got to the outside world. He wouldn't let it.

For a clever person Verity was remarkably blind. She never asked what *he* wanted, just assumed, like all her class, that he was happy with his lot. No university for him. She'd mentioned in her letters that she was applying to Oxford to read History, her father's subject. He had an image of her, a black gown flying out behind her, late for a class, clattering on cobbled streets, among high spires. He thought of *Jude the Obscure,* which he had read at the grammar. He could see her there, toasting crumpets on a fire in an ancient room, a foppish youth fawning at her, she with an open book reclining on a sofa. There was a stubborn determination about her that could make it happen, as unlikely as it seemed, and he admired it; it was what he'd always loved about her. But him? No, not now, he'd had to give that up. National Service had been his university. And a funny kind of education that had been. She never seemed to see that he had once shared her dream.

'Where've you been?' His mother was drying her hands on a tea towel by the little kitchen window, silhouetted in the late afternoon light. Since he had been home he had noticed how small she was. She seemed to have shrunk. He didn't remember towering over her as he did now, and he was not a particularly tall man. Compared to the Frosts of Howe Farm, all tall and tree-like, rooted to the land, he and his mother were the last shrunken remnants of an old family, washed up in this quiet seaside town on the edge of a county, not even their own.

'Just went for a walk.'

She gave him a long look of distrust. 'You smell of beer,' she said. He couldn't tell her he had seen Verity, not because she wouldn't approve but because she would approve too much.

It had not always been like this. Long ago when he was a boy, a half-Jewish evacuee, standing under the sign for WELLS-ON-SEA, Mrs Frost had appeared, looked down at him, taken his hand and driven him – the first car he'd ever been in – to her home. It hadn't mattered that Mr Frost barely saw him, or that the children initially thought him alien, or that Mrs Timms gave him less food than she gave Verity and Peter (he was used to far less). All that mattered was that this magical woman found a space for him and loved him. And in return, he had loved them all.

Once, Mrs Frost in a diaphanous white dress had been waiting on the lawn when he and Verity had careered back to the house, laughing and sandy, and Peter was sulkily throwing balls at the dog. She'd insisted on taking their photograph with the tiny aluminium camera she carried around with her. Verity and Peter had grumbled but she had a way of getting them to do as she asked and, with her quiet, terse little smile, they lined up dutifully underneath the oak tree. He remembered the photograph clearly. For a while it hung in a silver frame in the front room – the drawing room – and he would catch sight of it every day. In the picture, Verity was staring straight ahead defiantly. Peter had a sarcastic, silly smile on his face. Arthur, though, looked as if he'd been shot. His mouth was open, vaguely smiling, and rather than looking at the camera, he was gazing at Verity and if you looked really closely, you could see that the tips of their fingers were touching.

But Mrs Frost was dead now. And with her death, some wire that had bound him to Howe Farm and the Frosts had been cut. They were still there but he wasn't part of them any more. So much was obvious from the awful tea embarrassment. He guessed they were having a tea in her memory but no one had invited him – neither Peter nor Verity. He understood. A grocer's son – and a Jew – it just wouldn't do. He was fine as a childhood playmate but Mr Frost had made it quite clear that Arthur could no more consider himself a suitor to Verity than a fisherman could. Since Mrs Frost's death, no one at Howe Farm considered him family. It had been immediately apparent at the excruciating wake in the aftermath of her drowning. None of them knew what to do about him without her there.

He set the kitchen table for tea, in silence. From the wireless came the irritating rum-de-dum of a big band. His mother cut the bread, humming along to the music. He felt her lack of comment, waited for the judgement to come. Each morsel of bread, a mere scraping of margarine and jam to wet it, was dry in his mouth.

'I'm glad you're back,' she said finally.

His shoulders felt heavy with the weight of her need. It was a miracle, the way she'd uprooted herself to this rural backwater after living her entire life in the East End of London. When she'd stepped off the train in Wells during the war, her face was open in wonder. She hadn't come with him when he was evacuated. Couldn't leave the tailor's, she said, but she'd visited, just that one time. He remembered the telephone call from his mother telling him his father was MIA, shot down over Germany. Mr Frost's large hand on his shoulder and Mrs Frost, gasping, rushing to him, crying, 'Poor boy!' He never went back to London. It had been his mother's idea to come to Norfolk herself. *A fresh start*, she said. But he hadn't foreseen how much she would rely on him, how much her expectations for him were a load on his back.

'Now you're here, you can help me with the shop. It's been hard without you. I had to get a young lad from the prefabs to do the deliveries. I'll let him go now. He's been filching I'm sure.'

His eyes ached. 'I said I'd see Peter tomorrow, Mother. A round of golf.'

'Golf? I see.' There was a pause. 'How's that poor boy? After the terrible way his mother passed away. They were lucky to get the vicar's blessing for a Christian funeral.'

Arthur creased his forehead in pain. How could she be so cruel? 'Why wouldn't they? It was just gossip.'

His mother pursed her lips and stirred her tea vigorously.

'I thought we might check the stock.' She left a heavy pause, sipped her tea. 'But that's fine. You need a day of rest. I'll go to church.'

'I can help on Monday, Mother. But I should get a job. I can't stay here forever.'

'Monday. Thank you, Arthur.'

In the evening they sat in the front room, overlooking the harbour, and listened to the wireless. At least, his mother listened, the click clack of her knitting needles the background music to the evening play: a George Bernard Shaw, which was typical of the radio. There was rarely anything new and the theatre itself wasn't much better – just farces and sentimental musicals, nothing that reflected real life. He stared out of the window at the twilight. The purple bruising of the sky was silvering, boats turning to black shapes, the sea into mist. He wished he was in one of the planes he'd seen and that he could fly away from here.

More than ever he felt that this place was a sickness, a sleeping sickness in the head.

And it had killed Mrs Frost. He could not forgive it for that. He'd been on leave at the time, a few rushed days before returning to the camp. He remembered her body, a collapsed form washed up on the beach below the farm. No one understood how she could have drowned; she'd been a competent swimmer. There were whispers, rumours. He knew it, that this place had drained her of vitality with its endless sky, its slow attrition, the salt that killed everything. It had dragged her out to sea and thrown her back again. He'd known. She'd had on a nightdress when they found her. Grey and clinging to her, indecent. On the train back to the camp, he'd found he couldn't stop thinking about the way the folds of the material made ripples like the patterns in the wet sand all over her.

But he wouldn't let it kill him too. He would get out, he would see the world, report on it, and he would take Verity with him.

At this moment, looking out over the cold sea, he knew why he'd come back. He was here for her. That was all.

3.

Deep into the veins of the east saltmarshes, Muriel sailed her dad's old crabbing boat. The water was just high enough to manoeuvre it through the creeks to Blakeney Pit but it took skill to navigate. The boat's underside could easily catch on the mud and marsh grass and if you timed the tide wrong, you'd be stuck and that was that. Like a warning, she passed the rotting skeleton of an old abandoned boat, sacrificed to the sea.

An eel thrashed in the beak of a cormorant and dozens of tiny terns screamed. Muriel dropped her baited pot into the creek. There wouldn't be many crabs but she liked it here. Few fishermen came this far into the marshes.

She'd seen the planes arriving and felt the change in the air. The town was stirring again.

Muriel pulled up her crab pot. Writhing at the bottom were two green shore crabs and a beautiful brown. She lifted them out, placed them in her saltwater bucket and lowered the pot once more into the muddy creek. She was feeling lucky.

4.

A stranger was leaning on the gate to the grazing field. He was wearing a white shirt with the sleeves rolled up, revealing tanned forearms covered with golden down. His red hair was sticking up at the front, shining with grease, his mouth too big, his nose at an odd angle. Verity's first impression was of something altogether too bright and uncomfortable to look at. And at the same time, impossible not to.

The sun, at its zenith, had burned through the cloud and now shone hot on the back of her neck. She had fed the chickens. She'd groomed her horse, Gypsy, nuzzled and whispered into his hair and left him sheltering in the shade at the edge of the paddock. Gyps had been her mother's gift to her. He was the only living being with whom she felt fully at ease.

'Hey, you must be Pete's sister.' The stranger was smoking. He looked directly at her, with an odd, arrogant smile.

He was obviously American. Verity lowered her eyes and felt her chest flush hot with something like anger. Boys she knew would never look at you like that.

'Yes, I've come to fetch him. Father wants him.'

'He'll be here any minute now, he's just over in that field.'

He indicated the field down to the right of the gate, but offered no explanation or apology as to why he might be there, standing so casually on their land.

'You want one?' He proffered a cigarette and she took it off him, then stood, foolishly holding it between her fingers.

He laughed and held out a silver lighter. Her hand shook as she tried to light the cigarette. She felt his eyes on her again.

'I gotta tell you, you're a lot better looking than your brother, Miss Frost.'

It was a terrible line but its effect on her was physical and immediate. Her throat constricted and she couldn't breathe. No one had ever spoken to her like this. It was intolerable. She knew she should say something or do something but her throat was caught, she was so unused to the attention. She sucked deeply on the smoke for some relief.

'Hey, sorry, I didn't mean to alarm you.' He was still smiling, not in the least sorry. She realised she must have been frowning and tried to relax her face. *Say something*, she told herself.

Her laugh came out as a croak. 'No, not at all, it's very flattering. I'm just not used to such high praise.' She sucked on the cigarette again. It rasped against her throat and made her cough. 'I'm actually engaged anyway.' Why had she said that? It wasn't even true. There had been some talk between her father and another gentleman farmer but she was definitely not engaged. Later she realised that she had thought of Arthur when she said that and it had been an unwelcome thought.

'Yeah? Pete didn't mention it. Shouldn't you be used to compliments then?' She must have made a face because he extended his hand, saying, 'Look, I'm just teasing. I'm Jack by the way, pleased to meet you.' She hesitated but took it; it was warm and unnervingly strong. He didn't let go and she found herself holding the stranger's hand for longer than she wanted. She caught his eye and noticed they were an unusual colour – hazel flecked with gold, framed with flickering pale eyelashes, disconcertingly transfixing, almost vulpine. How long they stood like that she didn't know. It was enough for the impression of his hand to seep into her skin and remain after he took it away.

'How do you do. Have you just arrived, Mr—?' she said.

There was a slight hesitation. 'Doherty,' he said. 'Sure. Just arrived.'

She thought of the plane she'd seen on the day of the tea and pictured this American sitting in it, seeing her in the barley field. It made her shiver.

'How do you know my brother?'

'He's taken me under his wing. Said he'd show me the sights.'

She raised her eyebrows. Whatever Peter was up to, it was certainly not anything to do with acting as a tour guide for this overconfident man.

'Jack! Where the devil are you?' Peter was calling from beyond the gate, out of sight down the far end of the field. His voice was big and open and full of a joy rarely heard.

Verity stiffened and took a step back away from him but he took hold of her hand and held onto it. He pulled her towards him, brought his face to her ear and said, 'Can I see you again?'

'Excuse me?'

His mouth touched her neck just below her ear. 'Please,' he breathed out.

'No!'

In a second he had released her and was standing back at the gate, lighting up another cigarette. She thrust her hands in the pockets of her dress for something to do with them.

As Peter came into view, she called out to him, her voice too loud for her own ears, 'I was sent to tell you – Father wants you at the house!'

Peter's expression soured. 'Oh for God's sake, what now?' She shrugged.

'Fine, fine, tell him I'll be along in a minute. Oh, this is Jack, Ver. He's an airman at the base. Jack, Verity. My little sister.'

'I introduced myself,' said Jack, smiling as if they shared a secret. 'Will you be coming to the dance we're holding, Miss Frost?'

'I don't know, I hadn't thought about it.'

'You said you were dying to go,' said Peter.

'I might go,' she said, wishing her brother dead. She began to stalk away from them, trying not to break into a run.

'See you there!' called the American and she turned and gave an awkward wave and saw him wink at her. At least she thought he did, but it was hard to believe.

Fleeing back to the house, a blur of images ran through her head: his mouth breathing into her ear, those strange golden eyes and the bright, red hair. What an oddity he was. It was funny now he was gone. Such a presumptuous, rude young man.

Her father grunted at her knock.

His study was in shadow, barely any light coming in

from the north-facing bay window, which looked out over the fields to the woods. His chair was turned away from the desk, and he was sitting with his pipe. When she entered he turned to look at her.

'Father, I've brought you a cup of tea.'

He nodded his thanks. She hesitated in the doorway. Once, he had encouraged her, ordered her books from London and boasted about her. He used to call her his little bluestocking, but she was a fool to think he cared now. He seemed bemused by her desire to sit the Oxford entrance although he was an Oxford man himself. She wanted to shout at him, *You made me think it was possible.* He'd stood up for her against her mother's wishes when Verity had come home from school glowing with her schoolmistresses' reports. Her mother had always said 'Well done, dear' in that way she had of suggesting that it was just a passing phase, but Father had been proud of his clever girl. Verity was destined to be presented as a debutante, as her mother and her grandmother had been, but he'd seemed relieved when she resisted being a deb after Mother died. This March, she'd not been among the girls in their elaborate frocks and hats trotting through the palace gates towards the very new queen. Thank God. There was no money anyway. She hadn't realised that it would be her only sanctioned rebellion.

Peter said that when Father first took on the farm he hadn't any idea what to do – he had no background in it and their farmworkers, especially the ploughman, Billy, used to tell Father, 'You'll larn.' Verity couldn't imagine anyone speaking to Father like that. She remembered Billy as a kind, red-faced man. Real Norfolk. Deferential but blunt. He'd saved the farm in '30 according to Father. Then he went off to war and they turned more of the land to arable for the war effort. They'd had land girls to help and money from the Ministry for crops, but since Mother's death, it had all languished. Verity was just one more worry. She suspected he wanted to get her off his hands and the only way he knew how to do this was through marriage. As if she exhausted him, as everything now did.

'Where's your brother?' Her father was staring at her with his disconcerting, pale, heavy-lidded eyes.

'I don't know,' she said, and this was true. She didn't know *exactly* where he was. 'I gave him your message.'

Her father murmured acknowledgement and she turned to go.

'Verity,' he said, peering past her at the door. 'I've arranged a visit with the De Veres next week. For you to spend time with Richard.'

She felt her whole body tense. 'Please, Daddy, not that again.'

He gripped the side of his chair and seemed to be about to spring out of it to strike her. But then he sank back into the leather folds and closed his eyes. 'We don't have a choice. The farm – the farm cannot keep you.'

'But I'm going to university.'

He looked at her with a kind of despair. 'It's not practical, Verity. And what is the point of all that time and effort if you are going to marry?' So that was it then. The reality of what she was to him now – chattel he couldn't afford.

She looked down at the floor, her head boiling. 'I'll pay my way. I'll work—'

'It's not just about the money,' he spat.

'And I'll work afterwards. They need people like me in

– in government or – the arts!'

He sighed. 'The arts,' he said, as if she had told him she was going to the moon. 'And how will that help with finding a husband?'

'Can't it wait?' She was wailing now.

'It's what your mother wanted for you. I made a mistake, giving you ideas that couldn't—' He was cut off by a fit of coughing, wracking his hulking form.

She ran over to him but he waved her off. 'Daddy, please,' she said, not sure what she was asking for. But he raised his hand wearily as if she should leave.

Away from her father, Verity intended to study as a form of rebellion – that would show him she was serious. She would ace her exams and get in despite him. She had to. But when she was actually out in the garden, instead of studying, she sketched out a furious picture of the house with deep, black strokes in charcoal and a gloomy, lowering sky.

5.

The flat was his mother's world, her kingdom, the repository of years of collected knick-knacks of the Silver family, which she obsessively dusted and polished.

National Service had been six hellish weeks of basic training – endless square-bashing, being screamed at by the sergeant, lunging bayonets into straw dummies – followed by months of numbing boredom and deprivation, broken only by the odd lurch into thrilling danger. It had been the smell of other men's sweat and slops in canteens; day after day of card games or reading on your barrack bed; the permanent reek of engine oil; the numbing cold in the freezing barracks. Once, the sudden rush upwards, away from the earth in a Tiger Moth. And early on, the inert body of a boy his age, then eighteen, hanging by a rope from the toilet cistern. He hadn't written about that to his mother, nor to Verity.

Hating it, he had yearned for Verity and, by extension, the woods and the sea, but never this flat. Arthur saw the five (six if you included the WC) draughty little rooms above the shop as nothing to do with him. He slipped into the same routines as before: stirred the porridge in the kitchen at the back, which overlooked the rooftops of the cottages on Red Lion Yard, and, breakfast over, set up the shop. But if his mother wasn't looking, he peered through the nets of the tiny front parlour from where, on a clear day, he could see right across the harbour and the saltmarshes to the line of pine trees in the far distance, and could imagine Verity there.

His mother expected her tea. Her room was, if anything, even more crammed with gimcracks than the rest of the flat. All he ever snatched sight of confirmed it as a shrine to femininity, all lace and costume jewellery. The scent of floral perfume and lemons pervaded the room. She was already in her work dress, hair pinned and make-up done.

'What have you done to your hair? It's sticking up,' she said, taking the cup from him. In her voice, just the trace of the east London accent she'd striven to lose.

'It's supposed to be like that. It's the style.'

He turned, quickly, before she could collar him about anything else, catching only a glimpse of her pursed lips.

'I don't like it, Arthur,' she called down the stairs. 'It's common. Like a Yankee.'

Out on the quay he opened up the shop. It was quiet, apart from the odd fisherman and his boat, and the sky was grey, tinged with the pale yellow haze of the coming day.

It had all seemed clear enough when he was staring at the bare iron ceiling of the barracks or pointlessly disassembling and reassembling a Bren gun: articles for the local press, a lucky break, London, travel. The world. And yet somehow, now he had returned, the seaside town had sucked him back in. The salt air itself seemed to get in his nose, his eyes and his brain and lull him to inertia. He'd written little. Done little. He was putting off everything because of Verity and it scared him, because each time she left him in the woods, she became less real. They'd only ever been together here, in this cut-off place, and that was why it filled him with dread and pulled him in. They needed to get away from here, both of them together. They needed to get to London where he could write them both free, free from this soul-sapping end of the bloody world.

Arthur looked up at the shopfront with his usual combination of familiarity and loathing. Above the awning *Silver's Grocers* was written in red paint. But it was also a tobacconist's, a sweet shop, a newsagent's, even a chemist's, as they stocked a selection of women's beauty products and Knight's Castile soap for men. The tins and boxes of non-perishables were in tall columns on two sides, the produce was arranged outside, and on the floor behind the long counter were the sacks of flour and grains. Even now, when sugar was still on rations, his mother had a way of making the shop feel full. The only thing they didn't have was meat. For that you had to go to Thurgood's. Thurgood himself was skinny, which didn't seem right for a butcher, and Arthur knew for certain he was up to something with the meat rations, selling the choicest cuts on the black market. But he was local. His was a local name and Arthur had the impression that the Thurgoods had been here, on the Norfolk marshes, forever. *Silver*, though. It was only marginally better than *Feinsilver*. His grandfather, Ivan Feinsilver, changed his name when he came to London from Warsaw. Now both he and Arthur's father were gone, but the name remained, with its whiff of foreignness. It still sounded Jewish, Arthur thought, with a twinge of discomfort and then shame at the discomfort. He wasn't even Jewish officially as Mary Silver, his mother, was from an old East End family of tailors, all dead, but he felt his difference. The half counted.

He spent as much time as possible out the back in the storeroom spinning his own dreams, jotting down ideas for the article that was forming in his mind about the atomic world, about the nuclear threat and war between the Soviets and America. It was sitting on his own doorstep – the story that would get him out of here. If he could get a couple of pieces published in the local rag, he could take them to the national papers. If he'd learned one thing from service, it was that what was coming would be worse than anything they could imagine – worse than Hiroshima or Nagasaki. The RAF and the rest of the British military were desperate to keep up with the Yanks who, if anything, were even keener on retaliation. But this sinister new war was nothing like the last. It was being fought under a cloak of secrecy and lies. He wanted to tear it down and reveal it for what it was – a deadly game of decimation. His working title: *What Nuclear War Means for Us*. He should be grateful rather than resentful that he'd dodged military action, but this war wouldn't be like the last. The enemy was their own government as much as the Soviets. He was scribbling when he heard the bell tingle and then a girl's voice:

'Hello? Anyone here?'

In the orange half light of the shop, reflected from the translucent plastic they put in the windows, he blinked at a vision: a girl was standing with a basket in the hazy glow. Muriel. When he thought of Muriel, he still thought of her as the girl on the beach. A scrap of a thing, fair hair blowing about her face, gathering clams in her old net in the shallows, running wild on the mussel beds at low tide. Not much to laugh about, you'd have thought, but she always did.

Mother was nowhere to be seen. Her position was usually at the cash register, where she sat on a stool with her knitting all day long, interrogating the customers, weaving their complaints and stories into her endless scarves for one of her 'causes'. In an effort to overcome the twin negatives of her married name and the obscure shame of his missing father, she joined everything. Church, WI, parish committee, she did them all.

'Hello, Arthur, what you gawping at? Never seen a girl afore?' Curling out from under a green headscarf, Muriel's hair shone gold, her pouting lips were bright red and her narrow eyes were laughing at him.

He looked down immediately. 'Sorry.'

'Are you going to just stand there like a great lummox or are you going to serve me?'

He took her list and her ration book. Close up, he could smell the seasalt on her hair.

Up on the ladder, fetching tins, he felt her sharp gaze on his back and his neck burned.

'I heard you'd come home. She told me, your Verity.'

He stiffened, half turned to face her, aware of the heat on his neck. 'She's not *mine*. I didn't know you were still friends.'

Muriel's smile was large in her face. Her lips were very red. 'We're not. I bumped into her down Askey's milk bar a couple of weeks ago. Where's your mother then?'

She *is* mine. She's mine. She's mine.

'Right here, young lady.'

Arthur jerked round and nearly fell off the ladder. Mother's eyes were like daggers.

'Let me have that, Arthur, I'll put it through the till. How's your mother and the baby, Miss Gittings? Any more on the way?' It was his mother's acid-polite voice, the one she used with people she thought below her.

Muriel's mother was constantly either pregnant or nursing. Her father was always out at sea, preferring the waves and the fish to the cries and the grime of the eight children crammed into their ramshackle old cottage down the East End.

'Good morning, Mrs Silver,' said Muriel. There was a hint of mockery in her voice.

Arthur, up the ladder, with his back to them both, tensed.

'Freddie's seven months now, got a mind to start crawling, I reckon. Mother don't want any more, that's for sure, but that hint exactly her choice.'

His mother tsked. Privately and often publicly too, she aired her opinions on the breeding of the poor and felt it was an affront to everyone else that they couldn't 'find a way' of stopping. She was in her early forties and her time had come and gone. He heard her whispering the names of the babies she'd lost at her bedtime prayers through the wall, but neither of them ever mentioned the ones that had gone before. Nor his vanished father. She only had him now, him and the shop.

She sometimes slipped in something for the little ones, a twist of sugar, an egg, to other families that she felt deserved it. But not for Muriel's family, breeding like rabbits and only the dwindling fish stocks to support them. Arthur wrapped up the meagre portion of flour and weighed the pathetic handful of greens Muriel had picked and tried to signal with his eyes his regret, his shame.

'What do you think about the Americans then, Arthur?' said Muriel, eyes glittering.

'What do you mean?' he said.

His mother made a sound in her throat like a squawk. He knew exactly how *she* felt.

'Well, I think it's *fantastic*,' said Muriel. 'Bring a bit of life to this dull old town. Mind how you go, Arthur,' she called, as she tied her scarf tighter round her hair. Mother had settled back to her knitting. He hoped she didn't see Muriel winking at him as she turned and left, holding the door open for old Mrs Hatchet.

'I like your hair like that,' she called as she disappeared out of the door.

'She's trouble that girl,' said his mother.

Arthur saw his mother's pinched mouth and grabbed a paper twist of sugar.

'She's forgotten something,' he called and disappeared out of the door, before his mother or Mrs Hatchet could say anything.

Muriel was still on the quay, one hand holding onto her scarf in the gusty wind. She turned at his voice and waited. He handed her the paper twist.

'I... She should have...'

'Thanks, Arthur,' she said, and put it in her basket. The wind was flapping at the furled sails of the boats behind her in the harbour. He noticed she had a large cloth bag as well as her basket. She saw him looking. 'Just on my way back from the Buttlands. Collecting laundry. Mum does some of them posh ones' washing. She's got me slaving for her as usual.' There was resentment but no embarrassment.

A wash of grief fell over him for what they had once been. It was strange now, to think of the four of them together as they used to be. He, Muriel and the Frost children. It had all gone, their childhood: he had been cast out and so had she. Since he had been away he could see it more clearly.

Blinking, he tried to think of something to say. 'I've not seen you for an age.'

'You've been away,' she said. He'd been back from National Service for a week now but he'd hardly seen Muriel since he'd gone to the grammar. 'How was it then?'

'Dull, like you wouldn't believe. Didn't see any fighting.' He wondered why he always did that, incapable of putting a positive spin on anything.

'I never saw you as the fighting type anyway. You looked dapper in your uniform, though. Your mother showed everyone a picture of you next to a plane. She kept saying how much you looked like your father when he was in the RAF. You were flying, weren't you?' She squeezed his arm.

He felt heat rise again up his neck. She'd always been direct and it had always caught him out. He had an image of Muriel, hair flying, jumping over the ditches that criss-crossed the grazing marsh with her bucket full of wriggling creatures.

'Only once,' he said, remembering the vertiginous feeling of rising through the air and the smell of the fuel at the back of the plane. 'I was a clerk.' It was only the public school boys who got commissions and went on to become airmen, while people like him, grammar school boys who could type and file – they were given desk jobs. He moved a step back.

She stayed where she was. 'You going to the dance the Americans are putting on?'

'I don't know anything about it.'

'It's going to be at the Hall. Everyone's going.'

'I'm a terrible dancer, Muriel.'

'I don't believe it,' she said, and he heard the chime of laughter in her voice. 'See you there, Arthur!'

She turned to go and he listened to the click of her heels on the pavement as she went down past the Shipwright's pub towards the warren of little cottages down the east. He watched her skirt swishing as she walked. He had no intention of going to Harborough Hall. The last thing he wanted to do was go to some dance with a lot of arrogant Americans.

Arthur and Peter cycled out to the golf course, south of the town, passing the body of a dead badger and what looked like the red pelt of a fox. In the shadow of the scrub under the hedge, the animals' bodies appeared as if they were sleeping.

As they rode, another of the planes he'd seen at the beginning of May flew overhead. It was an American jet bomber, everyone knew that now, but no one knew why they were here. It was like a futuristic rocket, incongruous in the flat Norfolk countryside. With its deep rumble and flashy brilliance, it seemed to say that whatever the British had done in the war was not enough in this new, atomic world. Arthur wondered why more of the town weren't resentful of their presence.

The golfing was a write-off. On the ninth, he got stuck in a bunker, sweating, while Peter leaned on his clubs above him offering unhelpful instructions. Peter was in the full regalia: plus fours, shirt and tie, but he didn't seem bothered by the heat. Arthur loathed golf but he did it for his friend's sake.

After the tenth, there was a long walk to the next hole. A funny pair they must look – he stocky and dark, Peter tall and fair. Peter offered him a cigarette. Camels.

'Where did you get those from?' he said, taking one.

'Ah, that reminds me. Fellow's joining us in a tick. One of the Americans. Said he'd be late so I didn't expect him at the first. Reckon he'll be here soon, though.'

'What American? Why didn't you mention it earlier?' He sounded piqued but it was odd. No one else ever joined them on their golfing days.

Peter looked surprised. 'I should have, old man. Just clear forgot about it to be honest. Been up to my ears in farm business. The accounts aren't squaring. Ver doesn't know this, so keep it under your hat, but I think Father's been off on one of his jaunts again and I can only think he's gambled some of the profits. Feed costs are going up all the time and we have less and less to cover it. I don't know what to do.'

'Have you confronted him about it?'

'How can I? You know what he's like. It'd push him over the edge.'

Arthur did know. Mr Frost had always been a drinker but since Mrs Frost had died, Peter seemed to be taking on more and more of the farm business and putting off making any decisions.

'Look, there he is. Lucky I remembered, otherwise I'd have looked like quite a fool.' Peter looked away, tugging at his collar, and, for once, appeared uncomfortable. Arthur realised that he was actually embarrassed about introducing someone new to him.

Away across the fairway, a speck in the distance, a figure was walking towards them. When the figure was close enough, Arthur saw he was strolling, relaxed, in pale yellow trousers and a dark navy polo shirt, his golf bag slung over his shoulder.

'Jack!' Peter walked forward towards the newcomer with his hand held out in greeting. Arthur stayed back and surveyed the interloper. He was medium height, probably about as tall as he was, but with a litheness and a swagger that spoke of complete confidence. His face was slim and with a pointed chin and eyes that creased with his wide grin. But the most obvious thing about him was the strange red-gold of his hair. It shone like a beacon against the green of the range and the pale blue of the sky – a flash of deep orange, drawing attention to itself, demanding that they all look. He felt a shiver of something close to dislike and, aware of it, he consciously readied his own face to brighten into welcome.

'You must be the famous Art,' said the American and Arthur wondered where the man had got that nickname from. No one called him that. Arthur wasn't the sort of person to give others nicknames and was irked if anyone shortened his, with the exception of Verity and Peter. Even in the service where everyone had a nickname, he was still known as Arthur. He extended his hand and Jack took it. The hand was small and cool but with an insistent grip and he felt the American's almond eyes focus on him until he had to look away.

'Pleased to meet you,' he said.

'Let battle commence,' declared the American.

For the rest of the course, Arthur became more and more frustrated and with each duff shot his irritation grew and he became careless. Jack would shout encouragement, which only put him off. He let more shots go until he was so far over par he felt like giving the whole thing up. But he couldn't do that. Instead he had to watch Peter, with his long, slow arm and his careful, hunter's eye, find the hole more times than not. Worse still was the American with his easy, casual swing that hid, Arthur suspected, as keen an eye as Peter's. Thoroughly discouraged, his shirt stuck to his back with sweat, his entirely wrong, badly fitting shoes dug into his feet and he dreamt of swinging the club into the American's satisfied face.

Finally, they arrived at the eighteenth. With the relief of the ordeal nearly over, he relaxed. Peter was up first and hit straight to the green.

'Magnificent shot, Pete!' Jack was leaning on his club, with a cigarette in his fingers, his large mouth beaming. Arthur had a vision of a Hollywood star in some sunshine-drenched film from the last decade and it made the American unreal, even ridiculous, which was rather comforting.

On his turn, he no longer cared whether the ball ended up anywhere near the damn hole. He took a wild swing.

'Watch it go!' blared the American twang behind him, and he looked up to see the ball carving a beautiful, soaring arc along the range heading magically straight for the flag.

He watched in bemused awe as the white ball plummeted to earth, falling straight for the hole. He thought, *I've done it*. But in a blink it had bounced off the edge of the green and into a bunker.

Behind him, the old windows of the clubhouse gleamed mockingly in the afternoon sunshine.

In the shady, faded bar, deserted apart from a couple of old gents and the barman himself, Jack bought a round of beers. They took their drinks back out into the light and stood on the terrace overlooking the course, toasting Peter's triumph.

'Jack's at the base,' said Peter, smiling at the American with pride as if he was showing off a prize.

'Just trying out some new planes,' said Jack.

'What kind of planes?' He might as well show him that he wouldn't be diverted.

'B-45 Tornado,' Peter answered for him, like a kid collecting cigarette cards.

'What exactly are you here for?' He loathed this pretence, the easy sham of it all.

'Art, old boy, they can't divulge—' Peter's hand was on his shoulder, as if to restrain him.

But Jack's smile seemed to take them both in. 'Pete's right, I'm afraid, I can't really say, but it's joint operations with the RAF, and I'm sure you realise that this part of the world is a strategic base.'

'Yes, you're using England as a convenient spot – from which to do what exactly?'

'Art fancies himself as a roving reporter, Jack. Not much going on around here usually.' Arthur winced. He wished Peter hadn't exposed him like that.

Jack slightly raised an eyebrow but kept smiling. 'The Brits want us here as far as I know.'

'More's the pity,' said Arthur.

He wanted to ask more because Jack's answer was no answer at all, but he realised two things simultaneously: that this wasn't the whole story and that Jack would only tell them what he wanted to and no more. Well, he would do his damnedest to find out.

'What state are you from?'

'Arizona,' said Jack, with a slight hesitation.

'That's funny, you sound like someone I met on service. He was from the East. Near New York City.' This wasn't quite true – the visiting GI had been from Pennsylvania – but Jack's voice was odd. He'd seen enough Westerns at the flicks, and Jack sounded nothing like those cowboys.

Jack shrugged and smiled as if it meant nothing. 'Pete told me you're a flying man.'

'Not really. I was just with the RAF for National Service. Demobbed now.' His guts tightened and he couldn't bear to tell this interloper that he was his mother's delivery boy. 'I'm thinking of going to London, after the summer.'

'Are you?' said Peter, his eyebrows raised.

'Can't stay here forever,' Arthur said.

'I suppose not,' said Peter, truculent. 'Though I don't seem to have a choice over that.'

Jack was looking from one to the other, a slight smile curling up from one side of his mouth. 'Is it so awful here?'

'Oh no,' said Peter. 'Best place in the world really. Best shooting and birding in the country. You'll see. We complain about it but we love it truly, don't we, Arty?'

It was easy to reply yes, because if he thought of her, it was true.

He'd been enthralled by her, right from the beginning. When Arthur first saw them they were in the garden. The boy was practising cricket and throwing a ball, a game of toss at the dog. The girl was sitting reading on the swing they had back then, strung up between two towering sycamores. She looked up from the book when her mother called her name and stared at him from under a dark fringe as if he had arisen from the sea carrying a trident. The swing slowed and stopped and the little girl jumped off, revealing herself to be his height even though she was only six and he was eight. She thrust her hand out and peered at him. When he said, 'How do you do,' as he had been taught by his mother, the girl let out a blast of laughter before shutting her mouth firmly. But it was still in her eyes, sparkling.

A ball flew at him, which, blessed miracle, he caught. 'Come and play,' demanded Peter, and with deep gratitude Arthur turned his back on the priggish little sister.

It was funny how he had resolved to hate her.

Determined to keep up with their games, she would appear, eyes narrowed with satisfaction, pouncing on their latest den in the pine trees or the dunes.

He would catch her looking at him over Peter's shoulder and a small smile of victory would twitch at the corner of her mouth. Sometimes she would say mean things. If she'd been a boy he would have punched her, but she was just a little girl. He wanted to say something horrid too but when he opened his mouth to speak there was a hard defiance on her face which looked like it could burst and it made him uneasy. He often caught her peering at him from under the black fringe and he grew a kind of fondness for that fierce look of hers, the way her eyebrows furrowed into a deep frown. He found himself looking for her when they were playing, wanting her to find them and missing her when she didn't come.

Once, they were running together, he faster than her now he had grown, but he could hear her breathing behind him, the swish of the wheat as she pushed through it, just an arm's stretch behind him. Through the woods she kept up with him, then something caught at his foot as he scrabbled over the dunes and down he fell. Falling, sand flying. She banged up against his back and down they dropped, like two dominoes. She thrust against him as they fell. He remembered the thrilling feeling of the weight of her chest on his back, her cry in his ear. They landed with their legs sprawled on the side of the dunes, sand in his face.

'I've got you now,' she said, triumphant.

He manoeuvred himself round to push her off him and sit up but she took hold of his wrists and held them down in the sand and sat astride him. He thought he could break free but her grip was strong and his first effort failed. Her fringe had been cut back and the twin scythes of her black bob cut across her jaw. The sun created a halo glow on the top of her head. He squinted up at her, not wanting any more to release himself from her hold. It was then, he realised later, as he lay pinned down by her on the hot sand, that she had won. She had been trying, ever since he had arrived in their garden, to claim him as her own, playing a silent game with Peter over his loyalty and love. And now she had won, there on the dunes. She had won him forever.

From the golf course, you could see out over the fields to a faint sheen where the sea must be. They were the same twisted rope, Verity and this place. He couldn't unknot one from the other, and yet he knew that he must.

6.

June
Eight months before the flood

From the middle of June onwards, the heat kept rising to an almost unbearable level. Verity was the only one who liked it. Mrs Timms complained about the milk curdling. On the marsh, gnats multiplied, grass withered and mud dried and cracked. Peter kept moving the cows to find somewhere to graze and they slapped their tails against the flies and drooped their heavy heads. A heat haze shimmered between the land and the vast, oppressive sky. Beyond the parched fields and the wilted barley, the sea glittered a bright, blinding white.

But the languid, stifling days and hot nights suited her post-school mood. Her exams were over and she wore a floppy straw hat, one of her mother's old gardening ones, tried and mostly failed to sketch, left her legs bare and considered reading the pile of books her History mistress, Miss Gardiner, had recommended for cramming for the Oxford entrance in October.

Miss Gardiner. Oh, there was a crush. She was a slim, neat kind of woman, not much older than the students, with very straight hair always kept in a trim bun. She seemed impossibly glamorous and clever to Verity with her little berets and French cigarettes. Verity had wanted to be everything Miss Gardiner was: beautiful, erudite and educated. The mistress had taken her to her bosom and lent her all sorts of books and pictures of art. In the absence of close friends, Miss Gardiner was a worthy substitute.

Sometime in the winter, they had been taking tea in the rooms off the school where Miss Gardiner – 'Call me Cecily' – lodged. It had been late afternoon and getting dark. The teacher was leaning over the grill, toasting bread, and in the inadequate yellow light of the primitive kitchen area, Verity noticed the lines around Miss Gardiner's eyes. She had thought of her as someone romantic, her lover killed in the war (his picture was on the mantelpiece, staring into the camera, serious and very young), and rather glorious in a ballet dancer kind of way. Though they had no proof whatsoever, the girls at school had often speculated that the mistress had been in the Resistance or something else exciting.

'Miss Gardiner – Cecily,' she said, plunging forward, 'do you ever feel as if there is more to life than being stuck out here in Norfolk?'

At first, Miss Gardiner didn't move. There was the slightest contraction in her thin neck. She turned and said cheerfully, 'Oh, but my dear, I know there is. I have travelled, you know. Before the war. To Paris and Florence and Rome. It was our Grand Tour. My friends and I were rather intrepid, you know. The Uffizi, the Louvre. All of it.'

'God, I wish I could do that. Father would never let me.'

'Then you must find another way.'

For a while they were silent, eating toast and drinking tea.

Daringly, because this was her old teacher after all, Verity lit a cigarette and sat happily sated in a warm fug of smoke.

'But why did you end up *here* of all places?'

'My family found me the position, after the war.'

A veil had come down. Verity was stupid to have asked. Then the mistress reached over and held Verity's hand hard as if she was going to embrace it.

'You really should go and see the world, my dear. Don't wait.'

There was a hunger and a desperation in Miss Gardiner's primly lovely face. Suddenly, Verity wanted to jump up and leave, as if the sadness of lost chances she smelt on the mistress would catch and infect her too.

It was a late afternoon of swooning heat. She hadn't been to tea at Cecily Gardiner's for months now. She felt guilty but dismissed it, shucking off any sense of obligation she couldn't bear to feel. Her mother had made her like this – unable to connect with anyone, unable to find a real friend. There was some coldness, some distancing in her that had contaminated Verity too. Only Arthur had ever come close, and now, what was he?

She was lying on her stomach under the tree, eyes closed, feeling the prickles of dry grass under her legs and the heat of the afternoon sun on the backs of her calves. The textbook about the French Revolution was lying face down on the grass. Her sketchbook was open but she'd abandoned her attempt at a charcoal landscape. The image of the red-haired American with the sly, fox-like grin flitted across her vision but she shook it away. It was replaced by the burning sensation of his hand on hers. Like slow waves, the sensations fell over her prone, sun-warmed body.

From somewhere nearby, the revving of an engine, a rough and shocking noise, tore through the low hum of the hot summer's afternoon. Curious, she slipped into the house via the kitchen back door and heard voices in the hallway. With an ear to the door, she could hear Mrs Timms was clucking around Peter, but another voice chimed in, lower than the others, with a distinctive twang: foreign, assured. She took the back stairs to the landing. A rainbow of diffuse light filtered through the stained glass of the porch door into the hall but she was hidden in the shadows and could observe, unseen, the unexpected visitor from above. Through the banisters she tried to work out who it was. She could only see the tops of their heads and couldn't be sure of the colour in the washed-out light.

'Are you sure you won't stay for supper, Peter? And your guest…'

'Jack,' said the other man. 'A pleasure to meet you, ma'am,' and he stepped forward into Verity's line of vision and took the housekeeper's plump hand in both of his.

Verity swallowed. It was the American. Of course – Peter talked of no one else. Mrs Timms must be bristling at his impertinence but he didn't seem to notice. Verity leaned forward to try to see him more clearly, but he had his back to her.

'That's awfully kind of you, Mrs T,' said Peter. 'Maybe a drink or two would do the trick. Show this uncouth fellow how we do things in the old world. Can't stay long, though.'

'Peter? Is that you?' Father's voice cut through the hallway from his study at the back of the house. Verity stiffened.

Her father came out to the entrance hall. He was tall and used to commanding the attention of the workers on his farm and his family, but from her position on the landing he appeared to stoop. He moved slowly as if he had all the time in the world – or as if he was in pain.

'And who are you, young man?'

Jack sprang forward and shook her father's hand before Peter could introduce him. 'Jack Doherty, sir. So great to meet you.'

'Is it? I can't think why.'

Jack laughed and Verity thought her father would be horrified at the crude sound of it, shattering the usual hush of the house, but instead he let out a bark, which turned into a cough.

'Father, Jack has been helping me with the herd. He's a fine herder, you know – he was brought up on a ranch.'

'A ranch? Cattle man, are you? Dairy or stock?'

Verity thought Jack twitched slightly. There was a small hesitation before he said, 'Both.'

'You sound American. Well, at least you're making yourself useful here. Unlike the rest of your lot. Don't know why you still need to be here. War's over, after all.'

'Father…' said Peter, hopping about.

'It's all right, Peter,' their father waved a hand at him, 'I shan't go on.'

'Mr Frost, you may have a point there. I don't suppose we'll be here for much longer. But there is a war, sir. It's just playing out a little differently. You know, I sure have been surprised by the welcome I've received. You have a beautiful country.'

Father grunted again but Verity saw how his back seemed to straighten.

What had Arthur said to her? The planes they had were bombers. She remembered the Pathé footage she'd seen showing the mushroom clouds somewhere in Australia, and the voiceover man pronouncing, 'It seems that by the possession of such deadly weapons, peace can be maintained in this troubled world.' That was a twisted way of looking at it.

'I was just going to get Jack a drink, Father, can we…'

'Yes, yes,' her father said, 'go ahead. You youngsters will drink a man dry.' He waved them into the front room. 'Mrs Timms, fetch Verity.'

Before Verity could scuttle back to her room, Jack lifted his eyes to the banisters. Although surely he couldn't possibly know that she was there, he smiled in the direction of the landing where she was crouching in the shadows as if he could sense her watching him. Quickly, she jerked back and tiptoed to her room.

Her mind was all over the place. She had taken something of a dislike to the American and his secret war but for some reason she had the stupid thought that he was here to see her. It was important, she decided, to let him understand that not only was she not interested in his advances if that's what they were, but that they were actually rather unwelcome.

Despite the summons, she absolutely could not go downstairs in her current state, hair dishevelled and face all crumpled from lying in the garden for hours. At her dressing table, adorned with her mother's pearl-inlaid hair brush and hand mirror, Verity smoothed her hair at the glass and rubbed just a hint of rouge into her cheeks to add some colour into her skin. Her face had a light tan from the sun but in the gloom of the house it looked yellow, like jaundice. Her mother would have known how to handle Americans. She would have disarmed this one with her trilling laugh. All men had loved her. She'd known how to flatter them, to make them feel special and, unlike Verity, she had been a fragile, delicate thing and it made men want to protect her too. Father said once that her brothers had worshipped her and been protective and he'd had to reassure them that he was good enough for her. Verity dabbed a spot of her mother's precious L'Air du Temps on her wrists. None of them had protected her, though, it turned out, had they?

A pale light suffused the east-facing drawing room but did not fully illuminate it. Her father and Jack sat either side of the cold fireplace. Peter stood next to the drinks cabinet. As Verity entered the room, the door creaked and they all turned to see her. She was warm with embarrassment, but her father just said, 'Come in, come in,' and waved at her impatiently. Peter helped himself to a generous measure of whisky. He winked at her.

'Creep,' she mouthed.

Her father did not offer her a drink. Instead, he was intent on listening to the American's tales of breaking in horses on a ranch in Arizona. Verity perched on the edge of an armchair and studied their guest. His hair was the colour of pale wood. Or was it a peach? Yes, that was it. But there was copper too. It seemed to change and shift when he moved and his golden head caught the light from the reading lamps. And his face was strange too: it was strictly rather ugly but undeniably compelling. She imagined drawing the line of his profile in pencil, down along the thin nose, twisted slightly to the left to his large mouth and his hard little chin. As she was recreating his image, the portrait himself turned and looked at her.

'Hello there.'

She almost fell back into the chair. But as he turned back to her brother she found herself looking at him again, studying the lines and contours of his form.

As if aware of her gaze, Jack shot back a searching glance. He wandered over to the other side of the room and asked about the telescope in the corner, positioned by the window. Her father was only too delighted to show the American his collection of optical instruments. His 'star-gazers' as he called them.

She watched as Jack's pale fingers clicked the pieces into place and he leaned down to look through the eye-piece. Her father looked on proudly. 'Have you ever done any of this yourself, young man?'

Jack gave him a white-toothed smile. 'Some. For the services, you see. What's this?' He was holding up a camera in his hand, cradling it in his palm as if it was a precious bird's egg. 'It's beautiful.'

The air in the room cooled. It had been her mother's. It was a shiny metal camera that could fit in the palm of your hand. It had an odd French name – LeCoultre Compass – and had been passed down to her mother by an old uncle. She had used it all the time, but since her death, no one had touched it. It remained on the corner table by the window, sat there like a useless ornament, stoppered, gathering dust.

No one spoke for a few seconds and she saw that Jack

noticed this but did not seem perturbed. Finally, Peter stepped in.

'It was Mother's,' he said. 'Photography was something of a family hobby. I think it was actually invented by a family member – one of Mother's aristocratic lot – apparently he took on a bet that you couldn't make a camera that would fit in a cigarette packet. Mother was an amateur, but very good.' He glanced at their father.

'Madmen, the lot of them,' Father grunted.

Jack set the camera down on the table gently. 'I've never seen anything like it,' he said. 'It's incredibly rare.' He had a dreamy look she hadn't seen before. None of them had ever paid much attention to her mother's interest. The American was saying something under his breath while his fingers nimbly caressed the levers and dials but she couldn't catch what it was.

'Father, Jack and I really need to get off,' said Peter, downing his drink.

Her father seemed to jolt himself into joviality. 'Yes, yes. You go and have your fun. One minute, though, Peter, I need to have a word with you.' Peter gave Jack a strangled look and Jack jumped out of his chair.

'Mr Frost, sir, would you mind if I took a look around your home? I've always had a great interest in English country houses but I haven't had the chance to take a good look at one as fantastic as this. Could Miss Frost show me?' Peter had his eyes raised to heaven but Jack took no notice.

'Yes, I see,' said her father. 'It's eighteenth century, quite old. But then I suppose everything must seem old to your lot. I would give you a tour myself but I must speak with Peter. Verity, please show Mr Doherty the house.'

'Me?' But it was no use complaining; she had no reasonable excuse. And perhaps this was her chance to see him off.

'Father, I can show Jack the house.' The colour had risen in Peter's face.

Realising that he desperately didn't want her anywhere near his precious Jack, she said, quite casually, 'Oh all right then, if I must.'

He followed her around the hushed and half-lit house, hardly a step behind her, admiring everything in a drawling voice that always seemed amused. The house was dark and gloomy and somehow *tired*. It was like a mausoleum, without Mother there. On the hallway stairs, he stopped in front of a framed photograph of her and Peter dressed up as Arabians in silk cloths. She winced.

'Mother took that. It was one of her things. Dressing us up, posing. I loathed it.'

He smiled. 'I love it,' he said, his fingertips touching the frame. 'I think I'd have got on well with your mother.'

'Oh, I'm sure,' she said in a withering tone but it sounded silly. It was true, what he'd said. Her mother, before her descent into – whatever it was – had been interested in people. Or at least she had appeared to be and had made everyone feel as if they were interesting. At parties, she would stand with a glass in her hand and cock her head to one side with wide eyes as if whatever dull nonsense the person was spouting was fascinating. Her mother would have been besotted by this odd American boy and he with her, and it made Verity feel strangely left out.

On the upstairs landing, they stood in front of some watery Norfolk landscapes.

'They're Cotman. Norwich school. Mother inherited them. Do you like them?'

'I—'

'I don't. Not any more. I'm fed up with old things. Sick of them. I'm supposed to be studying History, did you know that? But you know what's funny? I can't stand history. I hate it all. All the old stuff. I think I only chose it because of one of the mistresses at my school.'

'What *do* you like?'

Although she kept her eyes on the paintings, she was aware that he was looking at her. No one had ever asked her that. She had been angrily ranting and now he had wrong-footed her. She had to think quickly. 'I actually rather like the Americans, Mr Doherty, painters I mean—'

'Call me Jack,' he said.

But she carried on. 'People like… Rothko.' She knew very little about the artist aside from an exhibition brochure Miss Gardiner, who went down to London for the shows, had lent her. But it was new and strange and the opposite of the English landscapes and religious oils she had grown up on.

'Yeah, I know him. Big blocks of colour. Kinda strange.' Verity cast him a suspicious glance. 'No need to look surprised. I lived in New York before I came out here.'

'Did you?' This seemed improbable too but then she was starting to feel blindsided in her assumptions. 'Did you see them?' she asked.

'Oh no. I was kinda busy. New York's a wild kind of place. And I prefer photography anyway.' She flushed and fell away from him, suddenly aware of a tang of something unknown, sensual and alarming. Although he could have meant anything by it, she was sure he was determined to make a fool of her with his insinuations of a worldly life far away from Norfolk. And it was probably a lie about New York and the artists.

'Do you?' she said. 'What kind of photographs?'

He appeared to think. 'I like your mother's,' he said. 'You know, Miss Frost, despite what I said to your father, I don't really care about old English houses.' He was standing rather close to her and she was glad of the dim light because her face was burning. She wished he would stop. 'I think English people are funny, though. I think it's the way most of them never say what they really think but spend a lot of time pretending to be so proper about everything.'

'I see.' Was he mocking her? It was hard to tell. He probably thought she was stuck up and pretentious. She had made a fool of herself staring at him like that downstairs. 'Well, it was very nice to see you again, Mr Doherty, but I must get back to my books. Can you find your own way down?' Her voice was high and too loud. She turned awkwardly and took the few steps needed to get to her bedroom without looking back.

But when she opened the door he was standing next to her. He put his hand on the door.

'I'm only teasing you. I'm not really such an ass.' Even in the dull light of the landing she could see the whites of his eyes.

'You mean you just can't help being one,' she said, her tone horribly prim and hard. Good grief, he was so provoking.

'Well, I guess I deserved that.' He paused, seeming to

consider something. 'I really did live in New York City. It's not a lie.'

She blushed. 'I never said it was,' she said, in a voice of hurt. 'Now I would appreciate it if you could let me get into my room, Mr Doherty.'

He stood back to let her go in but, as she passed him, her arm brushed against his chest and for a few seconds she didn't move: they were touching, and she could almost imagine falling against him. But then the tip of his finger ran along her back and she pushed past him and into the safety of the room, her back on fire.

'I'll be seeing you, Miss Frost,' he said.

'Will you?' she said.

'At the Midsummer dance,' he said, 'I already invited you.' There was the hint of a question in his voice and that gave her great satisfaction. He did not *know* she would go to the blessed dance. That was the key.

She wanted to shout back that she had no intention of going but he had gone and she was left slumped on her bed, her heart beating far too fast.

7.

Midsummer's Night

'You look smart, Arthur.'

He glanced at his mother, reddened and took refuge in his bread and jam. Mother leaned back in her chair with a teacup in her hand, peering at him across the table. Her hair was in rollers ready for the night. Though she still had her 'face' on as she called it, she was in slippers and housecoat and she looked settled for the evening. It made him feel restless. He was wearing a tight-fitting shirt that dug into his neck and had combed his hair up into a quiff. He expected another comment on his hairstyle but none came. Through the open window he heard the seagulls calling. A male voice rang up from the street.

'That's Peter,' he said, scraping his own chair back. He was hitching a ride on Peter's bike to the Midsummer dance. He was only going because Verity would be there.

'Don't speak with your mouth full.'

He swallowed the bread and washed it down with a slurp of tea.

'Have a nice evening, Mother.'

She was sitting with her teacup poised in the air.

Something wasn't right about her but he didn't know what it was except that the lines under her eyes looked deeper, there were streaks of grey in her once black hair, and she was always tired. In the background of all their interactions was the unspoken assumption that she was seriously ill. She gave him a thin smile but seemed to be gazing into a space beyond him.

'Yes,' she said, as if she hadn't heard him.

Peter rang his bike bell. Arthur bent to kiss her cheek and she grasped his hand.

'You're a good boy, Arthur,' she said, her powdery face near his cheek, her hand digging into his. 'You look after me.'

He hesitated in the kitchen doorway with a question about how she was but he could feel the summer air wafting up from the street and wanted to be gone.

Out on the quay, away from the cool of the dark flat, the air was thick and heavy; the sky was white with heat and reflected off the still water in the harbour. The boats slumped, deflated, like punctured balloons, from the lack of wind.

'Finally,' said Peter. He was leaning against a street lamp, looking crumpled and hot, cigarette dangling from his hand, his shirt loose at the neck, and his tie askew. 'Here, have some of this.' The cigarette balanced in his mouth, he took a flask out of his pocket and handed it to Arthur.

'I need this,' Arthur said, pouring the burning whisky down his throat. It buzzed through his brain and jarred his senses.

'Scared of a stupid dance?' said Peter, laughing.

'Nah,' said Arthur. Handing back the hip flask, he watched

a tiny drop of water fall onto his hand. He squinted up at the white cover of cloud. 'I think it might finally rain.'

'About bloody time,' said Peter, offering him a cigarette.

He lit up. 'Where's Jack?'

'Something at the base, he'll be along later. Reckons he's bringing his wretched motorcycle. The girls'll love that.' Peter sneered, as he always did at something alien, but Arthur could hear both the envy and pride in his voice. Jack was a trophy, something new and shiny to be wondered at and admired. Arthur felt a twinge of anxiety for Peter. He saw the way Peter reacted to Jack. More than the American's novelty he was held up as an object of admiration, the perfect image of manhood. Peter had placed a lot of faith in him, as if Jack was the answer to a question he had been asking for a long time. But neither of them really knew him. Neither of them knew if they could trust him.

They swigged the rest of the whisky and set off wobbling and guffawing down the Holkham Road towards Harborough Hall, a mile out of Wells. They were boys again.

In the hot summers of the war they played at pilots. They kept a keen eye on the course of the Battle of Britain and chanted Churchill's words to each other as their arms spun wide in the fields down to the woods and the North Sea, long after the real battle had been fought and won. Arthur was usually German, as he was younger. The two boys bashed into each other and hurtled, pell mell, into the wheat, laughing, legs flying.

As they cycled, he standing on the axle holding onto Peter's lanky frame, the sun burned through the haze and the rain held off. The evening sang with sound and life. They flew down the country lanes to the Hall and he closed his eyes, listening to birdsong and the squeak of the tyres. He wondered how Verity was going to get there but he couldn't ask, he had to concentrate on holding tight to Peter who swerved alarmingly close to the ditches on every corner they turned. He had his answer when they finally arrived at the entrance to a grand house at the end of a long gravel drive, flanked by poplar trees on either side. Gaggles of brightly dressed girls were emerging from two coaches, like princesses from carriages, in dresses of yellow and pink and green. He felt a violent desire to get off the bike and run back to the safety of the town. But Peter was veering in wide parabolas across the path. For a fleeting moment, it was the two of them on a bike freewheeling down Leafy Lane as children and he opened his mouth to whoop in the boyish joy of it.

Peter turned his head to shout back to Arthur, 'Look at those peacocks!' In the same moment, he lost control of the bike and they fell sideways, scraping onto the gravel, skidding into the line of poplars.

The two of them sprawled where they had fallen, legs under the wheels, bruised and groaning. They weren't boys any more. Someone came crunching over the gravel. 'Peter, is that you?' There was a pause. 'Oh, for goodness sake.'

Arthur tried to sit up. It was Verity. She was standing in a shiny blue ballgown, a gauzy shawl around her shoulders, staring at them both. 'What on earth have you done?'

'Oh there you are, Ver, help me up, will you?' Peter held out his arm.

'God, Peter, you stink of alcohol. They won't have it, you know.' But she knelt to help him.

'Poppycock, just a little stiffener, dear sister.' Peter straightened his long body and ran a hand through his sandy hair.

'So bloody dangerous, what if this had happened out on a proper road?'

'Blimey, Ver, you sound like an old woman. Let me have a bit of fun, will you?' Arthur cringed at the hurt in Peter's voice. He levered himself up, trying not to wince in pain. He avoided catching Verity's eye.

'I would have thought *you'd* know better,' she said to him and he was forced to look at her.

'He's worse than me, you know that,' said her brother.

'I do not. Come on, Arthur, you can take me in.'

He shrugged apologetically to Peter and, not quite believing it, took her arm. She turned to her brother, still standing with his bike. 'Girls won't dance with you, you know. Not if you're drunk.'

'I don't care!' Peter shouted at their backs.

'It's true,' Arthur said to her, 'he really doesn't care.'

'But you do, don't you?' she said, inching a tiny movement closer to him.

'I really can't dance, you know that,' he said.

'I don't care a fig. But you'll dance with me? I couldn't bear it if I had to sit out the whole time.'

'Yes, all right,' he said. The thought of her dancing with other men while he watched from the side was impossible. He smelled her perfume: something floral, heavy and rather alarming. A man dressed in a tailcoat took the men's coats and the ladies' little shawls and cardigans in the hallway. It was brightly decked in lanterns and candles, the kind of entrance hall he had only seen in pictures, with a swirling staircase rising from the far end. Numerous doors came off each side, and on the right, one enormous door opened onto a scene of flickering light and the sound of a big band striking up.

Without her shawl, Verity's long white neck glowed, a curve of smooth porcelain from her chin to her shoulder blades and a wide V falling to the silky blue neckline. The tops of her shoulders were hidden under the blue capped sleeves but her arms were bare, smooth and honey-coloured from the sun. All this Arthur saw in sidelong glances as he tried not to gape. She smiled at him, and pulled him towards the ballroom.

'You look terrified,' she said, but it was not terror. Her hand was hot and urgent in his and the promise it signalled buzzed through him like a shot of electricity.

8.

The boy – he said his name was Jack – Muriel was dancing with had a big, wide mouth that was sort of lop-sided, and pale orange eyelashes and eyebrows, and the way he was looking was burning right into her.

He held her in a tight squeeze, and his hands dug quite hard into her back.

'Bunch of squares, eh, beautiful?'

She laughed. 'I'm no square,' she said.

'No, I bet you're not,' he said.

But in the middle of the dance, his hands slackened, his gaze was roving about the room. Across the floor on the chairs, she saw where it rested. There was Arthur Silver, the son of that harridan of a grocer, and Peter's sister, Verity. Muriel and Miss La-di-da Frost had been friends of a sort when they were young but that hadn't lasted beyond the war. Back to their own worlds after that. She saw the way Arthur bent his head towards Verity and she could feel in her body the way that this American was drawn across the ballroom floor to the gawky girl in the pale blue dress. She wondered if Verity had any idea of his interest. Probably not. She was a haughty one, thought herself too good for round here. Well, they can't both have her. They'll realise soon enough that neither of them are from the right kind of world for her anyway.

Verity Frost reminded Muriel of one of the horses she rode, and she imagined the other girl dancing like a horse too, thudding up and down like a shire. The boys – they were like dogs chasing after her, wagging their tails. She'll kick them with her back hooves, Muriel thought gleefully.

But she, Muriel, was from the sea. She was nothing like any of them – she was moveable and fluid like water.

Oh, but it was Midsummer, dark green fritillaries plucked the nectar from the dune flowers, sea bindweed blushed pink in the dunes, black-beaked avocets sucked up bugs from the sand and shrieked over their chicks. And there went sweet, heartsick Arthur, with his puppy's eyes, out of the ballroom.

It was steaming and clammy among the sweaty bodies. She was hot and she needed some air.

9.

The band was attempting to play rock and roll songs with their fast beats. They sat out on one of the faster ones and watched some of the bolder couples jiving. Arthur didn't care that he couldn't do it for the life of him. He had a lemonade, spiked by Peter from his second hoard. He had a cigarette, and next to him he had Verity. They were not touching but she was flushed and happy from the dancing and close enough for him to smell her heady scent and to feel possessed of it.

Leaning back in his chair, he surveyed the dancers. In the throng he spotted Muriel, spinning around with one of the many Americans. He'd forgotten she'd told him she would be here. Peter was over with a group of them playing up to their idea of an English gentleman farmer. He seemed to be finding them as hilarious as they found him. Arthur imagined him talking about hunting, fishing and the wonder and mystery of Norfolk. Watching Peter's countryman act gave him again the twinge of fear for his friend. There was truth in it but it was a stereotype of the masculine country gent that hid the real Peter. This was the Peter who cared more about the cows he milked than killing animals for sport. He turned back to the dance.

Muriel's legs were moving so fast it hurt his eyes to watch them. She was wearing a white polka dot dress with a red sash, which matched her red lips. She caught his eye and waved at him. He raised a hand involuntarily.

'Is that Muriel Gittings?' said Verity.

'Yes,' he said, still watching.

'I'm surprised she's here.'

He smiled to himself. Verity's mouth twitched.

'I think they invited all the young people, Ver, not just the debutantes.'

'I'm not a deb.'

He laughed. 'No, but you act like one.'

She looked at him quickly, the pinkness in her cheeks heightened. 'I know you think I'm a frightful snob, Arty, but we are quite… different.'

'We didn't used to be.'

'Oh, I didn't mean you, you're…'

'What am I?'

She was quite pink now and he was rather enjoying her discomfort. 'You're very dear to me,' she said quietly and took out a packet of cigarettes from her little bag.

He pinched her arm. 'Am I dear enough to dance with?'

She laughed. 'Yes, but if you don't mind, I'm quite fagged. Happy just to sit out for a bit.'

Someone else was dancing with Muriel now. They whirled out of sight behind the other dancers but then they came back into view, the two of them laughing. He saw it was Jack. The American gave him an ironic salute and Arthur half raised a hand in reply.

'Funny how we're in thrall to them when we know they're up to something deadly.'

'In thrall to whom?'

'The Americans. "Sleepwalking into the Apocalypse." It would make a good headline, don't you think?'

Verity's face was stiff, her cigarette held hanging in the air.

'What is it?'

'Nothing,' she said. 'Shall we go and get a drink?' She stood up, the blue dress rustling, and held out her arm rigidly for him to take.

At the trestle table where the lemonades were set out, she found an old school friend and they started gossiping about mutual acquaintances. Arthur found Peter in a corner holding court to a group of American servicemen on the superior merits of cricket as opposed to baseball. Jack was talking to an older US officer. He spotted Arthur and hailed him but Arthur waved and slipped out to the hallway. It was subdued in comparison to the ballroom, no footmen waiting for them now.

Outside, it was still light, although it must have been past nine o'clock. All along the driveway and away to his right, he noticed there were glass bulbs strung up in the gardens, glowing pale yellow in the slight dimming of the night. Here and there, couples were strolling among them, drinks in their hands, lit up softly like people in a painting.

'Pretty, isn't it?' It was Muriel. She came and stood next to him in the porch. 'Midsummer's Night an' all.'

'Aren't you cold?' She was just in her dress, her thin white arms exposed. It was cooler now; a slight breeze was catching the trees and ruffling the young leaves.

'I'm fine, got this,' she said, and held up her cigarette. But he took his jacket off and put it around her shoulders.

'You're a gentleman, Arthur Silver, I always said you were.' How much easier it would be for him if he was a real gentleman. 'Now are you going to tell me about the service or do I have to make it up myself?'

'There's not much to tell—' He stopped himself. 'Sorry, it's just that I never went anywhere interesting. Just Yorkshire and Scotland. They did teach us to turn bed corners. And I know a lot about venereal disease.'

Her face burst open in a cackle of laughter. He smiled, pleased with the effect.

'Did you meet any girls then?'

'No,' he said quickly, but his face felt warm. It was as if she could see into his head and see him, flesh exposed, and the girl, the prostitute, on her back. Muriel narrowed her eyes. His mind flashed with images of the girl with the scar, the dim room, her stockings hanging over the chair. 'Never got the chance to put my learning into action,' he said, trying to make a joke of it.

'Now, Arthur, be honest, are you courting Miss Frost? I saw you with her, sitting out. Don't she like dancing?' She was looking up at him with a mock innocence, an almost-smirk at the corners of her mouth.

'We did dance, at the beginning. I'm not very good, you know. I did tell you.'

'All Englishmen say they can't dance. It's because they don't try. The Americans are no better but at least they give it a go. What about that Verity then? You always liked her.'

He wondered why she was so keen on finding out.

'We're not courting really, just friends. I've known her a long time. But you know that.'

He wanted to ask her about Jack. Why was she dancing with him?

'Pinnicky, that one.'

'What?'

'Gets her knickers in a twist. Oh, I don't mind her, she's all right. Don't think she cares much for me.'

'Oh no—' he started to say but Muriel dismissed him with a wave of her hand.

'Too good for the likes of me, she is. Maybe for you too.' He became aware of her eyes on him. 'What about you then? Go on. I don't believe the service was completely dull. You don't want to tell me, do you?' She was appraising him, her head slightly to one side, trying to work something out.

'What is it?'

'You look different. Older.'

'Do I?' He laughed awkwardly. With some relief he heard the door creak open and a blast of bright light and music fell on them both.

He was slow to turn, dulled by the uncomfortable penetration of Muriel's gaze. He thought she wanted to say more to him but it was too late now.

'There you are… Oh, hello, Muriel.' Verity was framed in the doorway, half in obscurity, half in brightness, her face shining.

The three of them stood still, and then all at once they moved and spoke at the same time. Muriel took off the jacket, handed it to Arthur and skipped back; Verity stepped forward and took her place on the step. Arthur was left hovering, holding his jacket.

'She's after you, you know,' said Verity, lighting up a cigarette.

'What? Muriel?'

'Yes, you dozy thing, Muriel.' She ruffled his hair and his scalp prickled. She gave him one of her indulgent smiles. 'It's glorious, isn't it?' she said, and stubbed out her cigarette with her heel. She took his hand, pulling him down off the porch into the garden. 'Come with me.' Her eyes were white in the twilit haze. He glanced back. Watching from the doorway was Muriel. She gave him a little wave and turned towards the ballroom. A figure came towards her from the shadows, but Verity was tugging on his hand and he was forced to look away.

'Look,' Verity said. 'There.' He saw that her finger was pointing above the bush. In the peach glow of the twilight, hundreds of moths were twirling, criss-crossing each other, their wings flickering light, fluttering like the girls' dresses inside. The sky above them hung like a swollen parachute waiting to collapse and he detected a faint smell of swimming pool chlorine. They watched the moths as he ran his fingers along the veins in her wrist. He felt Muriel's gaze tingle on the back of his neck. A faint rumble of thunder came from away towards the coast.

First a drop came, then another, until soon rain was falling, splashing gently onto the patio at the side of the house, darkening the stone, and onto the leaves of the trees and the glass bulbs, sending up haloes of light against the sudden dusk. Girls holding little jewelled bags above their heads ran shrieking, ahead of their stumbling partners, for the house.

'This way,' said Verity, grabbing his hand. He caught a spark of her wide, white eyes.

She led him back towards the drive, to a maze of trees. As

he was pulled along, the entire scene was lit up by lightning, caught in a neon, motionless flash. Instinctively, he looked back. There, standing in the doorway where Muriel had been a few moments before, was Jack. He was wearing a sly smile.

Arthur held on tight to Verity's hand. When they stopped running he heard her shallow breathing and felt it hot on his neck. They were standing in some kind of arboretum, trees twined above them, a bower of dripping green. It formed a cocoon, a verdant cave where they could hide, unseen, from the drive or the house. Jack surely couldn't see them in here. Above them now, a low, deep rumble of thunder. They were soaked, their clothes stuck to them, but her face was radiant with laughter. The rain dropped off the trees pitter-patter onto the leaves above them, and the sweet smell of earth suffused the arbour. She smelt faintly of something dark, less of the perfume now. She'd been drinking. He kissed her mouth and it tasted of whisky. She submitted to the kisses. It felt as if she returned them. He touched his lips along the line of her jaw and then down her beautiful, long neck and along her collarbone, damp with the heat and then the rain.

She put something cold into his hand. It was Peter's hip flask.

'Where'd you get that?'

'Stole it,' she said. 'Peter's too busy chattering away to Americans to notice. Go on, have some.'

He swallowed some of the whisky, let it slide down his throat and vibrate through his head. On the side of the flask it said, etched into the silver:

Peter John Frost
17th February 1951

'Peter's twenty-first,' Arthur said. He had a memory of Verity against the bark of a tree in her dark, moonless garden – kissing her cold mouth in the gloom, the smell of wet oak trees, the figures from the party silhouetted in the downstairs windows of the house. Peter's birthday party had been only a few months before Mrs Frost was found on a deserted stretch of beach by the bottom field, in nightclothes.

'Arthur,' Verity said, and he was immediately alert. Her voice was breathy and fevered, not arch and brittle as usual. It seemed to be a sign of a change; an end to the tortuous dance between childhood friendship and adult sex. What that actually meant beyond tonight and the immediate future he didn't care. She was not too good for him, like Muriel said.

In the distance he heard something humming. At first he thought it was the thunder echoing from far away and ignored it. But as his fingers fumbled with the back clasps of her dress, he realised she was not moving. She was concentrating, listening. He listened too, his fingers hovering. It was hard to tell if the rain had stopped as the bushes were still dripping with water. It wasn't thunder. It was an engine. The hum grew louder until there was no other sound, drowning out the drip drip of the raindrops. Then it stuttered and stopped.

Dappled light lay on Verity's hair and collarbone, like jewels. He stroked the nape of her neck but she twitched.

'What is it?' he whispered and he felt her shake her head.

He kissed her again and willed the silence to continue.

Surely the intruders would go inside. Against his mouth her veins pulsed.

'Arthur! Come out from where you've hidden yourself!' It was Peter's voice, booming through the stillness, followed by another male voice, distinctly American.

'Hey, Art, I got something to show you!'

Jack. He didn't move.

'They're calling for you,' she whispered.

'Ignore them. They can't find me,' he said, and kissed her shoulder. She shuddered and sighed. Her hand rested on his head and came down to his face. He took it, held it tight and reached for her mouth. All was quiet. The men must have gone into the house.

But as they kissed, a voice – Jack's – called out, 'Art!' and she pulled her mouth away. He held onto her hand, reluctant to allow the air to come between them.

'I can't. Not with them there. I can't.'

'Ignore them,' he whispered, close to her face.

'Where the hell are you, Art?' The sound reverberated through the trees.

'We can't,' she said, and that was final. 'You should go.'

His hand fell away from Verity's dress and he straightened up. 'I'll see you later then.'

She nodded, but she wasn't looking at him.

He wanted to kiss her again but he couldn't bring himself to.

'Sorry,' she said, into the dark green of the trees.

He left her in the hidden grove and, immune to the wet leaves brushing his face, burning with rage at his so-called friends who had interrupted him and at her for letting them, he came out to the driveway.

'Just grabbing some air,' he said, trying to slow down his breathing.

'Taking you for a spin, old chap,' said Jack, grinning at him as if he knew exactly what Arthur had been doing.

The motorcycle gleamed wet from rain and the lights on the driveway. A knot of onlookers had gathered at the door and on the gravel drive, admiring, as if at some spectacular show. Peter was in the shadow of the bike but Arthur caught his expression as Jack revved the engine. He looked wounded, as if he'd received a punch to the guts.

Alone in the trees, the memory of Arthur's mouth still on her lips, her tongue and her skin, Verity heard the roar of the engine fade into the night. She stayed where she was until she was sure the motorcyclists had disappeared and Peter had gone back inside.

She'd not been aware of the drop in temperature until now. Goosebumps covered her bare arms and her hair was hanging wet about her face. She found her sodden shawl under a bush, shook it out and pulled it, shivering, around her. It was strange to need clothes after so many long weeks of them clinging to her body, wet with perspiration, or flung off and left abandoned and crumpled. She must go back to the dance. The other girls might notice she had gone. Light had drained from the garden, leaving dark shapes and rain dripping off the glass bulbs that draped from the trees, and the sky was deepening into pink and grey streaks. A strong smell of earth rose with steam from the rain-soaked garden. The driveway was deserted, the gravel shining and a fine drizzle lit up sparkling in the hazy glow from the string of lights along it. It was black at the end of the drive. They were out there somewhere, Arthur and Jack, on the motorcycle. There was a kind of thrill at the thought of them roaring through the night, and a thrill at the thought of her hidden in the trees with Arthur's mouth on hers – but a fear too.

Returning to the ballroom, she felt on show at first, as if everyone must know where she had been, then she realised that no one had noticed her absence and she could watch them instead. For a few long minutes she stood shivering in a corner surveying the dancing. They were all there, the local girls and boys, the shiny pastels of the girls' dresses swirling round the boys' clumsy legs. Farmers and fishermen scrubbed up for the night. The uniforms of the Americans were a dashing navy, but none of them, she noted, as interesting as Jack. She felt far removed even from the girls she knew from her school days. For all their talk they were not the kind of girls to *do* anything. They would wait. And maybe one of the smarter boys, a vicar's son or something, would court them, or even one of the more educated Americans, but it would be the usual dull courtship, ending in the usual dull marriage.

Verity couldn't help but smile at her secrets. Yet she squirmed. Standing shivering in the dripping trees as the engine revved and faded, she recalled Jack catching sight of her, lit by the rectangle of golden yellow fallen across the drive from the open door. How long had he been there? Had Jack seen them together, her and Arthur? His face told her he had, that he'd seen right through the trees and caught her being kissed by Arthur. It gave her a terrible sense of nakedness as if he must know what she really was. But at the same time, maybe she wanted him to know; maybe she wanted to be known. She felt as if she was teetering on the edge of a cliff. About to fly or fall.

A muffled cry came from in front. Clutching onto Jack's back, Arthur couldn't make it out.

'What?'

Jack turned. Arthur caught the words 'Miss Frost', but the rest was lost in the roar of the wind rushing past his ears, the throb of the engine like a miniature aeroplane and the pounding of his own blood. His insides felt like they were flying out behind him and the cold air snapped on his face as they hurtled along deserted country lanes. Arthur had been on a motorbike before in basic training, but not like this. Not at this speed, on these roads. Jack took them out on the coast road towards Cromer, through the tiny villages of Stiffkey and Cley. In one of them, a man walked out of the pub and had to step back into the doorway as they sped past. 'Terribly sorry, sir!' Jack called.

With Verity listening in the shadows there, he felt he couldn't refuse getting on the bike. He felt bad for Peter – he clearly idolised Jack. But Peter was vulnerable.

As they drove back through Wells and out the other side, he forgot about his friend and remembered why people loved motorbiking. He'd taken a few rides on one of the other recruits' bikes back on the service. It was the freedom. So much more electrifying than his old pushbike. This was what flying felt like. He remembered the old game of pilots he had played with Peter and that one sickening, exhilarating trip on the plane in training – the smell of petrol mixed with his own sweat. Jack, of course, knew all about real flying. It seemed oddly fitting that the usurping American had all this experience, but he, an Englishman who had the misfortune not to be born into the right class, did not. Behind them, the sun had long since sunk into the Wash. It was that strange time on a Midsummer night when it should have been dark but wasn't. Grey rainclouds moved across a pale, cold sky and the flints of the buildings they flew past sparked golden in the leftover light.

Jack turned and winked at him. For God's sake, man, face front, stop showing off. Was he drunk? He bloody hoped not.

At Salthouse, the road opened to the sky, and to the left of them the marsh grasses swayed in the wind, rippling down to the sea. Arthur felt a surge of dizzying euphoria edged with fear.

A young American was asking Verity to dance. He was pimply and gauche, and the others were gone – she wanted to say no. But there was nothing for it, all the other girls she knew were dancing, she might as well warm up. The band was playing all the big band American favourites, Count Basie, Glenn Miller, that sort of thing. No more jiving.

After her second dance, she looked up at the clock. It was almost midnight. The band had switched to a slow beat and the shadowy dancers slumped onto each other, the lucky ones' arms entwined, the unlucky ones seeking solace in each other's company, determined not to show their disappointment. She no longer wanted to dance.

Arthur and Jack weren't back yet. They must still be

messing about outside with the stupid motorbike. It made her nervous, the thought of them on the machine together. The excitement she'd felt earlier lingered but it was souring. She slipped off to the powder room and inspected her reflection in the glass. She smoothed her hair and wiped a few dots of black from under her eyes where the rain had streaked her mascara and reapplied her lipstick. In the mirror she saw that her hand was shaking. They would surely be back by midnight. What *was* she so het up about? It was Jack's eyes when he looked right through the arbour to where she stood. In his eyes a challenge – but a challenge to what? Maybe she was imagining it. It had been half dark and she'd drunk too much. But she couldn't get it out of her head, that he was taunting her, daring her to respond. And now Arthur was out in the darkness with this madman. And she couldn't help but feel that she'd brought it all about herself.

Jack swerved, braked suddenly and veered right, inland. The lanes curled along the edges of fields, deeper into the countryside. Arthur was tired. He thought of Verity back in the garden of the Hall, her face damp with rain, droplets in her hair. He imagined her dancing, the blue dress creating an arc around her, another man touching her bare arms.

Jack turned his head to say something. With a high hedge blocking the wind, Arthur caught the words, 'You keen on Verity Frost?'

He clenched his jaw. 'No!' he shouted, without thinking.

Jack seemed to nod, then turned back with the flash of a grin. He revved the engine and though the road was even more twisty than along the coast, he sped up, faster and faster, cutting corners, low to the ground, almost skimming the tarmac. As they swung round each bend, with each lurch Arthur questioned what on earth Jack was doing. It was as if he was trying to throw them both off, trying to scare him. Trying to scare him off Verity. He didn't want to show his fear, but he couldn't help gripping Jack's back harder. They passed so close against the hedges, drops of water cascaded onto his knuckles. Birds flapped up from the trees in a rush of alarm. The light at the front of the bike swept out ahead of them, like a lighthouse beam in a rough sea. Back inland, hidden from the coast, darkness began to seep into the domain, fields merging with the sky. Arthur's hair was pushed back from his forehead by the force of the wind. His face was wet with fine mizzle. His arms ached with the effort of holding on. Each corner and jolt of the bike churned his stomach and made him tense for the impact of a fall.

Jack didn't slow down. Was he doing it deliberately? Arthur remembered his face in the door of the hall. What was Jack trying to prove? He didn't want to frighten Arthur. He wanted to damage, to hurt, to maim him.

On an empty lane, heading west, Arthur saw the Hall up ahead, sick with relief. He wanted to get off the bike alive. Jack wanted him dead.

Without warning, Jack swerved violently to the right. In the thin headlight beam a flash of movement and colour. Something orange flew across the road. The bike skidded, out of control, along the lane. There was no time to do anything. He braced himself to hit the ground, still clinging on tightly to Jack as if they would go down together. But at the last moment, he let go and fell alone, spinning, into darkness.

The clock said eleven forty-five. Something must have gone wrong. 'Just a short spin,' she'd heard Jack say to her brother, but they had been gone longer than that, too long, now. She picked at a pork pie and sipped her ginger beer, gazing at the door, willing them to return. The hip flask was empty and she was thinking how she would very much like another dose of her brother's whisky, when Peter himself streaked out of the room.

'Peter, what is it?' she called, running after him.

'Fellow told me there's been an accident.'

They ran together out onto the driveway. It was dark now and a steady drizzle fell. The driveway made a tunnel of darkness. The hanging lights looked forlorn without the chattering couples illuminated beneath. From inside the Hall came the low, slow hum of the final tunes of the night.

'What did he say?' She looked around her as if the empty scene could give her some answers.

Peter peered at her quizzically. She must sound desperate. 'Just that someone's been hurt. Two chaps, out on the road. Bad crash, apparently.'

'One of them or two of them?' She tried to make herself sound calm. One, Peter thought, but he didn't know which one. The man who found them, out for an evening drive in his recently purchased motorcar, was in the Hall now, making a telephone call. Someone else from the dance had run out to the scene of the crash. He was bringing them back, Peter said. There was nothing they could do. She had an image of a bloodied head and a broken, limping body. It alternated between the two of them. One of them. It was only one. It shouldn't matter which one it was. Yet she knew with a nauseous inevitability that she ought to be concerned about Arthur. She had been kissing him just a few hours ago! But the face of the injured man in her head would not rest on Arthur. It kept turning into the bright-haired American.

'God, will you stop pacing up and down, you're making me nervous,' said Peter.

'Shut up, Peter.' She lit a cigarette, hesitated, then offered one to her brother.

'Did you get these from Jack?' he said accusingly.

'I might have done. What do you care?'

His long body visibly bristled and she saw a flash of pain on his face. He *did* care. She scrambled in her head for something to say but nothing materialised. Then from the end of the driveway tunnel came the noise of feet on the gravel.

From the gloom, two men appeared on the drive. They were holding up another man, hanging down between them like the carcass of an animal. His hair hung limp, orange-red in the yellow pools of light. Blood dripped onto the gravel in neat red dots.

She must have called out his name because Peter grabbed hold of her. He held on fast and she remembered almost tipping forward but she didn't hear herself saying anything. One of the men carrying the body looked up. It was Arthur. She caught his eyes and there was anger and hurt in them. She saw immediately what she had done, in her thoughtless, idiotic way. A gust of rain blew across her face, clearing her head, and she knew she mustn't act like a fool. She broke from Peter's grasp and ran to Arthur and held onto his arm.

'What happened? Are you all right?' she garbled at him, more words tumbling out.

'Crash – he swerved – bike's in a ditch. Jack needs an ambulance.'

'Other fellow's already called. It's on its way. Let's get him inside,' Peter was saying. Thank God he was there to take charge. He didn't seem drunk any more.

Jack lifted his head, bloodied and streaked with dirt. She heard her own intake of breath. He looked up at her, his eyes shining and with a twisted smile on his gouged, red-streaked face.

A scattering of dancers were drawn to the scene. Peter, Arthur and a group of other men made their way through the throng and laid out the invalid on the floor of the hallway. Through the open door to the ballroom, the band was still playing and shadow couples were swaying, unaware of the commotion outside. Verity stayed with the group in the hallway, unable to leave the scene. Muriel was there too: she'd appeared with the others and barged through and started bossing them around. Verity could do nothing. She was torn with anger at Jack for his arrogance and at Arthur for letting him do it. But most of all, at herself, for shouting out the damned American's name. Why did she do that?

Arthur was bruised and cut, and his clothes torn but he was walking at least. He sat on a chair someone fetched for him and took a cigarette with trembling hands. Someone else brought him a drink of water. Jack, on the other hand, had clearly broken something. He was propped up against the gold-leafed vine-patterned wallpaper of the hallway.

There were trickling lines of blood from his face down his neck, and onto the blue collar of his uniform. He submitted cheerfully to Muriel's ministrations while the rest of them looked on uselessly. Muriel wiped Jack's face gently with a cloth and picked out gravel from his cheeks and Verity hated the busy, confident hand that touched his face. She knew she should go and sit with Arthur. It was the right thing to do. It should have been her who fetched him the chair and the drink. She tried to tell herself that he didn't need her, that he was fine. It was natural for her to be concerned for Jack. If she could just make light of it, it would be all right. It was a trifle. But instead she hovered at the back of the crowd, watching the American. Arthur turned away from her and she felt rejected even though she had failed to go to him. She knew what she should do but she couldn't do it. Her jaw was clenched so tightly, little jags of pain shot down her neck.

When the ambulance came, the crowd fell back and drifted into the ballroom. Peter went with the invalid and she hung back. The ambulance man was talking to her brother.

'Is he going to be all right?' she said, thinking of only a year before, running down to find Peter and him turning her back to the house. Knowing something was wrong but not believing him when he said their mother was dead. How did it happen? she'd asked him, and he said she must have got out of her depth.

Behind her, someone crunched on the gravel and she looked around expecting to see Arthur but no one was there. She watched the ambulance leave. In the ballroom, the band was striking up a rendition of a Perry Como song.

Someone asked her to dance and she shook her head. She looked around for Arthur and saw that another American was handing him a flask. She must do something. It was becoming harder to pretend nothing was wrong.

She moved over to him and touched him tentatively on the shoulder. 'Are you all right, Arty?'

'Couldn't be better,' he slurred.

'Don't be silly,' she said, alarmed at the bitter tone, as if it was directed at her. As if he *knew* the disloyal thoughts she'd had. A burst of anger flared through her that he should make her feel like this. 'You've had a shock. Why don't I take you home?' She sounded impatient. Her fingers touched his arm but instead of responding to her in kind, he shivered and she withdrew as if the tips of her fingers had been singed.

'I'm fine,' he said.

Helplessly, she cast about for something to say. Was it only that she had called out Jack's name? It did not seem, in itself, so very awful. Yet it was clear that she had done something terribly wrong and could not undo it. That she had somehow created this entire, disgusting mess. The moment that she and Arthur had shared under the trees was long gone, so far away it was like a different night. 'Arthur,' she started miserably, but couldn't finish. The recriminations and unsaid apologies hung in the air. She felt nauseous. 'Shall I help you get home?' she tried again. 'I really think you should go home.' She wanted to go home herself now, was all of a sudden overcome with tiredness and guilt and confusion.

'I'm worried about you,' she said, although she was just as worried about herself.

PART 2

FLOW

October
Four months before the flood

Deep depression
Early morning frost and fog
Squally showers followed by persistent rain in the evening
Waxing gibbous moon

1.

'Bloody hell, if he doesn't come soon, he can't come at all. There are rules, you know. They are there for a damned good reason.'

It was well into the shooting season and Arthur and Peter were in the boot room, strapping up for the day's shoot. Mr Frost and his group of local farmers were still in the dining room, discussing the prospects for the day over an early breakfast. Peter was jumpy. They were, once again, waiting for Jack.

'He'll be here,' Arthur said. He would be quite happy if he never saw Jack again. He had a bitter taste in his mouth at the mention of the American or the airbase. But it was only he who felt like that – everyone said that whatever they were doing must be for our own good – so he kept his thoughts to himself. The naïvety of it! And Jack was always present. Always the three of them, never just he and Peter, and the latter only seemed animated when Jack was there.

'You'll never guess what I found out about the base.' He waited for Peter to bite.

'They're all spies?' said Peter, laughing.

Arthur smiled to himself. Something like that. The local lad at the Shipwright's had been quite a talker when he'd had his tongue loosened with a free pint or three. 'My source tells me they're carrying atomic bombs.'

Peter stood up. 'Your source?' he said, amused.

'It's not funny. Do you know that most of the scientists who worked on the Manhattan Project are against nuclear armaments? Einstein himself has warned of the dangers. He talked about it on American TV a couple of years ago. He said the idea of security through nuclear weapons was a dangerous illusion. I know it sounds apocalyptic but it *is*. He's talking about the annihilation of life on earth for God's sake, Peter.'

'Is he?' He sighed theatrically. 'Though I'm sure I heard that the Americans think old Albert is something of a fellow traveller—'

'That's bloody ridiculous, Peter. They say that about anyone who gets in their way,' Arthur snapped.

Peter shrugged. 'I suppose you think Jack knows—'

'Of course he knows, Peter, he flies the bloody planes, doesn't he?'

'You're rather harsh on our mutual friend, Art old boy.'

'Don't call me Art, *Pete*,' he said petulantly. 'I think you're a bit smitten, *old boy*.' His teeth were clenched together.

Peter stared at him, his mouth twitching. For a horrible moment, the two of them faced each other as if across a trench.

'You sound envious, Arthur. It's not an attractive quality.' Then Peter smiled, his open, sweet smile that Arthur knew from childhood, and lightly punched Arthur on his shoulder. 'I'm sure you're right about the nefarious goings on at Holkham.'

'There's more, I think,' Arthur said, wanting to move

on from the awkwardness. 'There's something else. I think they're carrying bombs *and* they're spying on the Soviets—'

'Don't we want them to be doing that, old boy?'

'But if the Yanks have hidden all this, what else could they be hiding?'

'Christ, we're all doomed then, aren't we?' said Peter, sarcastically, running his hand through his hair.

'But Peter, don't you see? We *are*. It's real. The threat is real. We'll be a target for the Soviets. Think about it – how safe is Holkham? Can you imagine what might happen if there's an accident...' But he trailed off. It was pointless continuing. Peter didn't want to hear him or believe him. He must think he was paranoid.

'God, if he doesn't get here soon, his shoot'll be doomed.'

'Whose shoot?' Verity had appeared and was leaning against the doorway. She was wearing a dark polo neck which made her skin luminescent and her eyes darker. Although on the surface she gave nothing away, her body was arched towards Arthur, her breasts sticking out under the tight wool of her sweater just above his eyeline. But perhaps he was imagining it. He wanted everything to be how it had been before the dance at Harborough Hall, but in his worst moments, it felt as if everything had been destroyed.

The sudden summer storm had dissipated the heat and, with it, their closeness. He pictured her rain-soaked in the dripping blue dress. Such a strange night. He remembered feeling dizzy and sick after the crash. It was incredible to think they were all here as if nothing had happened.

And everyone was so concerned about Jack after the crash. Poor Jack, everyone said, and he, Arthur, was forgotten, because *he* had not broken his nose or twisted his ankle. The ass hadn't even *broken* his ankle. You'd have thought Jack had smashed all his bones the way people went on. And no one cared that he'd had to endure the wild, drunken driving of a lunatic on dark, wet country lanes. The idiot could have killed them both. Jack said, 'Forgive me,' but he never said sorry. No, *he* hadn't broken anything. It was galling how people like that always got away with everything.

'Jack,' Arthur told her and she raised her eyebrows a little, nothing more, but he felt a familiar nausea.

'Oh well, I can't stop, got to cram.'

'Do you really think they'll let you in?' said Peter, standing now, boots on. The Oxford entrance was imminent. Verity had passed all her exams with decent grades and seemed to have spent most of the summer cramming for the entrance exam.

'Oh bugger off,' she said to her brother, and to Arthur, 'See you at the lunch after.'

'You can't come to that,' said Peter. 'You're a girl and you're not shooting!'

'I shall be there. You can't stop me. Bye, Arthur!'

Outside, Peter grumbled on about the rules and whether he'd beat his father's tally this year. All Arthur could think about was feeling along the line of Verity's chest and down to the bottom of her sweater, lifting it up and touching the skin beneath. He was imagining her interest in Jack; she hadn't looked at all bothered about whether he was coming. If she failed to get in to Oxford – and of course he didn't want that, he was just imagining another scenario

– then he would take her to London. They would marry in secret, find digs, he would get a job as a cub reporter on a paper... but it was hard to keep this narrative going with the thin mist of a sea-fret in his face. God, how he wished himself back in the house with her rather than out in the dreary drizzle of the autumn morning, wearing a preposterous outfit cobbled together from Peter's cast-offs. Peter was well over six feet tall, rangy and thin. He, on the other hand, was significantly shorter and stockier. The cap was fine, but the bloody trousers had had to be turned up by his mother and she'd gone too high. They looked all wrong: tight round the thighs, flapping around his ankles. His shoes were wrong too. They were his black work shoes, polished to a high shine, whereas everyone else had old brown brogues.

They walked out into the stubble, and as they did, the weak morning sun broke through the cloud cover and cast the fields and woods in a sudden golden light, sparkling slightly where it met the sea mist. You could see the sea from up here, a silver streak in the distance.

'Peter?' Mr Frost's deep growl rang out across the quiet fields. He was in charge of the shoot and wouldn't want his son racing ahead to nab the best positions. He had always been competitive about Peter. Perhaps it didn't help that Peter had been a bit of a dunce at school, while his little sister had flourished. Once upon a time, Mr Frost had taunted Peter with Arthur's aptitude for numbers and word-puzzles, and when Arthur had passed his eleven plus and gone to the grammar, Mr Frost had presented him with a *Boys' Compendium of Useful Facts*. 'Keep it up, old boy,' he'd said, but it was rather like a sending off abroad – an exile from which he wouldn't return. You're on your own now, he seemed to say.

They trudged back to the house, where four whiskery old men in tweeds were gathered on the patio at the back of the dining room, their guns crooked under their arms, dogs snuffling at their feet. One of them was De Vere, a portly man with startling, bushy eyebrows. Peter had pointed him out as 'Ver's future father-in-law', which made Arthur want to trip him up and see him sprawled on the stone. A local man, Skitmore, with a wide, pink face in a lop-sided black hat, was acting as gamekeeper. He usually worked for Lord Crake of Harborough, but Mr Frost had a long-standing arrangement with the lord to borrow Skitmore for his little shoots. When Arthur had first seen one of these shoots at the farm, he had felt himself entirely out of place, and although he was used to it now – the language of 'guns' and 'coveys' and 'brace', the outlandish outfits and, inevitably, however bad the day's shoot, the death – he still didn't quite fit.

Verity was by the back door, smoking. Mr Frost bore down on them with a black look.

'What are your plans now then, young man, now you've done your National Service?'

Arthur thought he detected the tell-tale ochre-yellow of liver failure in the man's eyes, something his mother always liked to note in her customers. My mother needs me in the shop at the moment, Sir, but I don't want to stay there forever.'

'No, I should think not. No man should hang around his mother for too long. Seen a bit of the world now, haven't you?'

'Not really, sir. Just Yorkshire and Scotland.'

Mr Frost snorted loudly and a few specks of wine and food sprayed Arthur. 'Same thing. Like a bloody foreign country up there, what?'

Arthur laughed politely. 'But I'd like to. See the world I mean. I thought…' He hesitated. He didn't want to divulge his plans to Mr Frost, but he needed to say something. Verity was watching him closely from under her eyelashes, a possible hint of pink in her cheeks.

'Army,' said Mr Frost.

'What?'

'The Army. Or the Air Force. I heard you were with the RAF in service? Fine way to see the world. They need good men.'

'Keep the Empire going, eh, Father?' said Peter.

Arthur and Peter exchanged the smallest of smiles. This was a favourite hobby-horse of Mr Frost's.

'Whole new world we're in now of course,' continued the old man. 'Atomic warfare. Need to keep up with the damned Yanks and the Reds. Good men needed more than ever.' Arthur thought of the pictures of the cauliflower-shaped cloud over a faraway sea that the newspapers had printed earlier in the month, and then of the airbase up the road with their planes he suspected were carrying A-bombs. The lad at the pub was just a local boy, whose parents put up one of the servicemen in their village near the base. It was only a rumour. But it felt true, and the whole lot of them just allowing it to happen. His other theory, that they were keeping something else secret from the public, was only just forming in his mind. He'd been watching the planes, keeping a record of the comings and goings. Sometimes they flew at night but it made no sense, unless they had something to hide.

'You don't need many men to detonate an atom bomb,' said Arthur, but Mr Frost ignored him as if he hadn't spoken.

'Or finance. Banking. Plenty of your lot in banking. You could do worse.'

'My lot?' He couldn't think of anything to say to that; the words caught in his throat. It was funny how people continued to think of him as Jewish whatever his mother's efforts to blend in. He supposed he looked 'Jewish', whatever that meant.

'*Father*,' said both his children, and Peter grimaced to Arthur.

'I just meant that they do look after each other,' said Mr Frost to Arthur's dismay.

Verity closed her eyes.

Arthur coughed. 'Yes, sir, I'm sure that's true but I had thought of journalism. I always liked writing and I thought if I could find some stories, get some pieces in the local paper, perhaps...' Peter opened his mouth to say something but Mr Frost beat him to it.

'Rum lot, journalists. Liars and crooks, most of them.'

'I'm sure old Arthur here wouldn't be one of those, Father,' said Peter, eyes wide to Arthur, a pained expression on his face.

'No, of course not,' Mr Frost said. 'Still.'

'I think it's a marvellous idea.' Verity was smiling at him. He shot back one of gratitude.

'Yes, rather,' chimed in Peter, 'you should get a story in the *Post* about what the Yanks are up to over at Holkham.'

Arthur thought Verity glanced at Peter then but his friend didn't notice. If only they all knew.

'What's that?' said their father, but Mrs Timms came bustling out to tell them that the American had arrived.

'Ah, we can ask him ourselves. Get him kitted out, will you? We can't wait all day.'

The old men puffed on their pipes while he and Peter went back into the house. Verity disappeared. In the hall outside the boot room, they found her greeting Jack. She started when she saw them come in, and moved back a few inches.

'Sorry I'm late! You're lucky I'm here at all. I've been up all night.' There wasn't a trace of tiredness in Jack's lean face and he looked as alert as ever.

'Where exactly have you been, then?' Arthur blurted out.

Jack raised his pale, ginger eyebrows and gazed coolly at Arthur. He sensed Verity flinch next to him but Jack shrugged and smirked at her. 'Nowhere nearly as interesting as you're imagining, Art, I can assure you.'

'How do you know what I'm imagining, Mister Hillbilly Yankee?' His tone of jollity was strained. He wanted to wipe the satisfied smile off Jack's face. It stuck but the American's eyes widened and stared.

'I think it's fairly obvious you've got a bee in your bonnet about the base.'

'You don't know anything about me, Jack.'

'Nor you, me, *Art*.'

Arthur's fists clenched and he felt the veins in his neck strain. No one moved.

'Chaps, we need to get on with the shoot,' said Peter, hopping from one foot to the next.

'Well, I sure am ready to shoot some birds,' said Jack in a hokey American accent.

The moment had passed but Arthur was left impotent, head reeling, his blood still pumping fast. What was Jack? A redneck rancher or a Yankee? He was determined to ask the boy from the local pub about Jack directly. Get some dirt on him.

Trudging through the courtyard behind the other two, Arthur noted that Jack was wearing his golfing clothes again. This would go down badly with the old man with any luck. But frustratingly, Peter's father put it down to his foreignness and thought it amusing.

'The birds'll see you coming,' he guffawed and the rest of them laughed heartily along with him. 'Go on then, you youngsters, let's see what you can do. Guns aloft, remember. And aim for the cocks, not the hens. And keep quiet.'

They spread out across the fields, fanning out away from the farm until they came to their allotted pegs. The mizzle had evaporated and now a weak autumnal sun warmed Arthur's face. It was lonely shooting. You couldn't speak to anyone, apart from the odd shout, though sometimes it was a relief to be removed from the unspoken separation he felt from all of them. Along the line of guns, he could see Jack down by the pines, his red hair garish in the sun, and further away near the marsh, the long figure of Peter, alert like a bloodhound. In the middle, an old squire on his land, was the tall, imposing figure of Mr Frost. Arthur couldn't tell if the state of the farm's finances weighed him down, but certainly the farmer looked as commanding as he always had. Mr Frost never let them forget he'd seen service in the first war, and in the recent war he'd been on the Home

Guard, a platoon commander shooting at birds. Skitmore had disappeared, along with a few other farm workers, to beat out the partridge and now they were all waiting.

As Arthur looked along the line, Jack raised his hand, a kind of salute. He was thinking about how to respond, when there was a flap, a beating of wings and a flurry of grey in the sky, then a crack, crack, and the first birds fell, spiralling from the sky.

When Skitmore's whistle blew for the end of the first drive, Arthur had bagged six partridge. Not impressive, but at least he'd made a start. They swapped positions for the second drive, and moved down, further away from the farm, towards the most distant fields of barley and wheat. He was close to a line of beech trees, whose leaves were just beginning to yellow. He held his gun raised, waiting for the flutter of a bird to break the emptiness of the sky. But the wind had picked up and clouds were skimming across it, catching the light from the low sun, and the combination of the wind in the trees and the fluttering flashes of light was deceptive. It tricked the mind into thinking there was a bird where there wasn't. Repeatedly, he heard the pop of a gun and nothing fell. Clearly someone was either a bad shot or the light was playing tricks on them too. Ahead of him he saw a flicker of orange. Jack. He raised his gun and squinted along the sight line. The barrel of the gun was level with the back of Jack's head. His middle finger squeezed on the trigger. He heard his own breath. It would be so easy to shoot. Bang. A burst of red. Jack would be gone in a firework of colour. He was dizzy with the thought of it. No one would know. It would be an accident. Unfortunate. Tragic. His finger tingled. Then once, twice, three bundles of feathers flew up and he jerked his gun up and the trigger was pulled. An explosion in his ears and he fell, head spinning, into the scrub of the undergrowth. Another bang rang out, this time above him.

'Halt!'

On the ground, his head was still ringing with a high-pitched whine. The leaves of the beech trees were black silhouettes above him, swaying; the light pulsed, voices shouted. Then above him, a ruddy face. Skitmore.

'What you doin', boy? Shooting off yer gun like that? Coulda hurt someone.' He peered closer. 'You aright?'

He sat up and squinted at the peering, round face of the gamekeeper. 'What happened? The gun—'

'Only that your gun went off, almost had me head off. Oughta be more careful.' But his voice was kind. 'Don't reckon the other lot have noticed, mind. You get back t'the house now; reckon you done enough.'

Skitmore was covering for him and Arthur knew he should be grateful. The man clearly thought he had no idea what he was doing, even though Arthur had been shooting many times before. He thanked Skitmore, trying to take the roughness out of his voice, and started to walk back to the farm, a circuitous route by the beech wood and round to the west, quietly so as to avoid the beaters. As he left the wood, he looked back and saw the distinctive orange of Jack's hair. Even from the distance across the field, he knew Jack was looking straight at him.

'What on earth happened to you today?' Peter sat opposite him, his second or third sherry in his hand.

Arthur's food congealed, uneaten, in front of him. He swallowed the sherry and his thoughts swirled like the liquid and couldn't settle. 'Skitmore thought my gun went off. Something wrong with it.'

'Really? Skitmore knows his stuff. You should get him to look at it.'

He wanted to say to Peter, *I wished him dead*. Had he wanted that? All he could remember was the tremble of his finger on the trigger of the gun and the desire coursing through him to obliterate the American. But would he have done it? And had he even shot the gun?

Whatever had happened, the strength of his sudden rage was disturbing. He didn't understand the exact source of it. Perhaps if he said it out loud, the thick grey clouds of doubt would dissipate and disappear. He wished that he could at least confide in Peter, to tell him his suspicions, his disparate thoughts, coagulating into a sense that the RAF and the US Air Force were keeping things hidden at Holkham. But he'd already tried to tell him and got nowhere, so kept quiet. Peter would just think Arthur was envious of the men at the base, the men who had purpose, unlike him. He, like Peter, had missed his chance. Too young in the war and nothing real happening now, just this fake war with Russia. In stark contrast to Jack's experience, he'd not seen active service, had even managed to miss getting posted to Malaya or Kenya or Korea. Even Cyprus would have been better than the miserable RAF stations he'd spent his service holed up in. And now here he was, stuck in a seaside town with a sick mother. The world was spinning on without him. He needed to make a grab for it.

'Jack said we should go for a chaps' day out to Norwich soon. What do you reckon?' Peter was saying.

Arthur's head spun.

'What for?'

'I don't know.' Peter looked crestfallen at Arthur's distrustful tone. 'Does there have to be a reason?'

Arthur sneered. He knew with Jack there was always a motive. And probably a sleazy one.

At the other end of the table, Verity was sitting next to Jack. She seemed entirely absorbed, her head bent, listening. Arthur found his eyes caught by the picture: the dark head next to the red. As he watched, Jack looked up and smiled at him and Arthur was sure it was a smile of complicity as if they shared a secret. He took a draught of sherry and closed his eyes, imagining the gun going off and shattering the American into a thousand tiny pieces of pink flesh.

2.

The minute she got into the interview room, Verity knew it was doomed. The room was panelled and dark, not unlike her father's study, and the don was short – shorter than her – but he had the same distant air of disapproval that her father had. She tried to answer his questions on the great sweep of Modern History: the Renaissance, the Reformation, the Great Reform Bill. But he gazed at her from under his white eyebrows and his eyelids began to flicker, and finally close. Was he listening? She cared about history – at least, she remembered caring. The dates, all the years and years, the actions and the inactions and the consequences. The millions of dead, piling up, all the names and all the places and the names of the places. The long-dead men and the long-dead ideas lay one on top of the other in a higgledy pile in her head. The sense of order from which she had once taken comfort no longer seemed to be working. And she knew that all the hours over the hot summer when she had been drawing in her sketchbook were hours when the dates and the great men had receded and lost their power over her. She didn't yet know what would take their place.

She stopped talking.

The clock in the don's study ticked on. The don breathed through his nose. Behind him, the mullioned window framed a quadrangle. The leaves on the trees were yellowing and falling, and across the quad strode two students, their black gowns streaming out behind them. They were turned to each other, laughing silently with gaping mouths.

From somewhere came the sound of coughing. The clock ticked. In the window, the students had gone, and in their wake, yellow leaves fluttered in the wind.

A door slammed and the don's eyes flickered open.

'Yes, yes, that will do, Miss...?' And he looked down at the sheet on the table in front of him, to remind himself of her name.

In the train carriage, she looked out of the rain-spattered window and tried to squeeze the tears back in. A stout woman opposite her in an enormous hat offered her a handkerchief, but Verity took out her own and pushed herself closer to the window. The train passed two horses grazing in a field next to the sidings. When she got home, she would take Gyps out and ride and ride. She'd put her face into his mane, feel his unquestioning love for her. She would ride and not come back. This was nonsense of course, but the feeling of something bursting inside her was real.

Out of the window, her eye caught movement. One of the horses was chasing the train, his tail flying out behind him, the other following.

She thought of Jack speeding ahead of her on his bike the first time she saw him after the Midsummer party. It had been late July, after the town carnival. The holiday season was in full swing and she was avoiding the woods.

Sick of mooning about the house, she'd been at the end

of Leafy Lane, approaching the corner of Dogger Lane and the Pilchard pub. She was putting her cardigan around her shoulders when she saw Jack. He was standing side on to her, leaning against the wall of the pub, smoking, wearing a brown leather US Air Force jacket. He was an arresting sight, incongruous in his American clothes next to the old terraced houses. He was scratching the side of his nose and twitching it as if it irritated him. There was the terrible motorcycle, the cause of the destruction. How could he bear to get back on that thing after the accident? Instead of acting quickly and ducking back up the lane to hide, her feet stuck to the ground. What would he look like now? She remembered the bloodied face on the rain-slick driveway and, with grim curiosity, steeled herself to be repulsed. Would he look like one of those soldiers returned from the war with their faces half torn away, the kind one turned away from, too late? And as she was thinking this, her legs moved and brought her within two feet of him.

'Hey,' he said, turning to her with a wide grin, before she had a chance to say anything. 'I thought I might see you.' Across his nose and cheek, a purplish, jagged line had ripped his once unblemished flesh. Although it must have faded it was still so striking, so incredibly stark against his pale skin, she recoiled, and the smile that had responded automatically to his boyish grin stuck fast on her face like a mask.

'Look like the elephant man, don't I?'

'Oh. No. It's not that bad.' She looked away in embarrassment but her eyes were drawn back to him. It should have been unsightly, repellent even, but, perversely, it had the opposite effect. The scarred and torn skin was bizarrely mesmerising. It seemed to highlight the strange ugly-beauty of his face. And he wasn't ashamed either. He was like a tomcat, a pale ginger tom, rakish and battle-scarred, almost proud of his scrapes.

Confused, she said, 'What are you doing here?' She had meant to sound discouraging but she could feel the telltale heat on her cheeks.

'I have half a day's release from the base and was just taking her out for a spin.' He remained in an unconcerned pose, leaning against the motorcycle.

'I see,' she said. Now was the moment to leave, but she didn't move. She felt dizzy.

'Do you want a smoke?'

She took one without thinking and then had to stand and allow him to light it for her and then smoke it. All the time, she was acutely aware of his presence near to her, breathing in the distinct musky smell of his cologne and the petrol from the engine.

In the end, she gave in, as if it was inevitable. She slung her leg over the leather seat in an attempt at nonchalance. But as they sped along the Holkham Road, she clung on in terror. The wind rushed past her face and as long as he kept straight she could almost enjoy the sensation of movement. There was nothing but the sound of the engine in her ears. But then he swung the bike and she felt she was about to be flung off into the marsh.

'Stop!' she shouted into his back, the smell of the leather in her nostrils, but he didn't seem to hear.

Finally he did stop. He swerved to the side of a field and cut the engine. She wobbled and fell off the bike, landing with a thump on the verge.

'You nearly killed me!' she shouted, trying to stand up with shaking legs. It came back to her what Arthur had said at the Midsummer party about Jack trying to kill him.

But he was smiling down at her. He held a hand out and she took it automatically. They stood at the edge of the road facing each other. Behind them, the marsh was a haze of violet from sea aster and sea lavender. She glared at him. 'Sorry,' he said, but his eyes were bright and glittering. She couldn't stop looking at the scarred face.

'I wanted to show you something,' he said. He hadn't even asked if she was all right.

'I don't feel well,' she said, and she did feel nauseous and weak. She had an urge to sit down but there was nothing to lean on except the bike and she couldn't trust that machine. She closed her eyes and waited for the moment to pass. The nausea passed but, coming out of her daze, she was leaning against him and he was holding her up. She could smell Brylcreem underneath the tang of the cologne. Verity pulled back sharply and looked around her. The sun that had seemed so bright minutes ago had disappeared behind grey clouds, tinging them gold. Rain clouds. Deep shadows came across the marshes, turning them a dark blue. The dull light, the dizziness and the loss of control made her panic. How would she get home?

'Come on, I've got something to show you.' He was indicating across the marsh towards the sea. But she was afraid.

'I need to go home now, you promised me only a few minutes, and it's getting late.' She took off the scarf from her hair, tied it back round her neck and started walking away in the direction of the town.

'You're not even going to ask me what it is?'

He sounded young then, and it pulled at something inside her. She almost felt sorry for him. But she sensed this slight power that she had over him could easily be lost. Not on any account could she get back on that bike.

'Maybe you can show me another time,' she called and she was pleased with herself. Tired, aching, two miles from the town, she nonetheless felt a grim satisfaction as she walked. And even when he came up behind her on the road and asked if she was sure she didn't want a ride back to town, she shook her head.

'Another time then, I guess,' he said, looking straight at her in the disconcerting way he had, and she shrugged. 'I come here every week. Sundays usually.' He roared off. As his figure disappeared into the distance, already the incident with the bike was in the past and could be laughed at. She'd had a lucky escape.

'Where on earth have you been?' Mrs Timms had said, through a cloud of flour in the kitchen, when Verity sneaked in the back entrance at home. 'Your father wants a word with you.'

'Just for a walk,' she said.

The train came into Norwich station and she caught the connection for the line to Wells. She was supposed to be meeting Arthur at the hollow tree in the woods, but she didn't want to see him.

At the partridge shoot lunch the other week, Jack had sat next to her telling stories of hunting jackals in the desert. They sounded outlandish, unreal. But she liked listening to his stories anyway. Arthur had been sulky and she found herself wanting to punish him for his downturned mouth and the deep, ingrained ridge between his thick eyebrows. She wanted to make Arthur jealous, to say: *I'm not yours. I can do anything*.

She decided that she would tell Jack, the next time he asked if she'd meet him, that she'd go on the bike again.

3.

November

Verity sat at her mother's dressing table and played with the glittering treasures inside her mother's make-up box. She tried on a Chanel lipstick, a slick of deep red, the colour of glamour. Her lips startled her. Pouting in the glass, she marvelled at how much thicker they appeared, how very bright in her pale face. Joan Crawford in *Sudden Fear*. She didn't look like herself. In the mirror, as she tilted her head slightly to the side, there was a glimmer of her mother. She had grown up thinking they were nothing alike and she could never live up to her mother's delicate beauty. She smiled and it was gone, but it was still not her old self looking back in the glass. What exactly had changed? Perhaps it was failure. Hidden beneath her underwear was the letter from the college. At some point she would have to tell everyone but her shame wouldn't allow it, not yet. Her reflection scowled back. I shall just have to be beautiful, she thought, and that at least made her laugh. But the laugh turned to a sob and she had to gulp back tears. She had put everything into being clever and now she had nothing – no friends, no mother, no one to talk to. Grief came on her quickly. It would hit her on the back of the head and she was powerless to stop it gutting her from the inside out. But she was practised at fighting it back. There was nowhere for the grief to go – she might as well push it down. She soaked the tears up with her handkerchief, wiped her face and reapplied a dab of rouge to hide the blotchy pink patches on her cheeks. She had to get out.

In the long death of the afternoon, her father napped by the fire, drained brandy glass by his side, and Peter was God-knows-where, probably hurling wood onto the bonfire for later that evening, so no one noticed her slipping out. She'd primed them anyway by casually mentioning that she was taking Gyps for a ride. She led her horse out of the paddock as a deterrent against getting on Jack's machine, and was therefore irritatingly early. He was not there and she had a moment of doubt. He'd said two o'clock, Sunday, hadn't he? She was sure he had. Now she thought of it, the actual arrangement of this... *rendezvous* had been made in such haste she wasn't entirely sure *what* he'd said. In her post-interview funk, she'd contrived to speak to him one time he was down at the paddock with Peter.

'I've decided I'd like to have a go on your motorcycle after all,' she'd said under her breath. 'But not a word to anyone or they won't let me.'

He'd nodded, grinning, and said a time and day. But her heart had been beating so hard in her ears she wasn't certain of any of what he'd said now.

It was so quiet out on the Holkham Road. The only sounds, the caw of distant gulls and Gypsy's quiet snorts and tapping of his hooves. No sign of human life. And then the hush of the grey Sunday afternoon was rent by the screeching engine of Jack's motorbike. It came quickly and she only just had time to compose her features into a look of unconcern. She was very aware of the deep, pinky-red smear on her mouth.

He stopped in front of her and she was struck anew by the compelling, animal beauty of his face. He was smiling with wry amusement and his eyes glittered, his hair as bright and coppery as ever, even in the dullness of the day. On the left side of his face the trace of the scar.

'I knew you'd come,' he said, turning off the engine.

It was almost enough for her to spin on her heels and escape back up the lane. 'I wasn't going to...' she spluttered.

'I'm glad you came. You brought your *horse*? You're not going to be able to outride me on it.' He was understandably surprised. After all, she'd said she wanted to go on the bike. But his shock seemed out of place. It didn't square with his supposed familiarity and ease with horses.

'*Him*. I'm quite fast, actually,' she said.

'I bet you are,' he said, and an electric pulse ran through her. She wanted to be angry but she had no time to react as he had already started up the engine and was off down the street with a wave and a shout. 'Come on, I've got something to show you!'

She had to work poor Gyps hard to keep up with the figure disappearing into the distance but then gave in and slowed to a canter. It would be better to arrive unruffled than sweaty and red-faced. Away from the town, the sky opened up, a bleached-out, oppressive white-grey, wide over the flat, bare fields, the only colour the rust-brown rippling across distant trees. It made her temples ache to look at the sky. She hadn't ridden out in this direction for an age and she wondered why. There had not been enough of anything since her mother died. They were suspended, stuck. Despite the melancholy of the autumn landscape, it was good to feel the horse's flanks. The ache in her thighs from gripping Gyps, the sting on her cheeks and even the endless nothing of the land – it didn't matter. There was movement, towards something. Above her, a flock of migrant geese swooped, curved and disappeared out to sea.

When she saw him in the distance she almost didn't want to stop. She could have ridden on until the Wash and the sea and on forever across it. But he was lounging against the bike. He was waiting for her. For *her*. There was no point denying that this was a thrill. And the very fact of his existence, there in living flesh, was a pulsing beacon to which she was drawn. For a second she was reminded of Arthur, waiting for her by the woods back in the spring, and she gripped the reins hard. She wouldn't think about him.

'You look good on your horse,' he said. 'Like you belong together.'

She frowned at him. 'What is it you wanted to show me then? I can't imagine what there is out here.'

They crossed the road, he walking his motorbike, she leading Gyps, and they took a rough path by the side of a line of trees, flaring red. In the shade of the path, recent rain had turned the fallen leaves into a slippery mush and she was grateful she had her horse to hold on to to stop her sliding.

'Where are we going?'

'You'll see.'

The trees ended and he propped his bike where the path met the beginning of the saltmarsh. She tied Gyps up and patted his side. The line of the path headed straight ahead, soon dwindling and then disappearing on the horizon, and across the expanse of grasses, rushes and bog, and the glitter of creeks like veins on the skin of the marsh. As they walked, she thought he must be taking her to the beach, but as the grey sea grew closer, she saw a small thicket of stunted trees to the left of the path and she knew he was taking her there. Sprouting up from the marsh, the clump of trees was gnarled and twisted from years of seastorms. The track was barely wide enough for their feet. He walked ahead and she followed. It was impossible not to observe him, not to be snared by the way he moved, even here in a foreign place, on land that was hardly land, as if it was easy and natural to him. She kept her eyes on his sauntering figure ahead of her and could not have stopped her feet.

Behind the little copse was a rickety wooden shack, hidden from the road by the lone outcrop of old hawthorn trees.

'Is this it? Why have you brought me here?' A wave of panic shivered through her, an image of herself alone in the dark flashed into her head. It was silly and irrational but no one knew she was there.

'Hey, it's not that bad. It's not what you think...' He started to laugh and she realised she must look horrified.

'What are you laughing at? It's not funny. You don't know what I think.'

'You should see your face.' His laugh slowed and stopped. He came up to her and, in a swift movement that caught her out, touched her hair.

She froze, her scalp vibrating from the touch.

He took her gloved hand. 'Come on,' he said, 'this is the place I wanted to show you in the summer.'

She wondered, later that evening, safe at home in bed, why she went in. She could have stopped it right there and walked away. But she wanted to see what would happen. It was a strange little place, a marsher's shack she supposed, but it felt more like an abandoned beach house in a funny way and she always thought of it like that. It had pale blue paint peeling off its old wooden windowsills, a sign of brighter days. Weeds grew up to the grimy windows. Jack opened the door, holding back the tentacles of an overgrown climber that fell down in front of it. It was a gaping dark hole beyond the door and she hesitated. She had the sudden, terrible sensation of a tear in the fabric of her life, that she had already forsaken Arthur by coming here, and the dizzying sense that Jack had been promising this all along. She must have known, and yet now she was at the threshold of betrayal, it was shocking.

'Go on, go through.'

His voice was behind her, and she felt the presence of his body at her back. She wanted to go in. In any case, she couldn't go back. It smelled of old dust and damp and decay, but at the far end of the hallway was a chink of pale light. Picking her way down the narrow passage, she pushed open the door and beyond it was a bare room that overlooked the marsh, and beyond that, the silvery line of the sea. The soft autumn light filled the space. Her eyes were drawn outside at first, to the flat expanse of the marsh, but then she looked around. Jack had come into the room too and was watching her. On the right-hand side of the room was a heavy-looking old wardrobe and opposite it there was a low single bed and side table.

Her mouth was dry. There was a *bed*. 'I need to go back.'

Her voice was hoarse and ragged.

'Just stay for a minute. There's a kitchen. I can make coffee. Warm us up. Or tea?'

'No... thank you. I need to go.' Her head ached. She pushed past him out of the room. He stood at the door in partial silhouette, with a slightly lost look on his face.

'Let me make you a drink. It's cold.'

It *was* cold. Her fingers were numb, even in her leather riding gloves. She *would* quite like a drink.

'Come on, it'll warm you up.'

'All right then,' she said, 'just for a minute,' and he led her through to the so-called kitchen, a little room next to the bedroom.

It was a hob on a Primus stove and a chipped old earthenware sink. It too looked out over the marsh, slightly west, towards Holkham Bay, but the thin light threw only faint shadows. She drew a finger through the dust on the Formica table and watched him make coffee on the stove. His hands were almost delicate and belied the strong handshake he'd given her the first time she'd met him. She was reminded of the way he'd handled her mother's miniature camera – the way his long fingers worked quickly and deftly. It struck her as odd that he kept coffee here. The domesticity of it didn't fit. Had he brought other girls here? There were many things about him that didn't fit. A memory of Arthur and Jack facing each other in the courtyard last month sprang into her mind.

'What *is* this place? Doesn't anyone live here?' She had her breath back now and her control. It was obvious no one did live there, but she wanted him to explain it, to make it normal.

'I found it not long after I got here, on one of my rides on the bike. I get a bit stir crazy round here. It's the flatness, the lack of hills. All that sky, it drives a man nuts. And the goddamn base. All the rows and rows of Quonset huts and concrete and nothing else but barley and sugar beet fields. And the waiting. I get sick of that too. I saw the roof from the road, and I just wanted to see what it was.' He passed her an enamel cup of dark brown liquid. 'I shouldn't have taken you to that room, I wasn't thinking. I just wanted you to see this place. I think it's kind of special.'

The coffee was bitter but hot. He was pouring something from a bottle into his. 'Some of this?' He held up a bottle of bourbon, its liquid a deep, glossy black.

'All right. Just a little.'

It was hard to understand why an old shack would be special to him but she liked the way he was talking, as if he thought she understood him. It made her want to.

'But you get to fly. Isn't that an escape?' The drink was hot but she swallowed it down, blinking.

He laughed. 'Yeah, I guess, but that's work. Here, it's a kind of escape from people. I always liked that. I never had that at home, always a house full of family, people coming and going all times of the day. I always wanted space.'

'But I thought you grew up on a ranch. Surely there was lots of space.'

'Yeah – sure. And I miss that, finding a piece of land that could be yours, where you can see stuff from, where you can get a view of where you are. I miss it, you know, having that to myself.' He wasn't really looking at her but beyond her. Then he saw her watching him. 'I guess it's just me.'

'No, it's not. I think I understand. It's about having something of your own.'

'Yeah.' He was focused back on her now.

'I'd like that.' She told him about the farm, about how it didn't feel like hers any more because neither her father nor brother ever told her anything. How she wanted to get out of Norfolk. He put his head slightly to one side and she felt the impact of his gaze. 'When I was riding here, I thought I could just carry on riding...' She faltered and stopped.

'If you rode west and kept going you'd get to the Atlantic. And then you could go right on and get a boat. To America. Land of opportunity.' He was smiling but he seemed only half joking. It was as if he was offering it to her. She had a vision of cowboys on horseback, neon lights, rockets shooting through the sky. He drained his cup and put it in the sink. 'Listen, Verity – Vee – I can call you that, right?' She shrugged. No one had called her that before. It felt strange, like a code between them. 'I think you got the wrong impression of me. I joke around all the time, you think I'm messing with you. But I'm not.'

He came and sat down next to her, licked his lips and ran his tongue along the line of his teeth. She held tight to her cup. He looked straight at her and she felt skewered right through.

'I'd better get back now,' she said.

'Will you come again? I mean, just to talk. Have a cigarette, a drink, you know.'

'Maybe.' She got up quickly but stood in the kitchen doorway, not knowing how to say goodbye.

'You could paint here,' he said from his chair.

'Paint?' She wondered how he knew that she painted.

'Sketch, draw. I've seen you in your garden. You could do that here.'

'Oh.' It was as if he had opened up her rib cage and was poking around inside the flesh and the blood. She imagined him watching her in the private act of drawing. Her whole body prickled with heat. 'I barely… I just sketch sometimes.'

'Would you show me?'

'I really have hardly anything to show.'

'Just an idea. I don't want to pry. Hey, listen, wait a second.' He jumped up and plunged a hand into his Air-Force issue canvas bag that she now noticed was dumped in the corner. When he rose again, he'd drawn a black box out of the bag. It was a clunky, square camera, the kind you saw the press carrying about. His fingers began opening, flicking, turning and adjusting and he glanced up at her.

'Mind if I take your photograph?'

'What on earth for?' she said, flushed hot. But he'd already clicked the shutter and was removing the film holder from the side and sliding a new one in.

'Thank you, ma'am.'

She frowned at him. It was odd that he was a photographer. Why hadn't he said it back at the house when he'd picked up her mother's camera? Then again, she remembered that he'd held it as if it was precious.

'You didn't mention you took photographs,' she said, like an accusation.

He clicked the shutter again and took out the film holder before answering.

'It's just something I've been doing for a while,' he said. 'I got this one from work, but I've been taking shots of wherever I am for years. I've got to go to the city to get the plates developed, though. I'm going to take your brother to Norwich with me. Christmas shopping.' He was holding the camera in front of his face and adjusting the dials. Peter had already told her this, hardly able to contain his pleasure. What would he think if he knew she was here with Jack now? 'It's kinda like your painting.' One bright eye appeared around the side of the camera. 'I think we both want to interpret the world somehow, to put it down on paper. Sometimes it's easier to express ourselves that way. I get the impression that your mother would have understood that about you.' He reached forward and pushed the falling line of her hair behind her ear.

She didn't know how to respond. Once again, he seemed to be looking directly inside her brain and opening up parts of it that had always been there but she'd never noticed before. It was dizzying, disconcerting. Uncomfortable.

'Don't forget these,' he said. He stood, holding out her gloves, and when she reached to take them he kissed her lightly on the cheek. She was so flustered they dropped to the floor.

Immobilised by his nearness she stood still, looking down at the shapes on the floor. As she hesitated, he bent down and picked them up.

'Thank you,' she said, and it came out prickly, not thankful at all.

He didn't say anything, he just continued to look at her in his appraising way, as if he knew why she had come, as if he knew her more than she did herself.

'I really have to go now.'

'You'll come back?'

'I can't,' she said, and strode out of the cabin before she

said anything else. As she walked down the lane, trying to keep upright on the pockmarked track, she turned back and there he was. He waved to her from the door, looking like he belonged out there. As if the world belonged to him.

4.

Muriel saw the glow of the Howe Farm bonfire from all the way over by the East Fleet marshes and she thought, why shouldn't she have a bonfire too? She made one on the half-frozen marsh just to see the flames rise over the sea and watch the reflection of the fire, like goldfish flickering in the muddy creeks.

'Hey, is that safe?'

She whipped round, hearing the foreign accent. A man was standing on the quayside peering down at her. He was in darkness but from his voice she knew he was American.

'Why not?' she laughed. 'There's plenty of water round here.'

'Can I come down?' he said.

'If you want,' she said.

She watched him make his way across the gangway out to where she was. By the light of the fire she recognised him: the American with the scar, the one who'd danced with her at the Midsummer party. The bonfire cast a devilish glow, highlighting the thin jagged line across his face and she sensed a challenge in him, a dare.

'Jack,' he said, reaching out a hand. 'Have we met before?'

'No idea,' she lied. 'My name's Muriel. It means bright sea.' She shook his hand firmly.

'Hello, Muriel Bright Sea,' he said, 'would you like some fries?' He held out a bag of steaming chips he must have got from French's.

'Chips,' she corrected him. 'Yeah, if you don't mind.' She was empty with hunger, as usual, but she only took one.

'Go on,' he said, and she took a few more.

They sat on an upturned boat abandoned on the marsh and ate the chips and drank the pop he told her he could get at the base. He said he'd come from the Howe Farm bonfire and was heading to the pub for a nightcap. Did she want to come? But she couldn't go in the pub with an American. It was full of fishermen, including her own father.

'Was Arthur there?' she asked.

'Arthur Silver? Oh yeah,' he said, 'he's always there.' And it reminded her of the Midsummer dance and the crash the two of them had. She saw how it was, how they both were about Verity Frost. Dogs on heat, circling her.

'What do you say to a drink then, Miss Bright Sea?'

'I can't do that,' she said, but their faces were hot from the fire and close up.

He leaned forward and kissed her on her cheek, his lips greasy from the chips.

'I'm not like that,' she said, just so he didn't get ideas, but he told her he knew that and that she was pretty. And could she sit, *like that. Yes, perfect.* He positioned her sitting on the edge of the upturned boat and she turned to him in what she thought was quite a jaunty way, and pouted a bit like the girls on the front of *Life* magazine did. He smiled and she returned it and he held up his hands in the shape of a rectangle. It was nice to have the attention. She'd have to watch this one, though. He was a sly one.

'I'll bring my camera for real next time,' he said.

5.

Much as he wanted a day trip to Norwich with Jack on his own, Peter knew Arthur wouldn't forgive him if they went without him. He was his oldest and most loyal friend. He'd stood by him when all that bother at the school happened and after his mother died. Jack wanted to take photographs of the city and he had to get some developed. He turned up at the station with a chunky camera round his neck that made him look like a Hollywood press man. The day was overcast and bitterly cold, but as they chugged through the empty fields, Peter was certain it would somehow be different in the city. It was a boys' outing, a jaunt, each of them somehow with a sheen of glamour, in the anonymity of the train carriage. Jack, geed up at the idea of going to the city, was impossibly appealing with his scarred face and bright hair. Peter thought they probably made a funny-looking threesome – he with his tweed suit, Arthur wrapped up in his service greatcoat, looking rather like a throwback from the war, and Jack, altogether more modern, in his leather jacket. They drank steadily from hip flasks which they shared with Arthur, each of them matching the others shot for shot.

'To adventures in the city!' Jack raised his flask in a toast.

As the journey neared its end, Peter's body leaned closer to Jack's and he wished now that he hadn't asked Arthur along after all.

They arrived in a cloud of steam and the three of them stood in the middle of the station as the flow of people eddied around them. Peter was confused momentarily by the dimness of the light, the hoots of the trains, the scuffle of feet and the continual movement. His head hurt and his mouth was dry.

'Where on earth have we ended up?' said Jack. 'The goddamn underworld? Can we get out of here and get some air?'

But it was no better outside. In fact, it was worse. The steam of the trains mixed with the fog and was rising up the steps of the station and oozing over the whole of the city. It swirled and sucked around them, obscuring road signs and buildings and people. Only the eerie yellow headlights of the buses shone through the fog, eye holes in an empty face. Peter led them across the road, towards where he thought they could catch a bus to the city centre, but they couldn't find the bus stop. Each step felt as though they were heading into a labyrinth, each corner leading only to another and no sign of where they were. As they stumbled on, he could hear his companions' footsteps, muffled, and their breathing, rasping and hard. Eventually, a bus stop appeared like a lighthouse in a storm.

He turned to grab Jack and said, 'At last!' but his hand fell through the fog. There was nothing there.

'Pete?' It was Arthur's voice nearby. For a panicked moment he thought that Jack had disappeared.

'Hey guys.' Jack's face loomed up close and Peter's heart leapt.

Finally, when a bus came they sailed through the fog-shrouded city to where Jack said he had heard there were 'pubs and girls'. A sickness rose in Peter's throat. So that was the purpose of the day. He had hoped, foolishly, that it was just for them to be together, that it was Jack's way of creating a bond between them. A platonic bond, maybe more. He tried to think that this was just the sort of thing men did. Men talked of girls even if they didn't truly want them, didn't they? Hadn't Jack been his companion for all these months?

'Yes, let's,' he said, as if another man was speaking through his mouth.

In the little streets, Jack took photographs of people appearing through the misty air, but they were soon ensconced in a dingy pub on Lower Goat Lane drinking pints and eating pork scratchings. To Peter, each mouthful of the beer tasted sour. When they emerged, the cobbled street was still shrouded in fog. Arthur would be all right. He'd done National Service and Peter suspected he had done this before. Peter was exempt because of the farm but he sometimes wondered if it might have done him some good – helped him work out what kind of chap he really was. It might even have brought him an opportunity to meet someone like him. He'd sensed the tang of experience in Arthur when he came back to Norfolk, but Arthur hadn't said anything.

'Peter,' Arthur said, at his elbow, 'I don't really want to do this.'

Nor me, thought Peter, but Jack had stopped and was looking at both of them.

'What's up? You not keen on this plan, Art? You got a better idea?'

'You two do what you like, I'll find my own entertainment.'

'You got a special lady hidden somewhere?' Jack was baiting him.

'Arty,' Peter said, and he willed his friend back at the same time as he wished him gone. 'What will you do?'

But Arthur was hunched in his greatcoat. 'Don't worry about me.'

For a moment, he and Jack were alone, the fog swirling about them. Jack was close enough for Peter to see his copper hair, his pale eyelashes flickering. Peter reached out a hand and touched his arm. Perhaps they didn't need the cover of the girls now Arthur was gone. Jack didn't move but he gave Peter a look like he was working something out.

'You ever been with a girl, Pete?'

He couldn't answer; his throat was completely dry.

'Why don't you try it? You might like it.'

'Jack, I—'

'Hey, buddy,' he said kindly. 'We might as well try since we've come all this way, what do you say?'

Perhaps it was what they did in America – they used brothels as a cover for men being together. Or perhaps it was an initiation rite he had to undergo so Jack could accept him for what he was. The unsatisfactory, snatched encounters he'd had with other boys up to then meant he had little clue as to what men like him did beyond school.

Without waiting for an answer, Jack took his arm and walked him to a door along the street. There was no sign; he had no idea how Jack knew what it was.

It was dark inside, just a low, yellow lamp on a side table and a tatty velvet sofa. On it sat a deeply wrinkled woman with dyed red hair and legs that stuck out from under a voluminous skirt.

'Don't have no papers in here,' she said, eyeing Jack's camera, but he laughed and assured her he wasn't from the press. 'Just a little hobby,' he said, winking at her, and she shrugged.

'What can I get you boys then?'

'What have you got?'

She laughed a deep, gravelly laugh. 'Girls. That's what I got.'

Coughing, she heaved herself up from the chair. Peter almost went forward to offer her a hand but he was paralysed.

'Give us your best, ma'am.'

'Whatever you say, GI Joe,' she said, revealing missing teeth. 'What about him? Don't he talk?'

'Sure, he's just a bit nervous, that's all.'

'Jack—' he tried again, pleading with his eyes, but Jack was passing him a treacle-coloured liquid in a small smudged glass.

She waddled off through a curtain.

'Jack,' he said, with great effort. 'I don't want—'

'Just relax.' He put a hand on Peter's shoulder. If only they could stay like this. The drink was sherry, strong and sweet.

The woman came back with two girls. It was hard to tell their ages. They both had bags under their eyes and bad teeth but one was definitely younger and slighter and he knew, in an academic kind of way, that she was pretty, or had been once.

Before he had a chance to do or say anything, Jack had disappeared with the older one, and not knowing what else to do, Peter followed the girl, his head thick with the drink.

She sat on the edge of the bed and patted it. 'Come and sit here then.' But he stayed by the door.

'Can I please have a drink?'

'Course we can,' she said, and with a little sigh that made her seem much older, she got up and filled a glass with more of the same treacly liquid from a bottle on a sideboard. He gulped it down and got himself another one.

He slumped on the bed. The room was decked in pathetic bits of red and gold cloth, to make it seem exotic.

'Nice, ain't it?'

He regarded her blankly.

'You seem nice,' she said, more out of a sense of duty than truth. 'Come on, it's all right.'

From another part of the building came laughter. He thought of Jack. His wide mouth and long throat and the freckles on his nose. Jack's impossibly white, naked body. Something touched his leg and he flinched.

He didn't look at her. 'I can't,' he said. He felt her bristle next to him and waited for the mockery.

'You're one of them, ain't you? It's all right. I knew right off when I saw you.'

God, how did she know?

'I won't tell anyone,' she said, and, mutely, he accepted a cigarette from her. 'You want another drink?'

He nodded, drank one down and another. He had no idea what time it was. The room dimmed into a duller, darker red.

'I've got to go,' he said, staggering to his feet.

A hand snatched at his shirt sleeve, but he shook it off. He was aware that the girl had fallen back on the bed but he couldn't connect it with himself. He needed to find Jack. Out in the hallway it was dark. He stumbled down it towards where he thought Jack had gone. In one doorway, two girls leered at him with cold eyes. In another, an empty bed. The young girl's voice came calling, 'He went that way.'

Then a door opened. Jack appeared in shadow. He wanted to throw himself at him. He took hold of Jack's shoulders. 'Where were you?'

'Right here, Pete, right here.'

'Did you – did you—' He had an urge to know. Jack's face was a pale blur. He made himself focus on the silver scar cutting across the freckles.

'Pete,' said Jack's voice, 'Pete. I could be dead tomorrow. This is life.'

He wanted to tell him the truth. He leaned forward but couldn't get the words out, couldn't stay upright. He leaned against Jack's shoulder and closed his eyes. Jack's hands touched his back and Peter couldn't bear the feel of them. The touch ran through him and he lifted his head and pressed his mouth against Jack's blissful lips. And Jack kissed him back, he was sure of it. Then it was over and Jack pushed him gently away.

'You're blitzed, Pete. You don't mean it.'

I do, he wanted to say. *It's the only thing I mean.*

It was still daytime, though you wouldn't have known it. It was a day that felt more like one long, raddled nightmare.

Starving and half-cut after drinking all morning and missing lunch, the three of them ordered eggs, toast and sweet buns in the station café. The steam from the tea urn mixed with the mists from the trains and obscured them from enquiring eyes. Arthur was waiting for something but he didn't know what it was. When he'd returned to the brothel, Peter had been stumbling and leaning against Jack. His heart jumped in horror. How had Jack got poor Peter in such a state? He'd known this would happen – Jack's competitive drinking, his egging Peter on. Poor, dear Peter would do anything for that bastard, he could see that now.

Jack drained his tea. 'I have to run an errand.'

'So I'm expected to babysit?' Arthur indicated towards Peter who was slumped, piece of toast in hand, in a booth.

Jack shrugged and slapped him on the back. 'Christmas shopping,' he said.

Arthur watched Jack exit through the café door, and mentally followed him. His toast was dripping egg yolk onto his trousers and Peter's head was nodding and in danger of falling into the tea cake Arthur had bought for him. He was sick of this. Jumping up, he rubbed his trousers and left a shilling on the table. He had to find out what Jack was doing. In front of the station, he saw the American's distinctive figure with copper-coloured hair, disappearing into the fog down the Prince of Wales Road. He began to follow him.

The fog both helped and hindered. He kept losing him or his eyes would catch on a glimpse of orange which turned out to be someone's headscarf. But he found him each time.

They wound through dingy little back streets, the spire of the cathedral sticking out of the fog on their right. Jack's boots clopped on the cobblestones ahead of him as they emerged into Cathedral Close. Past the statue of Nelson, Jack exited through the vast gate opposite the cathedral. Arthur watched him cross Tombland and he thought he might have ducked into the pub on the corner, but there he was again, walking west down Princes Street towards the centre of the city. The fog here was lifting. Little wisps still curled around the guttering and the edges of the roofs but Jack's retreating back was now clearly in sight. Where on earth was he going?

He had his answer almost immediately, as Jack ducked into a shop on the left of the street. Arthur slowed his pace. Above the shopfront it said *J. Wilson Esq. Art Dealer*. Why Jack of all people would be interested in an art dealer's, he had no idea. Arthur slipped into a tobacconist's across the road and, in the guise of deciding what pipe to buy, watched Jack take something in a small paper bag from the shopkeeper and put it into his top left-hand pocket. Arthur turned his back as Jack left the shop and went into the next one, a toy shop. This was even more mystifying.

Arthur watched him re-emerge and continue on. Past a church on their right, Jack took a sudden right turn and, holding fast to the church wall, Arthur saw him go into a coffee shop in a medieval-looking building at the top of the road. He quickly stepped back and into the churchyard where he could position himself behind a tall headstone and see, unseen, into the café. It glowed invitingly with electric yellow light. Jack was sitting down at an empty table by the window. Condensation dripped down the windows and his back was facing the street, but Arthur could see it was him clear enough. On Jack's left, two women in furry hats were talking animatedly. On the right, Arthur could just see an older man, with a brown cap and a lean, shaven face, reading a newspaper. Nothing seemed to happen. He stamped his feet on the hard earth beneath him and pulled his greatcoat tighter around him. A waitress brought over a tray with a pot and a small china cup. Jack poured coffee and spooned sugar into his cup and drank. Then he pulled something from his pocket. Arthur strained forward to see what it was and his shoulders dropped, disappointed. It was a cigarette case, square and metal, which he laid on the table. Arthur waited. His legs ached from having to half crouch behind the headstone and his back was cold. Jack took something from the front pocket of his jacket. He lit up a cigarette, offered one to the man diagonally opposite him. The metal case Jack had lain on the table couldn't be a cigarette case.

Arthur's heart beat faster. Why didn't he have a camera or binoculars? He almost laughed. He was acting like he was in one of the boy's own adventures he'd read as a child. But he had no time to think about anything because Jack was already pushing back his chair. In a minute, he would be out of the coffee shop, and Arthur would have to be out of sight and ahead of him.

Back in the station café, breathing through his nose and affecting nonchalance, Arthur ordered a fresh pot of tea. Peter was fast asleep, his head on the table, his spittle pooling on the Formica. The shilling was gone, but otherwise no one seemed to be much bothered about him. When Jack sauntered in, minutes later, he didn't tell them where he had been other than to say, 'Got some Christmas gifts.'

Arthur nudged Peter, who woke with a start and, blinking, began tearing off bits of the crushed tea cake and chewing them slowly, like one of his cows.

'Get yourself a girl in the end, Art?' Jack said, helping himself to tea from the newly ordered pot. Arthur didn't bother replying. He would let Jack think what he liked. There was no need to tell him he'd gone to the library. It had been a waste of time anyway. He'd been trying to read up old newspapers, to see if he could find any clues, buried beneath a wave of copy, about the use of the Holkham airbase. But it was hopeless. He'd found nothing. A girl had sidled up to him on Lower Goat Lane, a red-haired one, surprisingly pretty. He'd imagined his hand under skirts, emptying himself into her. Like he had in Yorkshire, on service, that one time. He remembered the way she stood to take off her stockings, putting them carefully over a chair. He couldn't not look. The girl's hipbones stuck out sharply. He looked down at the dark between her legs and felt bilious and excited, in shock at the reality, the dreamt-of foreignness of it. But he couldn't leave, couldn't stop looking at the darkness. The girl had turned a bedside lamp on afterwards and it lit up the lines on her face, the creases round her eyes. He realised she was far older than him, almost as old as his mother. He was sick with himself, with the way he had cried out inside her, with the joy of the release. In the light there was nothing of Verity in her, nothing. He hadn't done it again. It was Verity he wanted. He made himself turn away from the red-haired girl, hovering on the corner he knew led to the library.

Into his head came an image of Jack, watching Verity, and he had to grip the table for support.

'You're a dark horse. I didn't think you were interested in that sort of thing.'

Arthur drank his tea and feigned disinterest. 'Why did you think that?'

'I had an idea you were courting Pete's little sister,' indicating the ravaged figure of Peter, who was slurping tea as if it was an elixir of health.

'You asked me that before,' said Arthur.

Peter, his mouth half full of tea cake, spat it out. 'For God's sake! Don't be vile.'

Arthur reddened. 'We're friends,' he said, 'that's all.' The lie hurt him, as if in the telling he had made it true.

'I should hope so,' said Peter, 'he's like our brother,' and smacked Arthur on the back. Then he groaned, bent forwards and vomited all over the table.

On the train, Peter slept again, or pretended to, his face squashed against the window. As they travelled north, the fog cleared and the flat landscape reappeared. Their carriage smelled of stale sick.

'What exactly happened to him? What did he do?' Arthur asked Jack.

'You should ask *him* that,' said Jack. 'Though I don't think he'll want to remember. He seemed to turn against her. Poor thing ran screaming through to me, saying he pushed her. And I find him like that.' He pointed at their stricken friend.

'Did he hurt her?' he asked, dreading the answer.

'She was going on as if he did. I got out of her that he shoved her and she tripped and fell against the bed post but I have no idea why he did it.'

Let's leave it like that, Arthur thought. 'Probably just too tight,' he said, lighting up a cigarette.

'He sure was,' said Jack, with an air of someone who has more to tell. Something else had happened. He thought of Peter making moon-eyes at Jack on the train, laughing at everything he said, and he wished he could protect his friend.

'What errand did you have to run, then?' He wanted to see how Jack would react, but there was nothing in his friendly, relaxed demeanour that gave anything away.

'A gift for a girl I'm seeing.'

'What did you get her? Is this girl here or in America?'

'Why do you want to know so much?'

'Why'd you lie about being from Arizona?'

Jack stared at him, his neck twitching, and for a second, Arthur thought he was going to punch him in the face. Then he opened his mouth wide, bared his teeth and laughed.

'Are you saying I'm not a hillbilly redneck now?' Jack took out his packet of Camels and offered one to Arthur.

He and Peter sat in the Shipwright's two weeks later.

Arthur wondered if Jack knew he'd followed him. If he did, what would he do about it? Peter maintained he had a blackout about the brothel. Arthur was afraid to ask his friend about it, afraid of things about him that were unsaid. He suspected it was something to do with Jack. They hadn't seen him recently and it was a relief to be rid of him. He had a wild thought that he should tell someone (who? The police?) about Jack handing over the metal case in the café, but as soon as he thought it, he dismissed it. He had no proof of anything.

'Ver didn't get in, you know. To Oxford. I heard her crying behind her bedroom door. There've been scenes at home,' Peter said, sipping his pint. 'Father's threatening her with the dreaded De Vere fellow again. To be honest, I can't see what choice she's got. We need their money.'

'What happened about that misunderstanding with your father about the farm finances?'

'Misunderstanding!' Peter snorted. 'There's a gaping hole in them but he pleads ignorance. Horses probably. It's dire. He'd already splurged on the bloody combine and, frankly, we need actual workers on the farm. He can't afford Ver to be knocking about at the farm any more, not pulling her weight.'

A flare of something like happiness went through Arthur and he felt immediately guilty. But this changed everything. She'd need him now. He wouldn't let her be sold off to some toff who didn't love her. It was like a reprieve. It wasn't fair, but her misfortune would be good for them both in the end.

6.

December

When Verity first went back to the saltmarsh shack she told herself it was from curiosity. On the back of Jack's bike, gripping onto his waist, she was another person, someone she only recognised from the glimpses she had in magazines, like the ones in *Picturegoer*. She wore her mother's red lipstick and tied a scarf round her head and imagined herself in Rome or Cannes or Paris. Or New York.

The wind scoured her legs and pulled back the skin on her face so it felt like it was coming off. The speed was intoxicating. As was the sense that she shouldn't do this and be this. Most exhilarating of all was the physical presence of the man she was holding onto – the buttery feel of the leather jacket, the slight scent of his cologne, even in the wind, and her legs, jammed up close to him. The idea of the two of them speeding through time and space to some-thing completely new.

Hiding out in what she imagined was a dead man's house was like a secret door onto another life. It was the home of a poacher or a crabber, judging by the rusted traps and dusty nets – alone on an empty marsh away from the eyes of others. She was amazed at herself, at her ability to shut off her doubts and disgust to create a kind of glamour out of such grime. It was funny how easy it was to put Arthur into a little box in the back of her mind, how when she saw Jack she could forget everything else.

On the bike, she didn't think about what would happen when they got to the shack, but when they were inside it was all there was. A secret, hidden world that had no meaning beyond the damp, misshapen walls. They sat and talked in the little kitchen, drinking his coffee laced with bourbon and smoking. The entire time she was waiting – waiting for him to pounce, willing it and yet afraid of it. When she said she had to go they stood by the door. She was wearing her coat, ready to leave, but she didn't move. He came up so close to her that she could see each freckle on his twisted nose and each silvery scale of the snake-like scar. He reached for the back of her head and she jerked hers to the side as he leaned forward, so he ended up kissing the end of her nose. She heard him breathe out in a laugh and then his mouth touched hers again. His tongue pushed her lips open and his mouth tasted of coffee and smoke. He stroked her back with one hand and the other was on her skirt. It crept up to her waist and towards her chest. Her whole body shivered. She knew she'd better stop it now or she was done for.

'Stop,' she said, but he kept kissing her as if he hadn't heard. His hand touched her left breast and in a rush of panic she pushed him away. He stumbled and almost fell back onto the kitchen floor.

'Hey, what is it?'

'You can't. I can't.'

'Why not?'

She didn't answer him, just shook her head, resisting the overwhelming temptation to give in.

After that, Verity brought her sketchbook as he suggested. She told her brother that she was sketching al fresco and he snorted as if he thought she was mad. She sat on a kitchen chair and drew what she saw out of the window: the rushes, the clumps of seablite, the geese and the waders, the spikes of grass and the line of the sea. Jack sat watching her, smoking. Slowly, he began to talk. He told her about the stars he'd seen from the desert, the cacti and the brutal heat. And cities with tall, shining buildings that reflected the sun. She allowed the words to cast their spell, watching his lips move while he talked, the flash of his teeth and the pale hairs on his arms, golden where the light caught them. He began to bring a camera to the cabin. It was a black rectangular shape with a plate that stuck out the bottom. Scratched on the side was a number and she assumed he'd somehow got it from the army surplus. Sometimes, he would get out the camera and take photographs from the window, sometimes turning it towards her. She found it embarrassing and flinched at first but then she began sketching him – the lines of his nose and jaw and cheekbones, filling page after page with bold, dark line drawings of his face and neck as he took photographs of her. It was a mutual gaze of recreation. She had never been looked at so much before in her life and it would have been unbearable except that she was also the looker. The way he focused on her as if every part of her was worth recording, was reciprocated in the way she drew every line and every crease and curve of his face. Sometimes her gaze snagged on his and she couldn't look away. It was like he was photographing *inside* her, as if he already knew what was in there.

Once she was making coffee in the kitchen and saw a newspaper, folded on the floor. It must have fallen from his pocket. She picked it up. It was the *New York Times* dated 17th November, eighteen days old. On the front there was a picture of an officer of some kind and then, on the left, the headline said:

Experiments for Hydrogen Bomb Held Successfully at Eniwetok.

Where was Eniwetok?

'Jack,' she said, holding the paper when he came in from the bedroom, where he'd set up his camera. His hair looked askew from where he'd been distractedly putting his hand through it. When she saw him, she almost didn't say anything. But it came out.

'Do you know anything about this? I haven't heard anything.'

'It was classified,' he said, not showing any sign of surprise. 'Nobody was supposed to know at first, but I guess they decided to leak some information to the public. Let them know we're ahead of the Soviets.'

'You make it sound like a game.'

'Pretty high stakes game,' he said, lighting up a Camel.

'It says it was the 1st of November. That's over a month ago, but there's been nothing in the British papers.'

Jack shrugged and took a slug of coffee.

Arthur's voice was in her head: his warnings about them *sleepwalking into apocalypse.* She only dimly remembered Hiroshima and the relief most people felt that the war in the East would end too. But a couple of years ago she'd seen newsreel of the city. The pictures of the children parading in their shorts and black bobbed hair made it seem as if all was well now, but at the end there was a scene of the people of Hiroshima's 'new city' bowing their heads in remembrance. It seemed to Verity as if no one else was remembering. Everyone was desperate to protect themselves from the devastation inflicted on Japan but how could they do that if these bombs were so prevalent, so common that they were sitting up the road in Holkham, waiting to be dropped over Siberia?

'Is this something to do with what you're up to at the base?' She held up the newspaper.

'That's classified too,' he said again, then laughed. 'Don't look so serious! Of course it's got nothing to do with it. This place is thousands of miles away in the Pacific. I'm here. But I guess it's all connected.' He paused. 'Look – what I do is preparation. Information. I can't say any more, you know that.' He put his hands up in helpless supplication.

'You could,' she said.

'But I'd have to kill you.' He had an irritating smirk on his face. It felt like he was playing a part. The American Rogue.

'Don't treat me like an idiot, Jack.'

'Vee, I'd tell you if I could but, really, it ain't so very exciting. I'm just doing what I'm good at. It's just a job, and a pretty boring one at that, stuck in a plane for ten hours at a time.'

'You're being disingenuous,' she said.

He sighed. 'It's hard to describe it, Vee.'

'You're not from Arizona, are you? All that chatter about horses, it's not true. I can tell you don't know anything about horses.'

He gazed at her, not smiling for once, and she suddenly felt afraid that he would snap and reveal himself to be something completely different. He drew his teeth over his bottom lip and then the cloud lifted and he brightened. 'I knew you were clever. I was trying to impress you. God, you make this so hard.'

'Make what hard? What's the matter?'

'You,' he said. He was leaning back against the table, cigarette half smoked and dangling in his hand. She was hot under his stare but neither of them looked away.

'Let me take your photograph,' he said.

She sat on the windowsill and he began the ritual. Open the shutter, turn the wind-up key, compose the shot, look through the viewfinder, drop in the film holder, pull the dark slide, pop the shutter, return the dark slide, remove the film holder. Repeat. Bored, her eyelids drooped and closed, then she felt his hands and woke up. He was gentle, but insistent. It was hard to keep saying no.

In their little wooden world they became just bodies. The kisses became more urgent. The two of them slid down to the kitchen floor, his hands roamed under her skirt, caressing the line of her thighs, the tender skin at the top, which made her shudder. She stopped it at lying on the floor, his weight on her, his hands on her, the dust and grime of the old cabin beneath her clothes. No, she said, again and again no.

Prone, she looked up at the chipped enamel on the yellow

stove-top kettle. She saw herself and could not believe it was her. What would Miss Gardiner, her old school friends, her family, think if they saw her now? She heard her own little moans and they were the sounds of someone else. They were the whimpers of an animal. At the last moment, she pushed him away and he relented. He didn't try to make her carry on and later she knew it was because he didn't need to. It was a game he was going to win.

But the line was crucial. She told herself that if she did not cross the line she had not sinned, she had not let herself fall.

At home, she stopped looking at the dressing table mirror for fear of what she would see. Her mother's face seemed to shimmer on the glass, watching her. She heard unidentified female voices. *Poor motherless child. Look at her. What would her poor, dead mother think?* She wandered into her mother's bedroom, kept pristine by Mrs Timms. She opened the wardrobe door. The empty white folds of her mother's wedding dress, hanging. Her fingers reached out and touched the silk but she took her hand away quickly as if stung. She closed the door and sat with her back to the wardrobe. Marriage. Babies. This was what her mother had wanted for her. Verity was no longer sure if it was true. In Verity's memory, her mother left an impression of gliding, of perfect, gilded beauty. She had not been the kind of mother you talked to. And now she was gone and she could never ask, *Were you happy? What did it all mean to you?* Her parents' marriage had been arranged, as marriages used to be. She'd been offered up, like a prize heifer, with farm attached, her father the lucky one, back from the Great War, in a country of few young men. The silky folds of the wedding dress, as creamy as the raw milk from the cows, hung as a warning of a life planned out and enclosed. It was meant to be every girl's dream – like the debs in their white gowns lined up for plucking by some suitable aristocrat. But it was not *her* dream. Her father said it was what her mother had wanted for her but that stultifying life had destroyed her. The photographs were the only signs of herself she'd left behind. Had they been her mother's attempt at some kind of autonomous life? Once, lying next to her mother on top of the quilt as she slept her dreamless, drugged sleep, Verity had taken hold of her thin, white, jewelled hand. 'Wake up,' she'd said, and had fervently wished that her mother would wake up, hold her and the two of them would tell each other their secrets.

When she was younger, a gauche, blundering thing in knee-high socks, her mother had gone away for the weekend. It was not long after the war. No one said where, or why. When she came back, Mrs Timms told her that her mother was sick. She stayed in bed. Verity stood outside the closed door and she could hear her mother crying. If only she'd gone in then, but she was afraid. Once she heard her father talking about *neurosis* and *excessive grief*. Eventually, her mother emerged from the bedroom and there were parties, teas, visitors again. But perhaps she had already disappeared. They had not been enough, her and Peter, to keep her from slipping into a state of distraction. And in the end, she'd left them, absolutely. No one knew if she'd meant to drown in the sea, or if it had been an accident, but it would always feel like an abandonment.

*

Their mother's birthday fell just after Christmas and still deep in winter. There'd been precious little festivities at the farm. As usual, they listened to the Christmas Day broadcast from Sandringham, but it was the new queen this year. She'd sounded so young, not much older than Peter was. 'Pray for me,' she'd said, and he thought it sounded like a cry for help. She talked of the Empire as a 'power for good' and their father had nodded along emphatically, but it seemed to Peter, with the Americans on their doorstep, that the old order was disintegrating.

Before breakfast and long before dawn, instead of returning to the house after milking the cows, Peter walked down Leafy Lane and across the Holkham Road to the chapel where Mother was buried. He didn't really know why. They didn't celebrate her birthday any more, certainly nothing had been said on the first birthday after her death.

On the grave was her name and the dates. *Loving wife and mother.* But was that true? It's just what people asked the stonemason to write. There were no flowers, it was the wrong time of year, but it looked so bald and bare. He should have brought something.

The graveyard was deserted. He began to talk, not aloud, there was no need. He spoke to the headstone and the bones six feet down in the cold earth.

At school it was quite normal. One never spoke about it much but it was done, that was all. Once, a sixth former whose fag he'd been took a shine to him, and there had been a boy – Farthing, his name was, like the money. Farthing was a vicar's son so from a poor, old family like his. Ironic that. Barely a farthing between them. Once, they had sought solace with each other. And there had been some comfort in it – just to know that someone was the same as you. He still thought about the smooth line of Farthing's back, an image of sad consolation. Even now he couldn't be angry at Farthing, despite what he had done, the bald fact of his absolute betrayal, the shame. He couldn't blame him because he understood the shame.

The sad business with Farthing should have prepared him for Jack. There was a moment, early on in their friendship, when he had wondered whether Jack was like him. The American had sought him out in the pub, beckoned him over. He'd looked at him slyly, willing him – or so Peter thought – to do something. There was a promiscuity about him, a look in his eyes that seemed to be always on the edge of something precarious. But Peter hadn't dared then and he kept on not daring until it was too late. He knew something had happened in Norwich but he didn't know what he had said or done except that Jack wasn't the same with him any more. He feared, more than anything, that he'd made some terrible pass at Jack, and the thought of that was worse because from the way that Jack was behaving now he knew that it hadn't been reciprocated. And now she, his clever little sister, who had always beaten him at everything, including Arthur, had done it again.

They still met in the Shipwright's sometimes but Jack didn't come on the shoots or to the golf course any more. Peter saw Verity go off every Sunday afternoon and he wondered if Jack had always meant to do this – to get her through him.

'Sorry,' he said, and it was aloud this time, although no one heard. An owl hooted. He wanted to kick the stupid headstone for its unresponsiveness. He wanted to say, *You knew*, to his mother, *you knew and you didn't help me*. But she couldn't help herself, let alone him. Indulged by her, he'd been naïve and was punished for it. Gresham's had a liberal reputation yet it also had the Honour System. All the students at the school had to sign an oath swearing 'Always to avoid impurity'. And if you didn't own up to your own impure thoughts or actions, other boys were encouraged to report on you. It was a licence to duplicity, to spying, to betrayal. It was no surprise to him that it had produced men like Maclean. But unlike most of the others, Peter hadn't been adept in the arts of secrecy, and had not learned quickly enough. He remembered the day that they'd sent him home from school after the fit he'd had, the fight with the boy. Someone (a nasty, pretty boy) had called him a fairy and Peter had punched him hard in the face. But in the Headmaster's office, there had been Farthing, chewing on his nails, telling them that Peter was a queer and that he'd seduced him. Peter remembered Mother (not Father, he was ever grateful for that) coming to collect him in the Jag, and she'd held his hand in the car while he cried and she hadn't told him to stop. She'd lied to Father for him so he still didn't know that he'd been expelled for sodomy (that word made him flinch), but his father had dismissed him years ago anyway. But he'd wanted, needed more and she'd not been there. It was never talked of again.

He'd found her once wandering on the beach. It was autumn and soon the cows would be brought into the cowshed but they were still grazing. He and the boy from the village who'd been helping with the cows had milked them and brought them back to the grazing field from the cowshed, their bulky forms grey and shadowy in the pre-dawn. A thin mist held to the ground and curled around their legs, making them seem as if they were half submerged in a sea of mist. He reached up a hand to pat the last heifer on the rump and turn back up the slight incline to the house. But when he did, a ghostly form appeared in the distance. Someone was walking along the beach. No one walked here, it was too remote for dog-walkers. He knew it was Mother by the slightness of the figure.

He left the cows chewing on the grass and ran down to the gate that led to the beach. She was standing on the dune, in only a grey silvery-looking nightdress and wellingtons, her hair down and a blank look on her face.

'Mother?' he said. 'What are you doing down here? You must be freezing.'

'Peter,' she said, and took his hand. 'It's so beautiful in the morning.' She gestured to the sea – a dark line behind her – and the fields and pine trees wreathed in mist.

He put his jacket round her shoulders and they walked back to the house, hand in hand.

On the day she died, he'd been down the bottom field. It was the same time of day. He'd already done the feed and was about to go back in for breakfast but decided instead to inspect the fence that separated the end fields from the woodland. So he was there when it happened. He could have saved her. Just a gate and a few yards of dune and beach to the sea. Dawn breaking, lightening the sky and colouring the fields, and there had been a cold, cutting eastern wind. He remembered the cold for some reason but he couldn't remember hearing anything out of the ordinary. Birds, wind, the sea. Nothing else. He'd fixed the hole in the fence and was returning to the house and Verity had come running at him in her dressing gown. His first thought was *Father*. He didn't remember what she said but it was something about Mother and the sea. He thought she must have got something wrong. Mother didn't have a habit of swimming in the sea. But his sister was insistent. He told her to go back to the house, that he would go to the beach.

Later, when he'd returned again to the house and called the police and the ambulance and they'd all arrived – Arthur on his bike as always, Mrs Timms, tear-streaked, his father, his face a block of stone and his hands shaking, and Ver completely white – only then, he had left them and gone to the pasture to feed the horses because he didn't know what else to do. She had gone from him by then. It was only her body down there on the beach. She belonged to all of them now. But before that, it had been just him and her on the wet sand, her body impossibly still and him shaking and shaking her and trying to breathe air back into her lungs and holding her, limp, and thinking she would wake, she must. She had to. She had loved him, above all others. But her eyes were like those of a stillborn calf.

7.

Verity's head was full of the image of Jack's tongue licking her arm, when she saw a man on a bicycle in the distance. She knew at once it was Arthur. Instinctively, she slowed Gyps to a canter, then a trot. What light there'd been was already leaching from the sky. Arthur on his bike was a charcoal smudge. As she neared him, she saw he had a pair of binoculars slung over his shoulder.

There was no way she could avoid him. She trotted up behind him and called. As he turned to her and squinted, she saw him in the half light as if for the first time: his old, beloved, kinked hair, the straightness of his nose, the darkness of his eyes, in shades of grey and black. She was so used to him that she rarely *saw* him but all she could think was how different he was to Jack. How moulded and still, where Jack was always quick and live to the touch even when he wasn't doing anything at all. She realised that she had never sketched Arthur.

'What are you doing here? Birdwatching?'

He glanced at the binoculars. 'Nothing,' he said.

It was too late to make an excuse. She dismounted Gyps. He lit up a cigarette and passed one to her and they smoked as they walked, she with her horse, he with his bike.

'Actually, I was watching the planes.'

He seemed tightly sprung, as if he would shoot off suddenly. It was an odd thing to be doing, spying on the Americans, but Arthur had been acting oddly for some time and it didn't surprise her.

'What on earth for?'

'Their planes are carrying atomic bombs,' he said finally, in a tone of defiance as if he didn't care if she believed him.

'Why do you think that?' she said. It sounded far-fetched, a conspiracy theory, as if he'd been reading too many spy stories, and it would be laughable were it not for the needling suspicion that this was something to do with Jack. When she'd asked Jack if the bomb tests were anything to do with the activities at the base, he'd said they were connected. It could be true.

He took a deep suck on his cigarette and glowered at her. 'I've thought it for months. I got some intelligence from a chap and I just needed proof. I've been tracking the types of plane they use and when they go out and I've noticed a pattern.'

'But they'd tell us, wouldn't they? They'd have to.'

'That's what I think. I'm right about this. I know I am. Anyway, I told the *Eastern Daily Press* about what I've found and they're interested in an article.' He sounded excited now.

'And there's a bomb store, Ver. Think about it. What if there was a crash? Boom!' His eyes were wild. 'Do you know how far the radiation zone goes out? Most people have no idea, but I did a day's training with the Civil Defence Corps – I mean they're cranks if they think we can defend ourselves against it – but it was illuminating I can tell you – the effects would be monstrous—'

'Stop.' She put her hands to her face. 'It's terrifying.'

She thought of Jack, dropping bombs over Russia, the mushroom cloud blooming up and engulfing him and the hydrogen bomb billowing out on the other side of the world. She curled her left hand into a tight fist and dug her nails into her palm to stop herself from saying the wrong thing. She should be horrified – and she was – but something like a thrilling fear flushed through her as well. What if he got shot down and never came back? It felt unbelievable.

'It *is* terrifying, but that's why I want to do something useful,' Arthur was saying. 'Write about what's happening right now in Russia, Korea, America. Things far away from here but right here too.'

'You should do it,' she said. It was like Arthur to do the right thing and a terrible part of her wished he could be worse so she wouldn't feel so wretched about her deception.

'And I think that to do anything useful, I need to go to London. If I can get this article accepted, I'll have something to take to the papers in the city. There's a new world coming, Ver, and I want to be a part of it. Not watching. Not on the sidelines.' He stopped and looked away and she thought he must be embarrassed for blurting out all his dreams. But he spoke again, much more quietly.

'I've been meaning to ask but I've not seen you.' He paused and she wished he wouldn't go on, aware, in a sudden wave of shivers, what he was going to say. He inhaled. 'I thought that you could come to London. With me.'

'Oh.' She tried to imagine marrying him, having children, at home forever, like her mother. And on the other side of the divide, the musty, damp marsh shack, Jack's body and hers, and risks she didn't even know. The silence of unspoken promises stretched.

'Why not? You're not going to Oxford and there's nothing here for you.'

'No, that's true,' she said, and she almost laughed. 'I don't know, Arthur.' Her voice sounded very cold. 'I have no idea what I'm going to do now.' This was at least some sort of truth. She felt his figure shrink beside her.

'I'm going to go anyway,' he said.

Go then, she wanted to say. But instead she said, 'Where? Where will you live?'

'I've saved up. I have enough for a month's rent in digs and I think I can get a job pretty quickly. I'm a decent writer.'

'You sound like you've got it all worked out.' She wondered how long he'd been planning this. 'It sounds wonderful,' she said, hating the sound of her deceit.

Darkness had now clothed them but she'd kept her eye trained on the turning for Leafy Lane. They walked in silence, with only Gyps snorting lightly next to her, and she could feel the words unsaid lying thickly on her tongue and the hurt radiating from him. Eventually, after a long minute without either of them saying another word, she saw the little sign for Howe Farm with a hand pointing up the lane.

'I've got to go,' she said, 'I'm late.' She gave his arm a squeeze and couldn't help running her hand through his hair. She felt him shiver next to her and, as she must have known he would, he pulled her to him and kissed her on the lips. The kiss felt strangely cool and mechanical. She wondered if he could smell Jack in her hair. She shouldn't be doing this. Her heart quickened and her groin and legs throbbed, but it was cruel. She pushed him lightly away.

'I really am going to be late,' she said, and remounted Gyps.

It was a relief when the lane bent and she could no longer feel his eyes on her back.

An RAF plane buzzed above her as she rode home. In school, they had studied the pollination of flowers by bees. The sticky stamen, the blooming petals, was all she could remember. She had a dim idea that as long as none of the white fluid – the *pollen* – was inside her body it would all be all right. The absolutely essential thing was to keep it out of her.

It was impossible to think about babies. They did not seem connected to the thing she was doing. She could not have a baby. University, she had been going to university, repeating it like a witch's chant to ward off evil. She was not like the other girls. In the absence of that one key difference she must replace it with something else, some other way of separating herself from her classmates. Unlike them, she was not naïve, like Pam and the others, set on marrying some dolt. When she was younger, she had been certain she would marry Arthur, but that was a long time ago. All of it seemed colourless, vague, someone else's life. The cabin on the marsh was all there was. Beyond it, she couldn't think. Even poor Arthur.

I have all these separate boxes inside me, she thought. And in all of them are bits of me but I don't know in which one is the important bit. I don't know how to choose the right box.

*

In the deep quiet of winter at the end of the year, Verity met Jack at the usual time. Unusually, he was already at the tumbling down shack. When she opened the door to the bedroom, he jumped back from the wardrobe. She was about to ask what he was doing but he said, 'Look,' and pointed out of the window.

The entire glass was filled with swirling black dots against a peach sky. It was dusk and pink-footed geese were returning from the inland fields to roost on the creeks and reed beds of the marsh, and the shack filled with the unk-unk of their call. Kneeling at the window ledge, he took photographs, then sat back on the bed next to her and they watched the whirling birds together, his arm around her. The geese wheeled and fell, swooping down to the horizon where they came up against the land and, in a flurry, came to rest. It filled her with a kind of exultation, recalled the waves of mind-obliterating intensity she felt on the floor with Jack.

'I've got something for you,' he said. 'Close your eyes.'

She glanced at the wardrobe, wondering if he'd hidden something in there for her, then did as he asked. Perhaps he would kiss her, give her some earrings, something romantic, sentimental but innocuous. Instead, he put a rectangle of card into her hand. She opened her eyes. It was a postcard of a Turner painting. At first, she was disappointed. Turner was last century. It was history and she was sick of history.

'It's called *Snow Storm*. It reminded me of here. I know you said you liked modern painting but I couldn't find anything. Anyway, look at it, it's crazy, wild.'

She did look. It was a snow storm at sea, a dark whoosh of paint above a floundering smudge of a boat. The sky was filled with dark and light. She turned it over. *To V love J* was written in black ink sprawled over the back.

'Thank you,' she said, strangely embarrassed.

'That's not all,' he said, like a magician, his hand behind his back. 'I thought you'd like this too.' It was a yellowed, crumpled exhibition guide from a Rothko show in New York the year before. The main picture was of a strange painting, with a creamy, sand-coloured background and two figures – for she was sure that's what they were – in geometric lines and curves, of red, green, blue and white.

'That one's called *Slow Swirl at the Edge of the Sea*. I liked the title.'

'How on earth did you find this?'

He smiled at her and touched his nose with his finger. 'You don't need to know none of that.'

She glared at him and he smiled disarmingly. 'Okay. I give in. I'm from near New York and a friend in the city found it for me.'

'Where near New York?' She wanted a place, a name.

'Schenectady. It's Nowheresville, USA.'

'It can't be worse than here,' she said.

'Ah, it is. It's industrial, ugly.'

She took his face in her hands and kissed his scarred cheek and twisted mouth. 'I don't understand anything about you,' she said. She had so many questions. This tiny crumb of truth was unsatisfying but it tasted sweet.

'You asked me what I do up there.' He gestured out of the window at the dark sky above the marsh. 'Imagine floating in the night sky, high above the world, up in the stars. Imagine it could suddenly end. Bang. Gone. That's how it is.' He clicked his fingers and she flinched.

He put his mouth near her ear and, breathing softly into it, reached behind her and unclasped her mother's pearls from around her neck.

In the dark of their isolation, with the sun gone down and the flickering of wisps on the marsh, they lay back down on the bed. There was something about how easy it was to lie down. Although the bed was cold and dusty like everything else, it was better than the floor. On a bed it somehow made it all right. Almost respectable. She shut her eyes and gripped his back while his embraces pressed into her. Even then, until the last moment she thought she might stop. But it all happened so quickly. He'd pulled down her knickers and himself on top of her before she knew the danger and by then it was too late, she was consumed. There was a sharp pain inside her and she cried out.

Afterwards, he slept, his pale eyelashes flickering, the tautness in his body slackened in sleep and his metal oval identification tags hung over his collarbone. Gingerly, she picked one up and held it in her hand. Punched in and set out in lines, she read:

DOHERTY, JOHN H.
20899970 AF
A NEG
CATHOLIC

It was for if he died, she knew. There was another chain too, with a tiny key attached and a small metal pendant shaped like a thin finger. She wondered what they were for but was afraid to touch them in case he woke.

She pulled up her knickers, put her vest back on and drew the old blanket up around her. Dazed and sore, her limbs were still burning. It was not romantic, it was a kind of glorious, awful violence. Even with him. That's what it felt like: something taken away from her and something given too. She wanted to dismiss it, to make it nothing, but she couldn't. It wasn't nothing. Her body was not the same, *she* was not the same, everything she touched, everything she looked at was left with a kind of mark. Before, she thought he was marking her body. Now it was inside her too. He was inside her. *This girl is no longer a virgin.* While he slept next to her she cried hot tears quietly into the pillow with the shame of allowing it to happen, that she had betrayed Arthur so thoroughly. But after a few minutes, she sniffed and wiped her eyes. Something had changed. And there was triumph in that, whatever other discomfort and doubt she might feel.

In the newspaper reports of the atom bomb test it said the heat was scorching and the power of the blast created a blinding light. If Russia bombed them, then all of Norfolk would be effaced, wiped out in a white-hot flash. Nothing else would matter then but that she and he had been here, in a damp marsh shack on the edge of the sea. It wasn't nothing.

8.

January 1953

'Y ou're late.'

Arthur stood on the threshold of Howe Farm and stared at Verity. 'But I'm so glad you're here. I can't bear all the rigmarole. You can keep me company while I sort out the breakfast.' She seemed hopped up on something, all twitchy and her words running on. Her face was flushed and shiny. She barely let him take off his coat before she dragged him by the sleeve through the hall towards the kitchen.

'I can't. I've got to go with them. I'd rather stay here.'

She stopped at the kitchen door, swung round and looked at him accusingly. 'What? Why? What on earth possessed you? You hate hunting.'

He shrugged. He didn't see why he should explain himself to her. And there was no easy way to explain the lust for destruction he was feeling. 'Peter asked,' he said. Something about the way her face creased in disgust made him want to hurt her. He thought about telling her about the man in the café and the metal case Jack had handed over. But it seemed like a scene from a thriller with no bearing on their lives.

'He took Peter to a prostitute in Norwich, you know.'

'Why are you telling me this?' She sounded bruised. He had a moment's doubt. What if he was wrong about her interest in Jack? But he'd started now. And he'd not forgotten her hesitancy when he asked her if she wanted to go to London with him.

'Because like everyone else he's got you fooled. You, Peter, the whole bloody town thinks he's so great. He's not what you think he is. If you knew what he was really like, you wouldn't hang onto his every word.'

'I don't know what you mean,' she said. Her voice was brittle and hard.

'Yes you do. You must see it. He's like it with all the girls, Verity. Not just you. You're not special.'

'I'm sure I don't know what you mean.' She had withdrawn, shrunk into the shadow of the wall.

'He's not a gentleman,' he said.

'And how would you know?'

'No,' he said, 'I have no idea.' He turned away from her.

'And what do I think he is?'

'A bloody hero.'

'Oh hardly,' she said, but her face was red. 'Go on then, tell me what *horrors* you've discovered.'

'He lied to us about where he's from,' he said. 'All that rot about deserts and horses and canyons. All rubbish. I've always thought it sounded too clichéd, like from a cowboy film. And his accent's all wrong. Well, I found out. He's from New York State.' Each word came out like a globule of spit that he wanted to get out of his mouth and he could feel his hatred bubbling up.

'I know about that,' she said, but he heard her voice catch. It served her right.

'We don't even know how old he is,' he went on.

'He's our age,' she said, but she didn't sound convinced. It hardly added up, couldn't she see? Jack had slipped out something about Korea and Germany to Peter, and although he'd backtracked, Arthur thought that if he'd seen that much service then he must be older than them.

He turned away from her and was going to leave when he stopped.

'I'm worried about you, Ver,' he said.

'I don't need you to look after me, Arthur.'

'Maybe you do. I mean, your mother needed help, didn't she, and no one helped her? I'm trying—'

'What do you mean?'

He frowned. He lowered his voice. 'You know it wasn't an accident, Ver,' he said, puncturing the bubble of pretence surrounding Mrs Frost's death.

She said nothing, just stood there trembling. He wanted to go to her and put his arms around her but her face was distorted in rage and horror. 'Ver—' he began again, but she recoiled from him.

'Please leave,' she said.

'I loved her too,' he said. Like a second mother. But Verity just stared at him more aghast. The kitchen door slammed behind him.

Outside, the cold air blasted his face. The sun hadn't yet risen and a low mist clung to the ground.

'There you are,' said Peter. 'Bloody glad you made it. Here, drink some of this.' He whacked Arthur on the back and handed him a tiny glass of something viscous and amber-coloured. Arthur downed the drink, the sweetness sliding into his throat. 'Nice little sherry,' said Peter. 'A fine pre-hunt tradition.' He seemed slightly drunk already, as if he was drowning out some frustration. He'd been increasingly reckless and maudlin since the awful trip to Norwich.

'Any chance of another?' Arthur asked. 'It'll shake off the cold.'

Peter filled up his glass and helped himself to another one too.

'No Jack?' Arthur said.

Peter's forehead creased in a frown. 'He was going to come but no sign so far. Probably something at the base.' He knocked back his sherry. 'Though I'm surprised he didn't come to see *her*.' He jerked his head to the house.

'Why would he?' Arthur said, his heart thumping painfully.

Peter rolled his eyes. Then he looked quizzically at Arthur. 'Come on, let's leave them to it and catch the beast.'

By the time they began to ride, Arthur was pleasingly drunk from three sherries in quick succession on an empty stomach. And Jack had not turned up. He was glad to be gone from the farmhouse, away from the awfulness of what he'd said. 'Don't let Ver see the body,' Peter had hissed urgently into his ear as Arthur had run down to the beach. He understood why when he saw her body. Mrs Frost was lying on the beach barely sheathed in a grey silk nightdress.

When they caught the fox, on a slight incline miles away from Howe Farm, the sun was rising behind them over the sea. Arthur held back at first, his hands stroking the horse's flank. But he couldn't keep away. He edged forward, a horrible curiosity propelling him. The animal was in the throes of death, clamped in the jaws of two hounds. A gash in its neck was open and bloody, the blood clotting its thick red fur. Its teeth were bared, black lips pulled back in a clown-like frown but its eyes were not yet dead. They shone, amber-coloured, jewel-like, gazing at him. He felt in his body a shiver of cold, and yet his hands, when he removed his gloves, were covered in a film of sweat.

Through the rest of the day, he couldn't rid himself of the image of the dying fox. He cycled furiously back home, barely seeing anything, and dumped his bike behind the shop. He aimed a vicious kick at the back wall of the yard. It was the way the fox had looked at him. Accusatory, as if it had seen something rotten in his heart. He had wanted to hurt Verity for putting up a barrier against him; and with a sick certainty he knew that he wanted to hurt Jack too.

Lying on her bed, with her mother's sampler above her – *Home Sweet Home* stitched in green – Verity felt again the cold, slow dribble of it down her thigh, Jack pulling back as if he had been burned. 'Jesus,' he would say. She turned away so as not to see it, the swollen, unnatural thing she tried not to look at, and pushed her face into the pillow until he drew near again and pressed against her back.

There must be something wrong with her, something immoral, and she imagined that it could be seen by other people, not like a giant red mark on her forehead like they used to give adulterers, but a stink, a reek, like a warning.

She told herself it was only once, it wouldn't happen again. It couldn't. It had been shocking, painful, and so reckless. But once the breach (that was how she thought of it) was made, it was easier for it to happen again. Her body started to respond to it and then to crave it. She began to think of her body as a different thing, something separate from the rest of her, something she had not known before and had not thought was possible. Now they went straight to bed, and only later she or he would make the bitter coffee. They would sit on the bed with their mugs and look at the changing light on the fields. Sometimes she would draw him, charcoal portraits with thick black lines, among the crumpled sheets and their bodies still smelling of each other. Sometimes he would take photographs of her lying in the bed and then he'd put the camera down and kiss her neck, his hands would be on her and it would start all over again.

On her side in bed, her body cooling, Verity watched the perfect curve of his sleeping back. The chains around his neck had fallen behind him. The tags, the tiny key and the cylinder dangled in front of her eyes. Tentatively, she reached out and felt the small metal ampoule between her fingers. She unscrewed it gently and tipped it up. Into her palm fell a creamy-white pill. She took a sharp intake of breath and almost dropped it. Jack breathed out and twisted slightly so he was further away from her. In a quick movement, she put the pill back in its case and screwed it shut tight.

On her back, hands shaking, it was as though she could feel the machinery of armies and governments whirring and moving through her. Of the world turning and her, helplessly caught up in a tide of change she didn't understand. Their lives – hers, Peter's, Arthur's – small and insignificant and disposable. And Jack – carrying a drug that could end it, from one heartbeat to the next.

When he woke, she would ask him finally. What are you doing when you leave me and fly east? Do you stop at the Baltic Sea, or do you fly over Moscow to Siberia? Through the Iron Curtain and beyond. Why? And in her heart the real question: Will you always come back?

But when he did wake he turned over and brought his face close to hers, and she said nothing because she didn't want it to stop.

Afterwards he stood above her, the black rectangle of the camera in front of his face, just a lick of flame-coloured hair above. She pulled the blanket over her head. It was both flattering and disquieting that she was being watched and studied. She wondered what the pictures would show of her, what iniquity looked like.

Friday, 30th January 1953
The day before the flood

Low Z depression, centre moving north-east
Further considerable deepening expected in LZ
in the next twenty-four hours

The old moon reflected bulbous and white on the East Fleet marsh. Muriel could hear the geese honking up a racket in the fields west of Beach Road. Every night in the winter, flocks of pink-footed geese returned to the west marshes to roost. But tonight they were still in the fields. They knew something was coming.

Down by the harbourmaster's house on the quay, Muriel took the weight off her feet. On the wall it marked the heights of the last ruinously high tides. 1930. 1912.

She'd come the long way back from the Buttlands, past the Pilchard on the Holkham Road, to drop off some laundry, when Verity Frost had ridden past her on her horse and off towards Harborough Hall. It occurred to Muriel that she was meeting the American. Muriel had been watching him. Yesterday she'd seen him leave the post office. Mrs Colman, the postmistress, was happy to tell her he sent a letter every week to an address in America. Arizona, she thought it was. He was very chatty, she said. Made her laugh, he did.

He was a right rummen, thought Muriel. She might ask him about who he was writing to when she next saw him.

10.

Afternoon

*North-westerly winds north of Scotland, driving
water from the Atlantic towards the North Sea
Gusts of up to 80 mph (Force 12: hurricane) in the Hebrides*

Jack was late, so late that soon it would be dark and her absence from home would be noticed. Verity had been waiting an hour. She smoked by the window of the shack, looking out over the empty, brown marsh. Dark grey clouds scudded across the sky, far away the pine trees shook and on the horizon the sea was churning. Tomorrow they were supposed to be going to a dance together, in the village hall. It was just a winter dance that the WI had organised, and all the servicemen from the airbase had been invited. They would be together, in public. But she kept thinking about what Arthur had said about other girls. She had been stupid, naïve. She had told Arthur she knew that Jack had lied about his upbringing, but she knew virtually nothing. *Schenectady*. She rolled the unfamiliar, foreign word around her mouth. Perhaps Arthur was just saying all of this out of jealousy, but what did he know? Why would Jack have concealed his origins anyway? It made no sense. A sharp pang of doubt stabbed her chest. Jack could be lying about all of it.

It was nearly three o'clock. She would have to go. She stood up and stubbed her cigarette out in the cup they used for an ashtray, but then she heard the creak of the damp, crooked front door and sat down again and lit up another cigarette as if nothing was wrong at all.

'Hey,' he said, standing in the doorway of the bedroom.

'Hello,' she said. 'I wondered where you'd got to.'

He just shook his head. She was expecting jokes, apologies, something. 'Come here,' he said, and she went to him, out of habit. He put his hand up her leg and unhooked the garter and they had sex quickly, without speaking.

'Aren't you going to tell me where you've been?' They lay with the cover over them, smoking his Camels. She hated the throb of doubt in her voice.

'I can't tell you and you know it,' he said.

'Is that because you were with a beautiful Russian spy?' She was trying to make a joke of it but failing.

'You know,' he said, 'when I first met you, you told me you were engaged to be married. Seems like I ain't the one with all the secrets.'

'I'm not marrying anyone,' Verity said. She was not a little girl any more, that was clear. And she would not marry her father's choice, whatever happened.

'Tell me anyway, I'm interested,' Jack said. She looked at him askance. He had the old, sly smile on his face. It was hard to know what he was thinking.

'There's nothing to tell,' she said, but he continued to

smirk at her. 'All right then. My father arranged it, the boy's a young farmer.'

'Rather than an old one.' Jack blew out a ring of smoke. She quite liked the tone of jealousy in his voice.

The smoke caught the pinkish twilight from the sun setting. From the bed, she could see the light bleeding out over the darkening marsh, catching the creeks in a final shimmer. The silhouettes of the pine trees swayed alarmingly at the far edge of the horizon. If she could get rid of everything apart from this – if she could suspend the moment, catch it, hold it and not ever let it go. If the light did not go out – if the thrashing sea rose and cut them off – they could stay here on an island of their own. But the sky continued to darken and the moment of terror and promise slipped away.

'Actually, I can't stand him, he's a horrible snob and a crashing bore, but he's very rich and that's what the farm needs. I'm like a nice parcel of land, you see, something to sell. I've put Father off but he told me if I don't decide what else I'm going to do, it's a fait accompli. He's insisting I meet him next week. Some tedious party. What do you care anyway?' She looked sideways at him to gauge his reaction.

'I care about anything to do with you.' He was still re-garding her with an intensity that made her feel uncomfort-able. 'If you're not going to marry this guy, what *are* you going to do?' he said after a while.

'I don't know any more,' she said. 'I was supposed to go to university.' She couldn't say more. It was too weighted with endings and decisions and difficulties. It seemed unbelievable that she could ever have thought she would be allowed to do such a thing. And what if, in some miracle, she'd been let in – she had no sense of how she would have lived, existed in an independent way. At the edge of her mind, she sensed that she was letting someone, or some concept of herself, down. Jack carried on smoking, idly caressing the back of her neck. She felt the heaviness of the air as they both waited for one of them to say something.

'There are other things you could do,' he drawled, which was true of course, but which one of those things was the right one, she had no idea.

'Your turn,' she said, afraid. 'Tell me what you're doing at the base. What's it all for.'

He sat up away from her. 'You know what we're doing. Keeping you all safe.' There was a tone of mockery and distance.

'But I don't, that's the point,' she persisted. 'It's all just rumour and conjecture. You can tell me. *I'm* not a Russian spy. Where were you today, for example?'

He gave her a long look and she thought he might actually tell her something real. But then in a sudden movement he stubbed out his cigarette and, underneath the blankets, drew his finger up her leg. She tensed. She was tired, would have liked to have slept, but her body responded anyway.

'Does Art do this to you?'

She jerked her head forward. 'What?'

He crawled under the covers. 'What about this?'

'Don't Jack, please.'

'You like it.'

'Don't tell me what I like.'

'I know you,' he said, and she wanted to slap him for his presumption. She drew back from him but not too far.

It was true. He did know something of her that no one else knew.

He kept going and kept asking. 'Please stop,' she said, but it was hard to concentrate.

Later, she did sleep and when she woke the room was dark and cold. She was alone in the bed. The kettle on the stove whistled from the kitchen. She got dressed quickly. Her stomach was empty and she felt sick, light-headed.

She was pulling on her coat from the pile on the floor when Jack came in with two mugs of coffee.

'Where are you going?'

She took the coffee from him, just for the warmth, but it was too hot and burned her tongue. The aftertaste was acrid, metallic. 'I need to get back, I need to go home. I'm horribly late.'

'Sure,' he said, 'let's just drink this.'

'No, I need to go now.'

'What's wrong?'

'Nothing,' she said, and tied her woollen scarf around her neck. But she wanted to speak, to make him have some kind of emotion. She wanted him to be honest with her, to tell her *something* she could hold onto. 'You shouldn't have said that about Arthur. He's your friend.' Her throat felt tight and she was afraid of crying. 'He's *my* friend.'

Jack snorted. 'He's no friend.'

'Don't be ridiculous, Jack, we've known each other since we were children.' Anger flared. 'He told me what you're like. He told me there were other girls.' Now it was out of her mouth, she was afraid of him telling her, afraid of knowing the truth.

'He did, did he? And why don't you ask yourself why he

said that to you? You really wanna have this conversation right now? Look at yourself, Verity, before you say anything about me.' His voice was low, almost a whisper. 'You're not so perfect. You with your old-money farmhouse and your *history* and your funny little English ways. All so very *proper* but you've not been honest with me. You've been stringing two guys along this whole time.'

'He also told me that you've been hiding things,' she said.

He stared at her. She was cold all over, detached from the person saying these things. And somewhere she felt the tingling burn of the truth, out in the cool, fresh air.

'Oh yeah, and how does he know so much?' he said, very quietly.

'I don't know.' It sounded pathetic.

He laughed. 'You even gonna tell me what I'm accused of lying about?'

'And you've never told us who you really are, who your family are, if you're not from the bloody desert, or a ranch. And what you're really doing here. Why does it all have to be so bloody cloak and dagger?' She was flushed and hot.

'And you're just gonna take this crap from a Jew? He's probably a bloody Zionist or a Commie for all we know.' His eyes were glinting with fire

'Don't be stupid, Jack. You can't say that. You're just a bloody liar who doesn't care about any of us.'

'A liar. That's rich. Cloak and dagger? You love all of that—' He waved his hand around the tiny room. 'All the subterfuge and hiding. I'm just someone to fuck before you get married to some pompous rich guy and disappear back to your real life. You don't really care about me.'

She flinched at his words and found her mouth twisting

into an ugly sneer. 'That shows how little you do know about me, then.' She turned and ran out of the house, careering along the dark lane on the black marsh.

A shout behind her. But she couldn't turn back and she ran, stumbling and crying, for the road. She heard the rumble of his machine coming up behind, the lights on her back illuminating a strip of road with her long shadow ahead. She turned to the glare.

'I never lied,' he said. 'You all created a version of me that suited you. Ask your brother. You wouldn't have looked at me twice if you thought I was a nobody from nowheresville. And you're wrong. I do care. I care about *you*, Vee, no one else,' he said. She wanted to believe it so much, to get on the bike and go back to the old marsh shack and for him to touch her and to do it all over again. She wanted to believe it so much that her body was already there.

'I don't believe you,' she said, wearily. 'I don't believe anything you say.'

'Screw you then,' he said. He revved the engine and drove off.

The lights of the bike receded into the distance towards the town as she half ran in a blur of rage and tears, until the rear light became a pinprick and then faded altogether. She ran all the way home, a harsh east wind against her face and it began to rain.

PART 3

HIGH TIDE

Saturday, 31st January 1953
The day of the flood

A vigorous trough of low pressure moving
east across the British Isles
Full moon, spring tide

1.

*Funnelling surge 8–10 ft above sea level
in the North Sea*

They used to kill witches by the incoming of the tide. Muriel's grandmother loved telling stories of the old days, delighting in the most gruesome of details. The old ladies, for they were usually old, were tied to a post on the ebb tide. Muriel imagined her own grandmother, stringy and sea-tanned, hair like iron filings, when she told her of the women, drowned as the tide came in over them, a crowd watching from the safety of the shore. Did this happen in Wells? she asked, eyes narrowed in suspicion. Oh yes, her grandmother said.

Muriel had always had a fascination with the foreshore. She was like a Victorian mud lark when a child, a cloth bag over her shoulder, hair wild about her face. A relic from another age. There was treasure here when the tide turned, when the storms came and left their bounty on the strand line.

Below the quay, hidden from the fishermen, the drunks and the children, by the old boat where she'd made the bonfire, she sat with the leftover chips Jack had brought her and licked the salt from her fingers. She could still smell his hair oil mingling with the chip fat. Chips and nylons for chaste kisses and posing. It seemed a fair exchange. He'd been distracted today and it made her afraid that the attention and the favours would be coming to an end. She knew him for a charlatan, a honey-voiced liar, but the things he offered were too good to resist. And it had been a laugh, putting herself in different poses for the camera. She had no idea what it was all for but she hadn't cared. Now, she sensed that change was coming and the change would bring her something new. She just didn't know what.

Away on the quayside she saw Arthur climb onto his bike and cycle off along Beach Road, a tiny moving figure. She ought to warn him. A storm was coming. She could feel it in the wind, in the greenish colour of the clouds. But he was too far away. She watched him pedal to the end of Beach Road, then she wiped her fingers on her skirt and jumped up. In the grey bowl of sky above the saltmarsh, the terns wheeled as if the wind had sucked them into a whirlpool. She drew her coat tight around her and climbed back onto the quay.

2.

Deepening Atlantic depression moving south-east
down to the North Sea

The wind buffeted Arthur as he pedalled. At the quay, boats bobbed up and down. The water in the harbour was flint-grey, the sky heavy. He struggled to keep steady, but it was good to be out of the shop. Mother had been in one of her funny moods again. She'd been to the doctor's surgery about a pain she referred to vaguely and he hadn't asked about it, though he knew he should.

As he cycled he mulled over his latest idea for a headline article to take his mind off Verity: *Nuclear Armageddon on Our Doorstep.* He would use the story to alert readers to the possibility of an accident or retaliation. He'd make them question why our government was allowing the Americans to use us as stooges in their hidden war.

The tide was coming in. Across the wide expanse of sand, the sky was now a strange yellow-grey, weighted with rain, and the sea was already halfway up the breakers. The wind whipped the trees to his left and created white tufts in the sea. The sky and wind seemed to be holding the water back. He turned away from the sea. It would be easier to take the route alongside the caravan park, skirting the edge of the wood. There was no way he could drag his bike along the sand on a day like this.

He cycled along the path, with the pond and the caravan park on one side, the wood on the other, and his heart beat faster than it should have done. Arthur had hardly seen Verity in the last couple of weeks. She'd been helping around the farm, or so she said. This was hard to believe. He suspected she was avoiding him. In fact, he hadn't seen her since the fox hunt, when all he could remember was her face, cold and closed-off to him in the kitchen before the hunt.

She was already there, her knees drawn up, just a few inches of stocking between her skirt and boots, with the tartan flask beside her on the rug. When he came upon her, he paused with the bike. She was gazing off into the distance, smoking, unaware of him. The sight of her caught his throat.

Then she saw him and started, like a deer. 'Oh, it's you. God, you gave me a fright. You were really staring.'

'What were you thinking about?'

'I've got something to tell you.' She fiddled with the hem of her skirt.

His heart lurched. It was over. He knew it.

'I've not been very good to you,' she said, and took a drag on the cigarette.

He sat down next to her. *No*, he thought, but he was too afraid to say anything.

'I've been thinking, that's all.' She was going to tell him she was in love with Jack. He realised that since the summer he had been waiting for this, waiting for her to say it. Over.

Finished. He should have left Wells when she had said no to coming to London. Why hadn't he? But he couldn't let go.

A crow cawed high up at the top of a pine tree. Her breath made white curls in the cold air. He watched a beetle crawl across his shoe.

'What?' he said, finally. Get it over with.

'Just… just that I'm sorry. I was wrong and I'm sorry.'

He tried not to smile and had to bite his lip. It wasn't over. Light-headed, he pulled her to him and fervently kissed her neck, her jaw, her mouth. Yes. She was his. Yes.

'Not here. We can't,' she murmured, looking up into the trees, but he already had his hand up her skirt. He had waited forever. He couldn't let it go again. Her hand pushed his away.

'There's nowhere else, Ver,' he said, touching her thigh. She twitched and he smoothed her hair, whispered into it, 'It'll be all right. We're as good as official.' There was no need to fear any more. She would marry him now – she must.

'I don't know, Arty.'

But *he* did. He laid her down on the rug over the damp ground and kissed her neck and then followed where his fingers went, kissing up her legs, feeling the smooth static of her stockings on his lips.

'What if someone comes? Oh.' But he heard her through treacle. The world had shrunk to her body and his.

No one appeared and she stopped talking, just let him touch her. He looked at her below him and noticed the dark shadows across her serious, intent face, from the canopy of the trees above them, swaying in the wind, and he drew her closer to him so he couldn't see her expression. Her eyes disturbed him and he pulled her into him so that she could not get away or turn into someone else.

Once, she moaned as if in pain and then nothing. She hardly moved, just lay still, frozen, gripping his back and he kept moving in and out, as gently as he could, expunging the memory of the woman in Yorkshire and the slick of guilt that covered him, until he stopped thinking and it was over, done. She was his.

He lay with her curled into him, her mouth in the crook of his neck, her legs twined around his.

'Are you OK?' he said, although he was afraid of the answer. Her silence made him scared he'd done something wrong. He'd thought about this moment for so long and in his imagining it had been different, slower, beautiful even. But his nerves had got the better of him.

'Yes,' she said, but her head was still buried into his neck and he couldn't tell if it was true or not.

'Come on,' he said, rubbing her back, 'we'll catch our death.' He caught a glimpse of the goosebumped, raw skin on her thigh.

Covered up again, wrapped in their layers, they huddled under the tree. He held her face in his hands. She seemed fragile; she was shivering. Verity was usually so sure of herself, so straight-backed, so queen-like, it was alarming to see her like this, white and pink and trembling like a child.

'Did I hurt you?' he said, but he couldn't look at her.

'It was just a… shock, that's all.'

He stroked her hair, at a loss for what to say. It was not how it should have been. What he'd done in Yorkshire had tainted it.

'I'd better go,' she said, 'it's a filthy day.' She squeezed his hand and smiled faintly. Her eyelids looked red and sore.

'Shall I walk you home?'

'No, no, you go. I'll be fine.' She brushed her skirt down, stood up and waited for him to stand. As he straightened himself he realised tears stood in the corners of her eyes.

'What is it? What have I done?' He had no idea what to do. A ripple of anger ran through him. With himself and with her, for ruining it. In dismay, he realised he must have hurt her. But what he could do about it now, he didn't know.

She wiped the back of her hand across her cheeks. 'Nothing. Nothing. Being stupid, that's all.'

In relief, he tried to take her face again, to kiss her mouth, the wetness on her cheeks, to kiss away the confusion, but she moved her head and pecked him on the forehead instead.

'I'll make it better,' he said, hardly knowing what he was saying. 'When we're together. It'll be better next time.' He wanted to make it true, to bring it into being by her acknowledgement that this is what would happen. But instead, she spoke matter-of-factly.

'It's fine, Arty, really. Sorry. Got to dash though.' She squeezed his hand again and walked away from him, but stopped and turned back. 'Are you – going to the winter dance tonight? It's at the village hall.'

'I can't. Deliveries. See you next week?' His breathing was loud.

She didn't answer. Instead she said, 'Do you love me?'

'Yes,' he called back. 'Always.' The wind took the words and whipped them away before he could unsay them. He didn't know what it meant but he had been saying it to himself for so long it was the only answer. She gave him a small, sad smile and walked off in the direction of the farm.

When she was gone, he became aware of the rain falling heavier now, dripping even through the thick canopy of pines and the wind howling out at sea. He realised he hadn't asked her if she loved him back.

3.

*Gales officially forecast in nearly all districts
of the British Isles*

All afternoon, as the rain fell unceasing outside her
window and the sky turned from dull to black, Verity
stayed shut up in her room. She alternated between lying on
the bed, face down, and pacing between the door and the
window. She was supposed to go to the dance in town but
how could she go now? When Jack had asked her, just over
a week ago, it had felt like a small but important victory.
The thing between them would no longer be hidden and
sordid but something else. But so much had happened since
then: the argument yesterday and then, today, Arthur. Now
it felt like a cruel, horrible joke she had played on herself.

Tea came and went. She couldn't face eating. The wind
began battering the windows and Peter stomped out into
the rainy afternoon to make sure the cows were secure in
the cowshed. Still, she didn't change, her face remained
bare. Finally, she stripped out of her clothes and sat in front
of the dressing table in her room. Her face was blotchy and
red, her hair a mess. It was hard to reconcile the image of the
girl in the glass with what she had done. She was a coward,

a craven coward. Unable to tell Arthur the truth, she had done something much much worse. Perhaps there was something wrong with her. She gagged and reached the sink in the corner of the room just in time to retch into it, a thin acid yellow stream of bile dripping into the sink. She sank to the floor and held onto the pink ceramic, her face pressed against its cool edge. The room darkened. Downstairs, she heard a door slam. Slowly, she pulled herself up, filled the sink and washed herself with her flannel, wiping the smell of the vomit away. She brushed her teeth. It felt good to be clean. Her heart was still beating too hard, as if it was waiting, getting ready to fight or flee.

The downpour became a patter and a drip and then stopped. The moon was rising and silver droplets covered the garden hedges. She looked at her bedside clock. Nearly five. The dance would already have started. She stood again by the glass in her slip and tried to see herself as Jack saw her – something worthy of attention. But she scowled at her image. In her dressing table drawer, poking out from beneath her underwear, the Turner postcard and the exhibition brochure he'd got from America. The fact that he'd found these precious things for her meant something. To decide what to do, she had to see him. She took them out and propped them against the mirror, then flung open the wardrobe.

Arthur felt the imprint of Verity's mouth on his, still tingling, as he rolled his bike back along the path, the sea a roar, black in the twilight. He could barely see the trees in the dark and was too stunned to cycle but clung to the line of the woods to make his way back. The night was closing in on him. He should have left earlier and he felt a physical relief when he reached the end of the path and pushed the bike up the slipway to the West Bank where he could see the lights of the village. The night was coming and Mother would expect him for his tea.

Behind him, the moon shone through the clouds, casting a silvery light on the boats in the harbour. There was the same strange yellow tinge to the twilight. The water in the harbour looked oily and black. With the wind up, Arthur could see the boats swaying on the water. His mac flapping and his cap pulled low over his ears, he rode hard for home.

As he neared the shop, a solitary old man in a peaked cap called out, 'Best watch out on that there bike, there's a foul old sou'wester coming.'

Arthur said he certainly would. But the old man stood motionless, staring out at the boats in the East Fleet as if he was waiting for them to give him the sign to do something.

'Tide's not ebbing,' said the man. 'Fair rummen.'

Mother was still in the shop, stock-taking, marking it all out in her blue notebook.

'I'm back,' Arthur said, poking his head round the door.

She looked up briefly, nodded. 'Set the table,' she said, and continued noting down stock.

He went back up to their quarters and laid the table for two, put on a pot of water for tea and buttered bread for their bread and jam. His mind was full of Verity.

'You look a mess,' said his mother. She switched on the radio and the Saturday big band concert was just coming to an end.

'Windy out,' he said.

'You're stopping in now, though.'

'Still got a couple of deliveries.' He couldn't stay in with Mother, just the two of them on a Saturday night. Other people were out, having fun, going to dances, that sort of thing. He had to get out.

'On a night like this? Don't be silly.'

'It's fine, Mother, I just need to do two more.'

'There was a ship went down near Ireland. I heard it on the wireless at the four o'clock bulletin. Nearly all of them drowned.'

'That's terrible,' he said. He wished she wouldn't do this.

'All the women and children. Imagine it.' She had a relish in the horror of it. It had been the same in all her letters throughout the war. A running tally of the dead, as if in cataloguing all the deaths she was remembering – or memorialising – every single one of those lost. Every lost child was one of hers. All the babies she'd never had; all the names of people he never knew from his father's side, killed in the camps; his father as good as dead. Only he and her left now. Arthur said nothing.

'Listen,' she said, and turned the radio up.

'*The full force of the gales is being felt in the extreme north of Scotland.*'

Her face was rapt. '*All sea and air services there are at a standstill, and from all parts of the islands there are reports of small boats sunk, roofs blown from houses, and trees uprooted.*' It went on for some minutes, detailing all the effects of the gales in Scotland and Northern England, but eventually it moved on to other news items and she turned it back down.

*

Strong north-westerly winds veering to northerly
Gales 120 mph

The hallway was dark, only the small orange glow of a single lamp by the telephone table providing any light. Verity was about to open the front door to slip out when she heard a hacking cough from behind her and the heavy footsteps of her father.

'Verity? Where are you going?'

She stiffened, but plastered on a smile and turned to face him. 'There's a dance in town, Father. I'm meeting some friends there.'

'Friends?' He spat this out as if he'd never heard of anything so ridiculous.

'Yes, school pals, that's all.'

'Your mother—' He stopped and seemed to sway as if a strong wind was battering him. Verity almost ran forward to save him, but he pulled himself up tall. 'Your mother would be worried about you if she was here. These dances, these parties. You need to meet the right sort of chap.'

Her fists closed, opened and closed.

'I could get a job,' she said. 'I could teach.' The words had blurted out. She sounded desperate, not even believing it herself, but there had to be some alternative to helping out at the farm until she married a member of the farming gentry, which is all she had to look forward to. She wanted to say more, to ask him to help her find a place in the world, to plead for him to understand, to tell him she missed the way he used to talk to her as if she was worthy of educated discussion. But he was far away at the other end of the hallway, wreathed in shadow, the circle of lamplight not reaching him.

'De Vere says his son would be willing to take you for a drive next week,' he said. 'For her sake, you could at least consider the boy.'

A scream rose in her throat but she clamped it down. 'I've got to go,' she said, and opened the door to gusts of wind from the cold night. She thought she heard a door slam upstairs.

'You're still a minor until you're twenty-one,' he said, his voice unexpectedly loud in the echoing hall, but she didn't reply and ran out, letting the door shut behind her.

On the way to the dance the rain returned, harder than before. She ran, collar up and head down, against the driving rain, her scarf scant protection against the wind and the bottom of her stockings damp. Glimpsing the harbour as she ran, she saw in the moonlight the water was bulging and swollen. It moved back and forth like an animal waiting to pounce. The tide was high, too high, threatening to spill over the quay wall. God, she hoped their land wouldn't be too affected if the tide overspilled tonight; salt was the enemy of the farmer.

Outside the door to the dance, she hesitated. In a puddle she glimpsed her reflection, shining, lipstick-bright, until a gust of rain fractured and scattered it. Under her mother's trench coat, she was wearing a purple silk dress her mother had made for her years ago, for a hunting party, and underneath the dress, nylons Jack had given her. The dress was too tight around her bust and it came a little higher over the knee than it used to, but it was her only good dress. She didn't count the blue she had worn at Midsummer; she'd made that one herself from cheap satin. For the purple, her mother had chosen everything – the material, the design – and Verity had hated it. Her mother cared about fashion and took all the magazines. She remembered an evening gown her mother had worn for a party early on in the war. It had been a pale gold colour that shimmered in the light. Her mother had answered a knock at the door. Then the sound of a glass smashing. The gramophone playing a jazz tune. Someone said, 'Nicholas, you'd better come,' to their father. Verity saw him kneeling by their mother's fallen form, the telegram in her hand, shattered glass by the hem of the gold gown and wine seeping into the floorboards.

This must have been Jeffrey, only nineteen, the last of the line. Her mother kept saying, 'What will happen to Felford?' As if the family estate was all that mattered. It was all gone now and the gold dress hung in the wardrobe, too small for Verity to ever wear. But she saw the purple dress now for what it was – an act of love her mother had been unable to express otherwise.

She was cold and the wet would ruin her hair, but she was paralysed on the threshold. What if he wasn't there? What if he *was* there? What if *Arthur* was there? God, no. But he had said he wasn't going. She had no sense of exactly what she was going to do, and it sent a shiver all over her. She swallowed. Her empty stomach growled.

She pushed open the door.

It was so bright inside, not like the moody, romantic atmosphere she had expected. She blinked in the doorway. Everyone was twirling each other, moving at speed around the floor, the band in full swing. The beat was fast and rhythmic. Teeth flashed as they spun past her. It was much livelier than the dance at Midsummer. The world had been smashed open since then. She took off her scarf and shook out her hair, trying to smooth it, scanning the dancers for him. No sign. She edged around the crowded floor and found the little bar, which was staffed by a brassy woman with piled-up hair whom she'd never seen before.

'Can I... could I please have a lemonade?'

The woman stared past her.

'I'm getting this one. Two whisky sours for me and the lady.' A hand was on her elbow, she was turned around and there was Jack, his smile inscrutable. She took all of him in in a daze: his hazel eyes, the freckles on his thin, crooked nose, the too-wide mouth. The familiar rush of heat spread up her body and prickled on her skin.

'Hey,' he said, holding her elbow. 'I thought you'd stood me up. But here you are, Aphrodite, come to life right here in front of me.'

She didn't want to but she smiled and blushed and took the drink with gratitude from the brassy woman. Her hand shook. She smiled her thanks at the woman too. Nasty cow.

'Don't be ridiculous, Jack,' she said, and blinked furiously, trying not to give in to him. Not yet.

'Let me take your coat, you can't sit here in a coat.' She passed him the mac and sat at a trestle table by the bar, shivering in her dress. She saw now the cut was far too low. He put her coat over the back of another chair and whistled.

'That is some dress.' She had to look down and take another large gulp of the bitter drink. It was important not to lose her resolve.

'I shouldn't be here,' she said.

'Who says? Pete? Art? They ain't your keepers—'

'My father, everyone. Me.' She tried to glare at him but looked fixedly at his ear.

'I don't believe you.' He sounded as if he was humouring a child and leaned back.

She took another sip of the whisky. He had not understood. She was trying to make it right. 'I can't be seen with you. I... love someone else.' This was not true. With a wrenching pull of sadness, she knew she didn't love Arthur. This morning she'd thought the only way out of this disaster was to return to him. Now she was here, in Jack's presence, it was falling apart.

Jack's smile was twisted in bitter amusement. He lowered his voice to a whisper. 'But you're happy to be with me when no one else is looking? You said this to Arthur too?'

She leaned back from him. 'No! And what about you? I don't even know if you mean anything you say. I don't know anything about you. I'm sorry about what I said but this still has to stop, Jack. It's wrong.' Even as she said it, she didn't believe herself. Oh, what a hideous mess she had created.

He was looking at her as if weighing something up. He leaned in again, close enough for her to see the specks of gold in his irises. 'I don't think this is *wrong*, Vee. Maybe, those other people, maybe they were wrong. Maybe we've both made mistakes. But this? It doesn't feel wrong to me. It feels right.' His hand came over and covered hers. She noticed how the freckles were sprayed over them like glitter. 'Listen. I'm not going anywhere – no flying tonight. Come with me—'

'Shouldn't we dance?' she said, standing up quickly, still with his hand in hers.

'Yeah, sure.' He put his arm around her waist and pulled her to the floor.

The next few minutes were a blur of feet and arms, Jack's face close to hers, holding her gaze. Together and out. Together again. His left hand gripped hers and his other was on her waist, a burning imprint through her dress onto her skin. She should pull away, release herself, but she couldn't do it. The beat of the music, pounding in her ears and in her stomach. All the time his grip on her never faltered.

After a few minutes, she felt dizzy and sick. They sat out the next one and she waited for the vertigo to pass. She watched the other dancers, only vaguely recognising a few of them from the town. She didn't mix with these people, they were people from Wells, not her sort. She thought they might know her but the dancing made her reckless and she didn't care. If only they knew what she had done! A bubble of laughter almost escaped before she swallowed it back down. Jack was wearing his uniform and she felt a rush of silly pride that she was with an American officer, the man with the most life in him. It was vain but she thought how handsome they must look, the two of them, the brightness of his hair against her dark – his uniform and her purple dress. An image formed of herself on his arm, a couple. On a ship to America, his arm tight around her waist.

He pulled her up again although her head hurt. He had his hand at the base of her spine. 'This is what flying feels like,' he said.

'Yes?' She was only half listening. She was looking at the whiteness of his teeth and the golden flecks in his hair, catching fire in the bright lights, and she realised that he was entirely beautiful to her now. Every single freckle, blemish and line was fascinating.

'I'd like to take you up in a plane. Take you away. Fly over the ocean and show you the mountains and the desert. The harshness of it, the brutality, not like here. Everything so *damp*. We could go riding together, you and me. You could teach me.'

She couldn't look at him.

'And I could take you to New York City and we could climb the Empire State Building and the Statue of Liberty and go to the Met to see those paintings you love.'

'They're in London too,' she said in a low whisper, trying not to smile.

'We'll go to London then. We'll go anywhere you want to go.'

'Stop it,' but she didn't want it to stop. 'I was supposed to go to university,' she said in desperation.

'I'm not stopping you doing anything,' he said. They twirled around and he brought her in close and breathed into her ear, 'How about it?'

'How about what?' she said, fighting the smile on her lips. 'It's just a dream you're spinning, a fairy tale, a mirage, an illusion.'

'It doesn't have to be—'

'But if it's all a lie... I have no idea who you *are*, Jack. Who you *really* are. I mean, I know you're a pilot. At least I think you're a pilot. And are the planes carrying atomic bombs? And you've never told me anything about your family. And I don't know if you're playing around with other girls. It's not fair.'

The tune came to an end and they were standing, facing each other. The band struck up another song but they stayed quite still.

'You know,' he said, stroking her wrist, 'last night when you walked out, that was a bad day. We lost someone, that night. I mean truly lost. That's why I was late. It wasn't another girl. I swear to you.'

She swallowed. 'But what about all the other lies, why can't you tell me—'

'None of it's a lie. I wanna tell you—'

A girl tapped Jack on the shoulder. Bewildered, Verity realised it was Muriel with orangey-red lipstick and her blonde hair done up in curls, a dark green dress clinging to her hips and bosom.

'Hello, soldier,' said Muriel, her eyes fixed on Jack.

Verity forced herself to smile at her old friend, remembering the polka dot dress at the Midsummer dance and the way Muriel's feet moved nimbly in her red shoes, while she had been clumsy and slow in that preposterous blue dress. 'Hello, Muriel, how are you?'

'Oh hello, Miss Frost, I didn't recognise you without your glasses.'

Verity scowled. She rarely wore her glasses these days, only for studying.

'Miss Frost? You two know each other?' Jack wore an expression of surprise and discomfort. The three of them stood in an awkward circle until he broke it. 'Let me get drinks.'

They both started to protest, but he moved swiftly to the bar, calling out, 'Whisky sours for three!'

'What about me, old boy, can I get one too?' They all

turned round and Verity felt herself flood with cold.

In front of them stood Peter, his hair plastered to his face with rain, dripping onto the dance floor in his long, waxed coat, his face a distorted picture of fury and love.

First breach of the sea wall, where the old ships' channel leaves Wells channel for Holkham Staithe

They ate their tea and she didn't mention it again or pressure him to stay in. After all, every Saturday was the same. Arthur never used to do his deliveries on Saturday afternoons as he always saw Verity, bothering away at the unbearable itch, and completed them later instead. Although he'd hardly seen her recently, his mother hadn't noticed.

His mother used to go to the cinema. They were showing the Clark Gable flick at the Regal, the sort of thing she would have loved. But she never seemed to go any more. There was something ailing with her but he couldn't bear to find out.

As he was leaving, she said, 'You enjoy yourself then.'

'What did the doctor say, Mother?' It came out tersely. He resented being pressured into asking and was guilty for it too.

She brightened. 'Just a little trouble with my insides,' she said, but he saw her thin hands were fluttering.

'Will you be all right?'

His mother tried to smile at him but it was a mere flicker. He knew the answer before she said it. Cancer. She didn't tell him where or how bad, which told him there was no hope. He leaned down to kiss her cold cheek and found it damp.

'I'll look after you,' he said, and he wanted to. But his head was screaming with the injustice of it. She had to get better so he could leave. He could feel the tentacles of her need suffocating him.

Out on the quay, it was dark. Rain drove into his face as he tied his packages onto the basket with rope. Down the street, a little crowd was cramped together under the protection of the awning from French's fish and chips, their coats pulled close around them, bathed in the amber glow.

It wasn't long past five. If he was quick with his deliveries he could see Verity at the dance. He could ask her to marry him. The sickness in the flat made him want even more to flee to her. He couldn't wait any more.

4.

Northerly gale of exceptional severity

'Pete, buddy. Have mine,' Jack said, beaming, handing Peter a drink. And he put his hand on her brother's back and led him to the bar. Verity stood, hovering, watching them, when Jack looked over his shoulder and winked at her. There was a movement at her arm and she whisked round to find... nothing. Muriel had gone. Verity had momentarily forgotten that Muriel had even been there.

Abandoned, she found a chair and took small sips of her whisky and watched the dancers. She wondered what they were talking about. Peter must be livid that Jack had brought her here. Or, more likely, he was livid with her. She looked over to the bar but could no longer see them. She began to feel stupid, sitting on her own. As they were still not at the bar, she might as well get a drink.

She was standing, sipping her whisky sour though each sip made her gag, when Peter came striding up to her. He looked furious. Had Jack gone off with Muriel? He wouldn't do that to her, surely? Not after all he'd said. No, that was impossible.

'That's enough, Cinderella, home time for you.'

'But I don't want to go,' she said. 'Just because you don't like other people, it doesn't mean I don't. I *like* dances and other people and—'

'Yes, I can see that,' said Peter and he had a nasty little smile at the corners of his mouth. Then he added, 'You don't know what you're getting into, Ver. Besides, it's foul outside, a storm is coming.'

She looked around desperately for Jack but couldn't see him.

'You're not my *father*, Peter,' she said, words tumbling out. 'You're just jealous!'

'I'm getting you out of here,' he said, his teeth gritted, grabbing her and hurting her arm. Under his breath he hissed, close to her face, 'Bloody disgrace.'

Where the hell was Jack? She scanned the bodies in the hall but could see no one with red hair. Peter had a hard grip on her arm and although she struggled against him, he propelled her out of the door.

Outside in the dark, she yelled, 'Get off me! Leave me alone!' but he ignored her, keeping a tight hold on her arm and looking grimly ahead until they got to his bike.

'Hitch up on the back. We need to get home to the farm. Father needs us. If you hadn't been such a silly *tart* then I wouldn't have had to come and get you.'

'You didn't *need* to come and get me. I am not a *child*,' she spat. 'If you were normal you'd understand.'

He stared at her coldly and just said, 'Get on.'

Glaring back at him, she did as she was told, afraid of his reaction. With a hollow thud, the realisation hit her that he was in love with Jack and had been from the beginning.

But he didn't say anything about Jack, he just said, 'Focus

on bloody holding on, you're going to have us both over in a minute. You're drunk, you stink of it. You'd better start sobering up before we get home.'

She clung onto his sodden trench coat on the back of one of the farm bikes, her face against the wet cloth as he wove as if drunk himself against the wind and the rain, towards home.

He was wrong. She wasn't blotto, she couldn't be. She'd hardly managed to drink anything before Jack had whisked her onto the dance floor and before Peter had turned up. Two whisky sours, hardly worth writing home about. She wished she *was* drunk.

'Bloody hell!' Peter shouted. 'Look at that.'

Water was already lapping over the quay wall, splashing onto the quayside.

'Christ, we need to get a move on. There must have been a breach already. Get *on*,' Peter shouted and she obeyed, perching herself back on the bike after slipping off.

For a suspended moment, before he began pedalling, she thought she could run back to the dance, to Jack. But her limbs were heavy and her head hurt and the water seemed as if it would swallow her. It didn't look like the usual high tide. It was unnatural. Wrong, somehow.

When they arrived at Leafy Lane, it was a wide, running stream already and they had to dismount and haul themselves and the bike through the cold water. It was up to their ankles and then, as they dragged on, up to their calves. Peter shouted, 'Come on, Ver!' as she fell behind but her legs were so slow. He held her hand and pulled her sometimes, until they finally stopped and clambered up a small bank on the corner to the farm where they could see, thank God, lights on in the farmhouse.

Breathing heavily, they looked at the water, ruining the winter-sown crops. She could smell it too – the smarting salt of the sea. Saltwater – *no place on the land*, she heard her father's voice – glistening in the moonlight, beautiful and destructive. Peter passed her a small silver flask in silence. She looked up at him but he wasn't looking at her. It made her think that Peter must be drinking more than she'd realised; that he was becoming like Father. She drank the whisky and spluttered, then drank again; the sweet, cloying, powerful liquid slipped down her throat.

'We'll need it,' Peter said, taking it back off her, and returning it to his pocket, already lowering his long legs back down into the dark water.

'Oh God,' she said, clutching her stomach. It heaved and buckled and she felt she had to hold onto it or she would explode.

'Bloody hell, Ver,' she heard him say, but she didn't care because she was doubled over, vomiting the whisky into a black hedge.

Later, all she remembered of the last part of the journey was the pain in her legs, the bitterness in her mouth, her tongue swollen. Something hard brushed against her in the water. Fear rose inexorably like the water.

At the house, the lights were off on the ground floor. Stumbling, splashing through the wavelets sloshing round the door, the water almost up to the letterbox, Peter said, 'You're here now, get him up to the top floor and stay there.'

'What about you?' she wailed. 'Aren't you coming too?'

'I've got to check on the animals.' He gave her hand a quick squeeze and she clung onto it.

'What about the house? All the furniture, *Mother's* things? And we don't know if Father is... How do you know he's not out there?'

'He won't be. But if he is, I'll find him. I can't wait. The livestock, Ver, the bloody cows. I've already been away too long. It's probably already too late, but I've got to try. We can't afford to lose them. We just can't.' His face was contorted in worry.

As if from high up in a hot air balloon, she saw what a precarious state the farm was in. It would only take one thing to sweep it away. As he started wading she was immobilised by helplessness.

Peter stopped, came back. 'Take this, you might need it. But eat something, for God's sake.' He put the silver hip flask into her cold, wet hand.

'You might need it too!' she shouted after him, but there was no sign of him in the darkness.

Second breach of the sea wall, halfway along the embankment

Rain was lashing the sails of the boats in the harbour and dripping off the guttering in Staithe Street when he emerged from the house of the spinster sisters, stuffed with the scones that they baked specially for his visit. He stood under the slight protection of their doorway lintel, peering down the street, which was lit from above by the yellow light from the sole street lamp, making strange shadows on the cobbles. It would have been easy to have dragged the bike round the corner to home but at the end of the street was the village hall. He could hear, just above the crash of the sea and the banging of Thurgood's sign against the wall, the bee-bop of a jive. It was later than he'd wanted, already after six. He must have missed most of it, chit-chatting with the old ladies in their dark and musty rooms, while his peers were flinging each other around. Whenever there was a jive on the radio, it would only be a few bars before his mother switched it over, tutting about 'black music'. He imagined the girls' skirts flung out like fans, their feet a blur of taps and kicks, Verity's dark hair swinging.

Arthur ran down the slippery street, past the dark windows of the milk bar and the butcher's, tripping over his bicycle and his own feet in haste. He slowed on sight of the village hall and leaned the bike against the wall opposite underneath the awning of the haberdasher's. He smoothed his hair, trying to catch his breath. The twang of the guitar floated over, through the rain. The music had changed. Now it was a crooning song. Inside, there would be slow, awkward dancing.

Before he pushed through the doors and into the bright space beyond, he needed courage. He felt in his pocket, pulled out a cigarette and sparked it up. He was smiling at the words as he took two steps across the street, to where the hall door, miraculously, was opened for him. In the seconds the door was open, he tried to adjust to the glare. He had just enough time to get the impression of figures in movement, when a blonde girl pushed past him, out of the door and onto the street. He barely turned his head. He stayed with his hand on the door, transfixed by the warmth and movement of the room, trying to make out Verity or

Peter. Then, something – the lingering breath of a familiar perfume, a clatter – made him turn and look back into the darkness of the rainy street. The girl was hurrying away, her coat billowing out behind her in the wind.

He realised, with a start, it was Muriel.

'Muriel, are you all right? What—'

He looked back to the hall but the light from the dance glowed momentarily and the door swung shut.

'Muriel, wait, I've got my bike...'

She turned and hesitated long enough for Arthur to pick up his fallen bike and run, dragging it down the street to draw level with her. Her hat was pulled down low over her hair and she looked past him, back to the hall. In the light of the moon, he saw that her face was shiny and flushed pink and her hair was falling out of the hat in bright blonde sprays, like the straw hair of a scarecrow.

'Got a cigarette?' she demanded and he produced one for her.

'What are you following me for?' she said, looking up at him with black smudges round her eyes, her red mouth smeared at the edges, her hand pushing her hair back under the hat.

'I... I don't know, I thought you looked upset... Has someone hurt you? Sorry.'

'I should've expected it. He were never going for me, not with her around. What are you always sorry for anyway, Arthur Silver, you've done nothing wrong. Why do you always say sorry for everything?' She seemed angry with him but he couldn't think what he'd done. 'She ent here, if that's what you're after.'

'No, I... I don't know... sorry.'

She laughed, showing her sharp little teeth. 'You don't know much, do you?'

'No, I suppose not,' he said, miserable that he hadn't seen Verity and he was now standing out in the rain with Muriel Gittings laughing at him. 'I was going to see you home, but I don't have to.'

She gave him a proper smile. 'No, I'm sorry, I was being raw, don't worry about me.'

He was struck by the redness of her cheeks and her mouth, the knowledge in her very green eyes. He leaned forward, almost toppling towards her. In the same instant she reached up towards him and kissed him on the cheek. He felt his breath catch and had to grip his bike to stop himself from falling forward.

'I best be off home, night's going something terrible.' She moved back a step.

'No, you can't, it's dangerous.'

People were hurrying past them, heads down against the wind and rain. An older woman shouted to them, 'Get off home, they've stopped the film, flood's coming,' and she pulled her headscarf tighter still round her neck, bent her head and scurried off down the High Street, splashing through the rain.

'See?' he said. 'You can't go on your own, there's a flood coming.'

'I can, Arthur. I know these streets better than you do. You get back to your mother.' Was she mocking him?

'I should take you home.'

'If you must,' she said, and strode off towards the East End.

Arthur thought for a moment, dumped the bike against

the house opposite and trotted awkwardly after her.

There was no one about now, everyone tucked up at home, sitting out the storm. She darted through the little streets and Arthur struggled to keep up against the rain. He was drenched to his skin, and almost blinded by the rain in his eyes. All he knew was that they were back now, close to the sea; the roar of the water was unnaturally loud, so loud that it crowded out all other thoughts from his head. Finally, she stopped, somewhere down near the East Quay.

'You can leave me here, it's all right. You go back. Water's rising, you better hurry,' Muriel called to him as he ran to catch up with her.

He had been so desperate to keep up, he hadn't noticed his wet feet. The street was flowing with pale brown water. It came down towards them in little rolling waves. There must have been a breach.

'I can't leave you,' he shouted at her through the rain.

She leaned in close to him and he could see the outline of her mouth and her eyes still shone.

'You have to. You get your mother. I'll be fine. I'm a mermaid, me.'

'Muriel, please.' He found himself gripping her shoulders.

She came in close and kissed him on the lips and his heart faltered at the boldness of it. 'You're a good one, Arthur Silver. Not like them other ones. I won't forget.'

And then she tore from his grasp and splashed into the water, hop-skipping through it as if it was a mere puddle, towards the shacks and cottages of the East End.

'What happened at the dance?' he shouted after her, but perhaps the wind took the shout because she only turned, very quickly, put her fingers to her lips and was gone. He

5.

19.27 train from Hunstanton hit by a bungalow at 19.32
Wells beach and woods cut off from the town by the flood

The front door wouldn't open, but one of the windows in the bay could be prised ajar, the wood old and brittle. It came away in Verity's hand and she tripped into cold water in the shadowy drawing room. It was up to her ankles here, not so bad. Thank God for the slight rise the house had been built on, the way it looked out from the top windows over the sea, thank God for that. But the rugs! The Queen Anne chairs! They'd been in her mother's family for years.

'Father!' she called. The only answer, the wind whining and rain pounding on the windows.

Again she called, wading through to the hallway. No answer. He must have left the house, but she went forward to his study anyway. She imagined Peter out there in the dark, the cold, the relentless rain, the rising water.

No light. She felt along the walls.

'Father,' she called out again, but quieter now, not expecting a response. In her throat a jagged pain.

But a sound came from ahead, a muffled sound, she

couldn't think of what, but hurried on and came to the study door at the end of the hallway.

The door seemed stuck. She pushed hard and water came rushing down around her legs when she got the door open. It was higher in here, nearly shin-height. Moonlight streamed through the bay windows illuminating a ghostly scene. A flooded room, sparkling. Shadowy bookshelves enclosed the walls, books from the lower shelves bobbed in the floodwater, and a figure was slumped onto the enormous desk, twitching, grumbling, but not awake. She had a pang of sorrow for the saltwater-swollen, lost books.

He'd been drinking so heavily the flood must have risen around him without him knowing. Was it because of her? Her rational self knew that this was how he'd been since her mother died, but she'd heard the catch in his voice when he said 'Your mother'. And she'd let the door shut on his face. When she tried to wake him to get him upstairs, he jerked and grouched and called her 'bloody woman' and she wondered if he'd spoken to her mother that way. She got him upstairs, with his arm around her neck, holding him up and cajoling him. Her arms ached with the weight of him. He was not an old man, and still strong from the farm, his arms ruddy and thick, but drink weakened him and he stumbled with slow effort up to his bedroom. They didn't need to retreat to the old servants' quarters in the attic to be safe from the flood, she decided. The house was strong, and with its position of power, the water could not get up there. She laid him down on the bed that had been his alone for the past year and a half, pulled a cover over him. He turned away from her, without a word, and slept.

For a minute after she shut the door on him she sank

down on the landing and had to hold onto the banister to keep herself from lying down. Why couldn't he look after her? Why did he have to make her feel so guilty?

Back down the stairs, she felt her way through the cold floodwater in the dark to the pantry. Leaning against the cool wall, she was overcome with nauseous hunger and took some bread and cheese in a napkin. Clutching it, she returned upstairs and along the landing to her own room, which overlooked the back fields to the sea. Through the window she could just see the sea above the pine trees, churning and foaming in the moonlight. Out in the fields somewhere was Peter. And somewhere else, Jack. Was he thinking of her? She closed her eyes in a silent prayer. For all that she was a hypocrite, maybe God would listen. Save Peter. Save us. Save the farm. Save Jack. And Arthur too, she added at the end. She sat down in the window seat and picked at her bread, looking down over the flood. A lookout in a crow's nest, watching a seastorm.

Her heart beat hard. There was a crazed beauty to the storm. It was almost miraculous, the way it took away all the mess of life, sweeping all in its path. A biblical flood. A kind of cleansing. She wondered if her mother had thought that when she'd swum into the sea for the last time.

*Third breach of the sea wall: close to the town
next to the old lifeboat house*

The bike was gone. Where it had been, there was now a river of water. It was up to his knees. He reached down to where he'd left it but there was nothing but freezing cold seawater. Then he saw it, the handlebars sticking up, across the street over by a closed shop on the corner of the Buttlands. He waded over and took the light off the front, pocketed it, then he turned down Staithe Street. There was no point taking it now. He needed a boat, not a bike. Figures huddled outside the village hall. The band were coming out with their instruments above their heads and he half laughed, they looked so ridiculous.

He tried to peer into the dance floor, but it had been abandoned and water was sloshing over the floor where the dancers had been. Someone must have evacuated them all.

A young policeman was directing stragglers up the street, away from the sea. Arthur tried to go past him.

'Not this way, sir, town's flooding, it's not safe down there.'

'But there's people down there... my mother...'

'Arthur!' And there was Jack, his uniform on, grinning at him as if it were all a great wheeze. 'Don't worry, officer, this chap is with me.'

'I see, sir. Well, mind how you go there. Look after your mother, Mr Silver,' he added.

'We will,' said Jack.

Arthur and Jack waded down the street towards the sea. Typical. The unfailing magic of a uniform. He considered his draft article on the base. *Nuclear Armageddon*. He had another possible title: *Revealed: Secrets of Atom-Bomb Base*. He'd hardly seen Jack but the one American airman he personally knew would never tell him anything. He had to rely on the ones who frequented the Shipwright's or the Crown, whose sense of secrecy waned after a few pints. He thought again about Norwich and what he'd seen through the misted café window. It could be nothing. And yet the feeling of distrust was almost physical. He wasn't going to mention the article.

'What the hell are you doing here, Jack? I've got to get to the shop.'

'I was at the dance. No point going back to the base. No flights tonight.'

Arthur stopped, floodwater rushing around his legs. Jack had been at the dance at the village hall. Verity had said she was going to the same one, hadn't she? His legs quivered in a strange way. He struggled to find the words to ask Jack about her, but the American was already talking.

'Listen, I've got an idea. Pete went back to the farm. He's going to need help with the animals. We should go out there.'

And Verity must be there. She'd be mad with worry for the horses. He wanted to go – the thought of her out there in that isolated farm, the sea raging all around – but his conscience tugged at him.

'Yes, we should. But my mother's in the shop, she'll need me.'

They were outside Thurgood's darkened shop window, shouting above the slap slap of the sign. Jack came up close to him. He had his hand on Arthur's arm.

'Is your apartment above the shop?'

'Yes, but—'

'Then she'll be fine. Come on, they need us.'

He thought of his mother alone and bitter with him for being out in it. 'No, I have to. She's my mother.'

'All right. I'll go on my own.'

'Don't be an idiot, Jack. You can't.' He couldn't let Jack do this, play the hero. It couldn't be him to save her. 'Come with me, I know where we can get a boat.'

They splashed down to the quay. The water was sweeping over the quay wall and it was slow work wading even the few yards to the shop. Clouds covered the moon and his bike light provided the only light, illuminating the patch of water in front of them. The shop window was dark and for a second he thought his mother was dead, drowned, saving her livelihood. The image of a drowned woman could only remind him of the mother he'd lost. In a cold rush of nausea and panic, he heaved himself at the door. Jack was next to him, his face taut with strain. Together, they edged the door open with their shoulders and found her, up to her waist in swirling water in her hair net and bedcoat, arms full of white bags of sugar and flour.

'Where have you been?' she said, her voice strangled and sour.

'Deliveries,' he said, staring at her stricken form. 'Sorry. I'm here now.'

'Well, help me then. Who's this?' She peered at Jack, standing next to him.

Her question propelled him forward and he half put an arm around her. 'This is Jack. From the American base. He's come to help. But we can't stay long, Mother, we just need to get you to safety.'

'The stock, Arthur. Just get the stock.'

He sighed. It was impossible. They took as much as they could but they soon saw it was hopeless. The water was rising fast and soon they wouldn't be able to wade to get a boat, to row to the farm. The harvest would already be ruined by the salt, the land leached of life for many years; there was nothing anyone could do about that now. But he imagined Peter trying to save the livestock and Verity rescuing her beloved Gyps. It knotted his stomach in pain at the thought of her out there in this storm.

In the kitchen, Arthur took his mother's arm. 'You've got to stay up here now, Mother. There's no alternative. We've done as much as we can.'

'You stay with me,' she said, pleading with him. The electrics had gone and she'd lit a candle next to the sink. The dark yellow light flickered on her face, throwing deep lines across it. Her small hand gripped onto his arm.

'I can't. I have to get a boat.'

'It's not safe. Oh Lord, Arthur, you can't leave me. I'm dying.'

'Mother, please. You're hysterical.'

'Art, it's getting worse down here!' Jack called up from the shop, and that was his cue. He bent down and kissed her on her thin, papery cheek and she dug her fingers into his arms.

'Don't leave me.'

'You'll be fine, just stay here.' He gently prised her fingers off his arm and pulled away. He heard the coldness in his voice and hated it. 'Please, Mother,' he said.

'We need to go, Art!' Jack shouted from below. He imagined Jack rowing out to Howe Farm like a hero and him here with his mother, and for all that it was a mad act, he couldn't let Jack do it.

He patted her hand, turned and left.

How long had they been? He didn't know but the harbour had overflowed the quay wall and they were now waist-deep in seawater. Little boats had broken their moorings and were out to sea or crashed into one another. All around them, what had once been solid ground was now a shining, silvery mass, glimmering in the moonlight.

He could hardly hear Jack above the roar of the wind. 'Boat?' he seemed to be shouting. Arthur laughed, mirthlessly. There were boats everywhere. Pulled along by the force of the current, the two of them blundered back towards Staithe Street where there were a couple of small rowing boats banging against the shops along the quay. He grabbed Jack's arm and led him towards one of them. He had to use all his strength to right the damn thing and get it steady. God knows how they would both get in it. And they needed oars.

'Oars!' he shouted and pointed at the freemasons' hall behind them. There was a set on hooks on the wall in the yard, a boat too, but he didn't fancy his chances in that old craft. The abandoned boat was sturdier. He indicated to Jack to keep hold of the boat and he plunged himself along with the current to the yard to grab the oars. There was a moment of nervous laughter as they almost tipped the boat over on itself as they tried to get in. He wondered if he would find it funny one day.

'Can you row?' he said, passing Jack one of the oars.

'Of course I can,' Jack shouted back.

It was said defiantly but he knew Jack would be lost out here on the flooded marsh with its creeks and banks and he knew it far better than the cocky American did. So in the end they agreed he would row first, and Jack would navigate.

They set off for Beach Road. Arthur attached the bike

light with his belt and used its pale, weak beam to guide them. He rowed while Jack knelt behind him at the stern, with a torch nabbed from the shop, holding it aloft like the captain of a ship on a raid. Thank God he could row. The water was black and the thought of going out in it was terrifying.

Wind rattled the window pane. Verity twitched, shivered, woke up. A light flicked on and off. For a moment she forgot why she was sitting in the window seat of her bedroom in the middle of the night. Her room was dark. In her hand, she was holding a silver flask, Peter's hip flask. On the seat in front of her, a crumpled napkin was flecked with crumbs. It came back to her: the flood, the struggle back to the farm, splashing vomit into the floodwater flowing down Leafy Lane. The nausea had gone but she was empty, hollowed out. Looking out of the window, the light flashed again, a distant starburst from the direction of the sea, then gone. *Come back*, she urged, but it didn't. Staring out into the night, she could see nothing reassuring. Cut off from the town, what would happen if they were engulfed? It felt as if the house was floating in the sea.

Father? Then she remembered he was safe, asleep down the corridor. She ran along the landing and looked in at him. Through the uncurtained window, moonlight fell on her father's ghostly shape, mouth gaped open, rasping. She breathed out, slowly.

But Peter was out there. It must have been his light she'd seen. In her bedroom, she looked at her bedside clock. Ten to midnight. Oh God, Peter had been out there so long. What time had they got back to the house? She didn't know. Hours. It must be hours. She thought of Peter wading through the water, leading a stranded cow to safety. It would be bellowing and thrashing. And the horses! With a lurch of anguish she remembered Gyps and then Peter's horse, Heather.

Quickly, before she lost her nerve, she took off the uncomfortable purple dress she was still wearing, changed into some jodhpurs and a thick sweater and ventured out onto the landing. At her father's door, she listened. Snoring. She wanted to ask him to help her, to do something, to be a child again and have him solve everything, but he couldn't help her. Not any more, and not in that state. She would just have to do it by herself. Get the horses to safe ground. Find Peter. Not drown. She laughed aloud at this last one as if defying herself not to give in. She would not end up like her mother, drowned in grief for all that she'd lost.

Near the bottom of the stairs, she stopped. The water was high above the skirting board. She noticed the strong smell of manure as if the fields had come into the house. They had. The whole of the downstairs had been infiltrated by a layer of the outside. To her right, the dining room, the old furniture, salt-ruined. All their history – her mother's history – desecrated.

But there was nothing she could do now. The horses needed her. She rolled up her jodhpurs and dipped her feet into the water. The cold made her gasp but she gritted her teeth and stepped in it up to her knees. She waded to the back door of the scullery where she found her old wellingtons floating. They would have to do. Standing on a chair, she pulled them on. Back at the front door, she took a mac off the peg. It was her mother's, the one she'd worn to the dance. She pulled it tight around her and it made her feel a little better somehow, as if her mother was with her. In the pocket she found the little cigarette case she had filched from her mother's drawer, and Jack's Zippo. To them she added her brother's hip flask and a small torch she'd found in the useful drawer in the scullery. These little preparations made her feel as if she had a plan, as if she was off on an adventure. She almost laughed at the absurdity.

Outside, the wind rushed around her and a bright, white full moon appeared from behind dark clouds. It shone on the glistening water, which was streaming away from her as if it was trying to escape back to the sea. Wading away from the farmhouse, towards the lower fields, she stopped and looked back. The old, imposing building was surrounded by a lake of water. It had become its own island, with her father in it, marooned. Like his whole generation, he was cut off now. Battle-scarred and exhausted, the tide of change threatened to engulf them.

For a moment she stood motionless. She had never been so alone. But she turned her back on the house and pushed on in the direction of the sea.

6.

Tidal surge receding on Norfolk coast
Tidal surge reaches Essex coast by 10 p.m.

The moon had quickly disappeared behind clouds once more. All Arthur could see, if he turned to look, was the patch of water in front of them, illuminated by the pale beam from the bike light and the golden one from the torch. His arms hurt with the effort of rowing against the current. The tide must have turned but the wind made the water a living thing, a surging, roaring beast crashing into their matchstick town.

Passing the shop, he saw a flicker of candlelight in the rooms and it both relieved him and confronted him with his absence.

As they tried to turn against the surge of water up to Beach Road, he heard calls. They must be coming from the prefabs down on the low-lying piece of land on the left-hand side of the road. His mother hated the prefabs. 'A scourge on the landscape' she called them and tsked each time she looked down at them from their flat above the shop. There were no lights on in any of the bungalows, but, craning round, Arthur could see their squat shapes in the dark. Down here, the wind seemed stronger, the night blacker and the calls eerie, like dogs or wolves. Maybe some of them were dogs. But then he thought he could hear children crying too and he shivered.

He twisted his neck round and shouted, 'There are people down there. Children.' The light illuminating his face, Jack nodded.

Arthur plunged his oars into the water and dragged the boat west, down towards the buildings. They bashed into the side of one of the prefabs and he realised that it was already almost fully submerged: the boat came up to its gutters.

'Help!' Arthur heard from what sounded like close by.

They were up against the side of the roof. He shipped the oars while Jack held onto the roof, leaned forward to his bike light and tried to tilt it to shine upwards. Jack did the same with his torch. The beams lit up a man's face, haggard and deep-lined.

'My wife,' he said. He was holding something in his arms. Arthur steadied the boat while Jack reached up and, legs braced, rocking, took the bundle from the old man. It was a thin, wretched woman, swaddled in a blanket, trembling, white with shock to match her hair, but alive. They manoeuvred the man down too and set back towards the town. As they were turning, a searchlight swept over the quayside and they rowed hard for it. The old couple were hunched in their blanket in between them. Jack kept up a steady stream of comforting talk. 'We'll get you a nice cup of tea soon enough,' he said. How could he possibly sound so smooth and charming when all Arthur could think about was how teeth-achingly cold it was? How they could easily drown out here in the dark.

They came up alongside the source of the searchlight, a rescue boat from the coastguard. A grizzled man took the old couple. 'Best get you fellas back to town now. You'll be better off at the rescue centre.'

But Jack shouted back, 'There are more old folk in the bungalows, sir. Children too,' as if it had been his idea. They exchanged a quick glance of shared purpose.

'We'll see about them, you've done enough,' said the man. Then he turned his boat around, sending spray over them and their little boat, and chugged off for the town.

'We can't stop now,' Jack said. He was in darkness, with the torch held low, but Arthur could hear the urgency in his voice.

'No,' he said. They were far past the point of stopping. He didn't think either of them wanted to – they were swept up by the tide themselves.

They tried to return to the prefabs but it was impossible to row. Each time Arthur tried to move the oars, the force of the wind and waves drove the little boat back towards the town. He knew there must have been multiple breaches of the embankment.

'We've got to walk,' he shouted to Jack.

This time, they each took a side of the boat and started to wade westwards. The water was up to their shoulders now, the bike light had disappeared, but Jack still held onto his torch. Now there was debris everywhere: when the moon broke through they could see pieces of wood, a fence post and the edge of a balcony floating past them. Once, the torch struck the snout and trotters of a dead pig sticking up.

They heard the rescue boat come chugging behind them but it must have been parallel to them, for its light never came but swung past and beyond them. They were still wading, trudging doggedly on, when he saw the other boat strike something and get stuck. One of their men lassoed a rope to the balcony.

Without speaking, Arthur and Jack pulled their little boat towards the stranded rescuers. Underneath them, the bungalow was falling apart, hunks of wood tearing off and floating away. The rescue vessel had sprung a leak and been abandoned. On the roof of the collapsing bungalow huddled a family, two girls and their father. One of the little girls was crying, the man's face was blank. Jack lifted the younger girl into the boat and Arthur held out his hand to the older one.

'Mother and Terence have gone,' she said, her face interested, curious. 'Drowned,' she told him.

Arthur didn't ask questions, but set the girl down in the boat. He couldn't look at the man and the sunken hollowness of his face again.

Verity could still see the house but she didn't know how to get back to it. The water was so much stronger than she'd thought. It was not coming in waves and was oddly calm. The greatest rush of the water must be elsewhere. Yet it was moving steadily away from the house, back out to the sea, pulling her with it. It was irresistible. She could imagine her mother being taken out with the current and not seeing the point of fighting it. But she wasn't her mother.

She crossed the garden and the first field, each step

tentative. The moon flickered in and out from behind the clouds, throwing silver flashes across the watery field and lighting up the black stick outlines of the pine trees ahead. She thought she was at the bottom of the first field, but it was hard to tell. All the winter-sown crops would be completely ruined. Please God, let Peter be all right. Let the cowshed hold. The floodwater was coming over her boots. Freezing cold water sloshed down inside the rubber to her bare feet. What a fool she'd been. The wellingtons were dragging her down. She pulled them off and sacrificed them to the water, and watched them float away.

She hesitated, unsure whether to go on. She strained to listen. Just the whine of the wind, the whoosh of the water. Then, very faint, the distressed bleating of cows. And there – the neigh of a horse. She was sure of it. Gyps? She focused all her energy on the sound of the horse, trying to work out where it was coming from and if there was a human sound too. But the rush of the flood was too loud.

Ahead, the torch picked out the glint of barbed wire. As she waded towards it, her left foot dropped into something. A fox hole? A badger sett? She fell forward, lunging for something, anything, and grabbed the fence. Her heart and stomach lurched. The wire cut into her and she screamed out, pain jarring through her hand and arm. She dropped down, pitching forward into the freezing water. Spluttering, she came up. Leaning gingerly on the wire, she inspected her hand by the light of the moon. A small tear, beads of blood. It was nothing much but, God, how it stung. Tears sprung to her eyes. How she wished, then, that she hadn't come out here. She could be with Jack now. Oh God, why had she ever left the dance? Her stomach was still fluttering as if there was a bird inside, flapping to get out.

'Peter!' she cried, her voice breaking on the word. There was no answer. Without logic or thought a word tore from her throat: 'Jack!'

Arthur sucked in the smoke and held it in his throat, feeling its warmth before blowing it out, slowly so as not to lose it too fast. They were smoking two of Jack's last Camels under the porch of the Golden Fleece at the top of Station Road, dirty water still up to their ankles. They'd taken an old woman who'd lost sight of her husband to the rescue centre, and had left the rowing boat down near the quayside. He knew it was past midnight as a policeman had told him. The worst must be over, surely. The tide had long since turned and the flood must be beyond the highest point. But there was no hope of going home. His bones ached and his feet and hands were numb. He glanced at the figure next to him. He was ashamed of the pettiness of his rivalry, standing with Jack now. Jack would leave, go back to America. There was no proof that anything had happened between him and Verity. They would forget about him. He thought of her, that morning, her cold skin against his. For all of the awkwardness of it, she had done it for him.

Jack breathed out a plume of smoke and said, 'We need to get out to the farm. Pete loves the farm. You saw that pig. He'd be devastated if they all go and die on him.'

'They don't have pigs, Jack. They have cattle. Arable. Can't do anything about that, it's too late.'

'Art.'

'Don't call me that.'

It seemed impossible. An act of madness. Yet, rowing out along the Beach Road embankment to the prefabs had made him realise where the breach – or breaches? – had happened. The farm would be cut off from the town. Even if they could row out to the farm, surely the force of the outgoing tide would be impossible to control, and would sweep them out to sea? But he couldn't leave her out there. He couldn't let Jack go alone. His marrow and soul were aching. Peter was his friend and Verity's brother. With a pierce of pain, the dance came back to him. She could have seen Jack at the dance. He opened his mouth to ask then closed it again. A chink of doubt had crept back in and he didn't want to give in to it. But now the image had lodged in his brain he couldn't cut it out. He saw her dancing at the village hall; he saw Jack holding her. Whatever happened, *he* had to find her. Not Jack.

'All right, but we better get on with it.' He didn't say, *because I'm frozen and tired and I can't go on for much longer.*

He was right about the high point: the flood was definitely receding. There was only dirty, lapping water on Staithe Street now.

'Jesus Christ!' Arthur looked to where Jack was pointing. Down to their right, looming up on the quayside, the huge bulk of a boat on the dockside, clearly lifted there by the rising waters. He recognised it: it was the Sea Scouts' torpedo boat, the *Terra Nova*. Its sheets dangled, useless. A group of men was gathered around it, shaking their heads. But they dragged their boat past the men, on towards Beach

Road, which was still underwater. He glanced at the shop as they passed, saw the windows broken and the night air streaming into the dark inside. There was no point worrying about that now.

Down on Beach Road, they climbed back into the boat. The water was still high out there, too high to wade. He wondered if anyone was left down in the prefabs but he couldn't hear anything apart from the wind. They rowed out towards the farm. Jack's torch provided a thin light to guide them. He hoped the batteries would last.

He was wrong, though; the worst wasn't over. When they reached about halfway along the road they were rowing down he saw water up to the telegraph wires and, as he'd guessed, rushing through a breach in what had been the embankment, towards the harbour.

'Jesus,' said Jack and they started to pull hard against the current.

But they couldn't stop it. The little boat was picked up by the gush of the torrent and pushed up to a bank of something, he didn't know what. Like a cork bobbing in the sea, round and round it went. Arthur thought they were bound to capsize and he gripped the sides. He braced himself, waiting to be upended into the dark, freezing water. But the boat kept upright and instead was swept up over the mud banks nearer to the beach, beyond the breach.

'Stop!' he called to Jack and they used the oars to drag the boat to a halt. He thought they could get out here. It would be safer to wade than to row with the mad uncertainty of the current. With the flood receding, he was afraid of the little boat being taken out to the open water. Arthur stepped over the gunwale. But instantly, sand and grit swirled round his legs and sucked him down. It swooshed over and into his boots and pulled him down. He felt himself falling, dragged down to the bottomless sea. The light of Jack's torch was in his eyes but he didn't know if he could reach him. He threw himself at the side of the boat.

'I'm sinking! Sand's bloody alive!'

Jack leaned out and grabbed his hand. Arthur felt his boots dragging him back to the water. He held on. A sucking sound and a sensation of release and he was hauled back in. He lay on the bottom of the boat breathing in great heaves.

'Got to keep rowing,' he panted. 'Ground's not safe.'

He grabbed the oars and pulled as hard as he could, away from the harbour and towards where he thought the farm must be.

7.

Before dawn, Sunday, 1st February

Tide abated
Much of the land still submerged

Soaking wet, and in pain, Verity squeezed her eyes shut and thought of her bed and home and safety. But the pull of the water was away from the farm, towards the pines and the trees. Another neigh from somewhere. To the east? Where was her Gyps? And where was Peter? He must be out here. If he'd got back to the house, he'd be wondering where she was.

In desperation, she swung her torch in an arc around her. There was something there, she could swear it. A dark mass. The figure of a horse above the water on a rise by the woods. It was Gypsy, it must be. Someone must have let him go. It had to be Peter.

'Gyps!' she shouted. 'Gypsy!' and the horse whinnied. Elation swept over her.

She tried to move towards the sound, using the barbed wire fence as a guide, gingerly holding onto it with her left, unhurt hand and her right arm held out for balance. The torchlight jumped and trembled in her outstretched hand. The bone-cold floodwater came up to her waist and the bottom half of her body was numb. When the fence came to an end, ahead was what looked like a copse of trees on a small rise. In the dark it was hard to tell the distance. If she could make it to those trees, she would be with Gyps. And she could climb up and see where they were. She might be able to see Peter. Anyone.

She let go of the fence, then tried to put her feet out to wade but there was nothing there. The ground fell away. Her legs thrashed and whirled on nothing. She tried to swim back to the fence, but the water took her in the other direction, away from the wire, away from safe ground. She tried to swim, but her swimming had never been as strong as Peter's. Flailing, the movement of the water was tugging her towards the sea, but she was too heavy. She could feel herself being dragged down. Above her, a black shadow, the branch of a tree. She was afraid to reach up in case she missed and the effort sent her under. But she flung her arm up and felt the hardness of the bark against her cut. Her scream resounded. Her fingers clung on. The branch bent into the water. It was thin, it could snap. But it was holding her back from the tidal sweep to the sea. She took a deep lungful of cold air and lurched with her left, unhurt hand to the thicker base of the branch and this time she got a firm hold. For long seconds she was suspended, arms hanging onto the branch, her body in the water. She imagined letting go and floating away to the sea. She saw her mother, sinking down, down to the seabed, her blonde hair flying out behind her. But her face in the picture was a twisted scream. A surge of horror propelled Verity back to the tree. She flexed her fingers. Inch by inch, she moved her hands along the branch to the trunk. Stopped, breathed. And finally, she pulled herself up, out of the water, and clambered up to a branch she hoped was strong enough to sit on. A cradle in the centre of the tree.

He had no way of telling what time it was beyond what the policeman had said. But that felt like hours ago. The wind had dropped and the water was no longer coming in waves. The moon fell on the shining surface illuminating the great glass sheet of submerged marshland and grazing fields, flooded between the town and the sea. He was at the stern, Jack rowing. Looking back at the lights pricking here and there in the town, he was sure that they must be near the farm. Ahead, the tops of trees sticking up in the water that must be the pine woods. Their woods. His and Verity's. Drowned.

'You cold?' Jack's voice sounded far away.

'Yeah.'

'Jesus, buddy, I can feel nothing down here. Goddamn, I'd kill for a smoke.'

A plaintive sound drifted back to him. It was Jack.

'What the hell are you doing?'

'Singing to keep myself warm. You should join in.'

But he couldn't. He listened as Jack's voice lifted out of the boat, singing about the moon breaking his heart and love blooming in the night, over the flood and out to the sea. It was a very strange thing to hear him. Then he couldn't bear it any more.

'Shut up!'

When Jack stopped singing, the quiet was disturbing. Sound had been dampened by the flood, like everything else. Just the shush shush of the water.

'I saw you in Norwich,' he blurted out. 'I saw you in a café with a man. You left a metal case on the table. At first I thought it was a cigarette case, but then I realised it couldn't have been.'

Jack was an outline at the other end of the boat. A dark shadow silhouetted by the full moon. He didn't say anything.

'What was it, Jack? What were you doing? Do your superiors in the Air Force know?'

From Jack's end of the boat came a burst of derisive laughter. 'You're imagining things, Art. What do you think this is, a kid's game, playing at spies?' He began to sing again.

'I did see you,' Arthur shouted in a blare of rage.

'All right. What did you see? Did you follow me?' He didn't sound angry, just tired. 'That's funny. Okay – so you saw me in a café. That's it. Nothing else. You've got this wrong, my friend. It ain't what you think. I ain't what you think I am.'

'What are you then? Because as far as I can see, you're not honourable, or honest, and none of us know a thing about you.'

But he was interrupted by a piercing cry. A fox? A trapped animal?

'What was that?' said Jack.

'God, I hope Verity's all right.' It came out without thought.

'Yeah, so do I.'

Arthur had a strange vision of Verity in many places all at once: with him in the woods, at the dance, in her house above the floods, safe, holding onto her horse in the flood. 'Yeah, so do I.' *So do I.* Jack's voice played in his head. He sounded hesitant. Or was he imagining it? In the dark it was hard to tell. If he asked, then it would be over.

In the dark, surrounded by seawater, the emptiness was overwhelming.

'Did you see her? At the dance.' He exhaled.

There was a pause.

'I did see her, yeah. She was there.'

'Who was she with?' As he said it, he heard the suspicion and knew there was never going to be a good ending to this. He could stop it right now.

'She was… say, do you think we're near their place yet?'

'Yes. We must be. Who was she with? At the dance.' He had gone too far. He had to know.

There was a pause. 'Listen, Art, I was going to tell you.'

'What do you mean?' He wanted to blot out the sheepish tone of Jack's voice.

'She was with me.'

'But she's…' The words came out slowly, each one hurting his throat. He couldn't say what she was.

'Look, Art, I don't know what she's told you—'

'Stop calling me that!' As he shouted, the sound came again. Thin and high. Arthur felt a thickness in his head. *Keep calm.*

Jack was speaking again. 'I like her. She's smart.'

'But Pete—' He didn't know why he said it, he was clutching desperately at something. It couldn't be true.

'Yeah, don't tell him, not yet. He's gonna blow a fuse.'

243

'But the others, it's not just her, is it?' Behind his eyes, Arthur's head throbbed. They had stopped rowing, and were drifting towards open water.

'There aren't any others. Not now.'

'You're lying.'

'You aren't still sweet on her, are you?' Jack's voice was falsely innocent. He knew.

Arthur breathed out an incoherent, rasping noise. He wanted to disappear, to sink into the darkness and never come back. He felt as if he might already have disappeared, he was so light, so weightless.

No one spoke. Jack made a kind of low whistle through his teeth but said nothing. Jack must know, from his silence, and that was almost worse than the treachery: the pity. Then he remembered her, out here somewhere in this endless night, and he shivered back into himself, felt the blood returning to his limbs, the anger simmering, and the pain sank into him like a stone.

It was funny, that this was the end of everything. That he could know it and yet keep on breathing.

In the tree, Verity took stock of herself: a cut, throbbing hand, blood trickling down her arm; jodhpurs ripped by the bark; her clothes, heavy and sodden with seawater. That was all. It could be worse. Next, she checked her pockets. She made the miraculous discovery of the hip flask, Jack's Zippo and two crumpled, slightly damp cigarettes, protected by the case. It was a small comfort to still have these things, these touchstones – little signs of normality, as if her mother and Peter were there in the tree with her. Jack too. She felt again in her pockets but they were empty. The torch had gone. The dark seemed to close in on her and smother her. She could no longer see her horse, stranded by the far trees. How would anyone know she was there?

For a few long minutes she cried for her loneliness, for her stupidity and her failure. For all the wretched things she had done. No one heard and she sniffed, and wiped her nose on the damp sleeve of her mac and her hand. She realised she had smeared her face with blood and licked the line of it down her wrist. The salty tang of her own blood was oddly warm and soothing. She tried to think what to do.

First, she would have a cigarette. The wind seemed to have moved eastwards so she turned her back to the land and looked out to the sea, holding the lighter close to her cupped, shaking hand. Once, twice, three times it sparked into light then was extinguished immediately. Then on the fourth go the tiny flame caught the end of the cigarette enough to light and she dragged on it, sucking and sucking, trying to keep the tar burning. But it couldn't last. When it was extinguished the loss of it hurt. She wanted to cry but forced herself to take a nip from the flask instead. She held the fiery liquid in her mouth, swilling it around.

Who was out there? Someone must be. And the person who came to her mind was Jack. She thought of him at the dance, his hand on her waist. In a wild moment, she decided that if she got out of this, she would go with him, to America, to the desert where it was dry and it hardly ever rained and to the skyscrapers where you could see for miles. They would ride horses together and he would show her his secret places and it wouldn't matter where he was from or who his family were. She wouldn't care. She would paint it all: the desert and the mountains and the sea. Nothing was real any more. She thought that not only was her world transformed by the water but she wanted to be too. It was insane, but it wasn't impossible. Either way, it was too late to go back now.

Groggy, she jerked and her stomach leapt like a hare. She was hanging precariously at the edge of her cradle in the middle of the tree. Below her, glowing in the moonlight, the water eddied and lapped, black and deadly. She must have closed her eyes, drifted off. Images of red mountains fled from behind her eyes. Her eyelids were like weights, her feet stung with cold. All she wanted was to sleep. She must not sleep. *Please God, don't let me sleep.*

Arthur groped with the oars, blind in the blackness, pulling, heavy and slow in the little boat through the floodwater. A deep ache jarred across his shoulder blades each time he pulled the oar back, as though he couldn't do it again. Yet he did, over and over. He was a body, that was all. The hatred he felt for Jack burned inside him like a fireball of pain. It hurt, and burned slowly, as if it could not be quenched. He saw Jack's red head in the autumn field interchanging with the barrel of his rifle, the explosion in his ears, the reverberation in his shoulder. Jack gone. He knew he was grinding his teeth and gripping the oars but he'd set himself on a path that he couldn't now get off. The original plan to row to the farm seemed like a parallel world of ideas and reasoning. All that was left now was this place of darkness.

A darkness that seemed to come from within him.

Jack's torch had died. Arthur's eyes had adjusted to the night and he could make out the deeper black of vegetation and the lighter grey sheen of the water. They relied on the intermittent moonlight, breaking through cloud cover, to cast a silver glow on the flooded fields they were crossing. Even with the moon, it was hard to tell which was the earth, and which the sky, it was all a smudgy shimmer of black, silver and grey. The flooded fields reflecting the sky and back again.

Neither of them spoke.

Out of the emptiness, Arthur heard a high, human voice – 'Peter!'

'Verity,' he said, in wonder, and then, 'Oh God.'

'Verity?' said Jack. 'You sure it's her?'

'She can't be out here, she can't.'

There it was again. Closer. It was impossible for it to be her voice and yet it was. They couldn't both be hearing things.

'It *is* her,' said Jack. 'Jeez, we've got to get her.'

There was a new tone in Jack's voice, a determination, and Arthur knew with absolute certainty that they would do anything to find her.

They both started shouting her name in chorus, their voices rising together and dying with the fierce cry of the wind, vying for supremacy.

On her small island of safety, perched like a rook in a tree on the edge of one of her father's fields, Verity was shaken awake by a cry and thought it was the wind or the sea. She must have fallen asleep again. She must not sleep. The moon illuminated the scene in a wash of light: a drowned world, what was her world, fields now rivers and lakes. Behind her, the pinpricks of yellow light from the house and inside, her father, safe and asleep. She clutched Peter's hip flask to her chest, like a talisman. Peter would come for her. She had to think it, although for all she knew, he hadn't made it back to the house. He might think she was safe in the house, on its rise above the sea. She was so cold, she had taken her arms out of the sleeves of the mac and was hunched inside it. She could no longer feel her toes.

There was no point in cursing herself for her idiocy in setting forth from the safety of the farmhouse, for the loss of her torch, the flailing, splashing in the bitter cold seawater, until – beautiful luck – the semi-submerged tree saved her. She was lucky. This had to be believed. She took a tiny sip of the whisky from the flask, careful not to glug it down. A part of her tried to imagine she was on a Girl Guide mission where she had to make her supplies last. If she thought like this, she wouldn't let the terror get to her. She was alive. The tide would ebb, maybe it was already ebbing. The image of her body, huddled, frozen stiff, found at dawn must be banished. The fire in her mouth distracted her, and burned its way down her insides. She had one cigarette left but so far had not been able to smoke it because of the impossibility of getting the Zippo to keep its flame in the wind. The Zippo had let her down. Why, she thought, if Jack loved her so much did he not come for her? Had he ever said he loved her? No. Stop it. Must stop it.

Where was Peter? Please let him come.

Gathering up her strength, she shouted again, 'Peter!'

*

'That's her. I tell you, Art, it's her, we're getting close.'

Arthur was concentrating on rowing and only now did he try to picture her – where? What on earth was she doing out here? It was absolute madness. And where the bloody hell was Peter? He'd forgotten they'd come to help Peter, or so they'd pretended. And still, even in the strangeness of the dark, all he could see was an image of Jack and Verity dancing, twirling round and round in his head.

They returned her cry with their own.

From somewhere out there, in the dark, Verity thought she heard her own name. Instantly, her body was alert. She flexed her aching fingers, tried and failed to flex her toes. They were numb and gone. She sat up, and, as much as she could, leaned out into the chasm of mute darkness and shouted with all the fear and loneliness of the night.

No sound returned to her.

Jack's face was white in the moonlight, lit up like a ghost. He was saying something Arthur didn't want to hear. He wanted to block his ears, black over Jack's bright moonface, blot him out. Shut him up. A scream from somewhere. Or the wind.

'Art, look, before we get to her, I have to tell you. I should have told you about Vee, I didn't realise you were—'

'I don't want to talk about it.'

'You know, I don't even think I wised up myself until

tonight, not truly. I mean about her. See, I've been messing about, but I stopped it, tonight. It's complicated, Art, I wish I could tell just how much. But that's it. I'm not going—'

The moon clouded over, plunging them into darkness, and at the same moment a spring snapped in Arthur's brain. Everything surged out. He gritted his teeth and ground them together. She hadn't given herself to him, had she? Why should Jack get away with what he'd done? He was a traitor. Nothing Arthur had ever wanted was going to come true. Nothing. Nothing. He lunged forward, throwing Jack against the prow of the boat.

'Shut up!'

He hit the hard bone of Jack's head.

Arthur was thrust back to the other end of the boat. He lay there, panting. Feeling came back to his body. His hand was throbbing and wet. Slowly, he realised that the boat had come to a stop. Cold water washed over his feet. They had hit something.

From the other end of the boat, where the slumped figure of the American lay, he heard a groan.

'Jack,' he said, whispering tentatively, 'can you believe it? The boat's taking in water. Jack?'

He didn't want to believe it. There was no way he could get into the floodwater. The boat was the only thing keeping him from certain death. He felt on the floor of the boat. Seawater lapped at his trouser legs. His hand twinged, his head throbbed. Out of the night came voices, distant, echoing.

'We'll have to swim. She can't be far.'

Silence in the blackness.

The water was up to his knees. He was sitting in it. He was covered with freezing seawater, something slimy around his legs. The smell of seaweed was mixed with something rotten.

Arthur imagined Jack grinning, though he couldn't see him. Why was he grinning?

'It won't be far. She's close. You heard her.' The voice was distorted, as if he was already underwater. He wasn't sure if he had spoken or Jack. It was true that when she had cried out, even given the wind and the darkness, he felt as if he could reach out and touch her. But he didn't trust his own senses. Between their voices a black void.

'Come on,' said another voice, a distorted echo of his own.

Arthur closed his eyes. Just a few strokes. He could swim. He had to swim. He plunged into the water, gasping. The coldest water he had ever felt. Cold everywhere, inside him. In his heart, in his lungs. He would die of the cold. Stop panicking. His arms splashed wildly. The boat. It was still there, behind him. It was sinking, but he wanted to cling to it, the only hard thing in a world of water. No. Splashing, his chin underwater. Don't open your mouth. Don't swallow. Don't go under. Can't go under. Move, he told himself. His limbs, in a spasmodic movement, smashed through the water. Don't think about the shadow in the boat. Don't think. Swim.

PART 4

EBB

———

Sunday, 1st February 1953
The morning after the flood

Low Z depression
Surge subsiding all along the coast
Full moon

1.

To most people there is something desolating about the ebb of the tide, but to Muriel it had always seemed the best possible time of day. This is when the richest pickings were to be had – when the cockles and mussels came out, when the waders, the curlews and the godwits fed, and the oystercatchers moved along the beach, waiting for mussels to open their shells so they could suck up the soft insides.

And she would never have said it, never have thought it consciously, but the time after a flood was always strangely full, teeming with life. Life had been undone, unmade, taken away by the sea. But what was left in its place? Her tiny brother was gone, his life barely begun. Her mother emptied out. There were other losses too; she felt them, like goosebumps all over her skin. But, but... she couldn't deny it. The truth was, there was always something left behind, when the tide turned, dragging itself over the sand. Life bloomed in the ebb. And so it was now.

Muriel sensed all this, in the aftermath of the flood, as the town reeled and the people reeled and rallied, and soon, out of the darkness of the night, she would find out what exactly had been lost and what was there to be taken.

2.

Thrashing, hot and wet, something clung to her, sticking. Verity surfaced, gasping for air. There was no air. Drowning. She was drowning in her own blood. Hot blood pulsed. In, out, in and out, in her head, in her body, deep down inside. Submerged, calm under water, she could see the green seaweed and it was her mother's hair, waving. *Mother*, she said, but there was no sound in the water. Bubbles formed and separated and her mother turned to face her but her eyes were creamy-white, shiny pearls. She opened her mouth to say *Mother* and nothing came out. No breath. Down, down, down. Dark.

White light, cold, shivering. Someone soothing. So cold. Mother? A cool hand on her hot-cold skin.

Back down in the deep. Dark red. Her blood. In front of her, a fish swimming. Pink translucent skin, fins for hands and a grey eye, a fish-foetus swimming.

3.

Tuesday, 3rd February

Verity had been asleep, on and off, for forty-eight hours. Or it could have been longer. The family doctor had been, felt her forehead and taken her temperature and said she needed to sleep it off. And so she did. She slept like a sated baby. On and on she slept, as if her body knew she needed sleep to save her energy, to feed it.

On the third day she'd recovered enough to take food. Mrs Timms fussed about her room, straightening the kicked-off bedcovers and tutting at the barely eaten breakfast on the tray. When she left, Verity drove herself further down in the covers and watched the sickly morning light play on the bedspread. In here, the flood was a distant horror. It had happened out there, beyond the known universe of her bedroom. She didn't know what day it was but knew from what Mrs Timms had told her that she had been in bed since the flood with a fever. The doctor said pneumonia. It was gone now and she was left wrung out like a dishcloth, her limbs soft and limp, her mind cloudy and prone to gazing at flecks of dust lit up in the light from her bedroom window. They told her she had been stranded in a tree half dead from hypothermia but it seemed incredible to her, as if it had only happened in a dream. Her dreams were watery and indistinct.

She remembered snatches: a boat, a man with a moustache, Arthur. They told her Arthur, anyway. He'd come to the house, they said. A woman's body upside down. But she wasn't sure if any of it had really happened. Dancing. She remembered dancing with Jack. Him winking at her as she left the village hall.

Something flashed in the corner of her eye. On the bedside table, the light had caught something silver. She reached over and picked it up. It was Jack's Zippo. Idly, she tried to light it but it was water damaged and couldn't spark. Still, she kept it in her hand, feeling the cool of the smooth metal in her palm. She wondered if Jack had also called to the house. Her body remembered him and she imagined him here in her bed, pulling up the white cotton of her nightdress and she shivered with an uneasy pleasure.

Mrs Timms had been feeding her titbits of information about the devastation wrought on the town but it was obvious she was keeping most of it back. The torpedo boat perched on the quayside, pigs found squealing in garden trees, even the gruesome discovery of the body of a poor child dangling from a bush. All these were told with hushed relish but nothing about the farm itself and the losses here. Her father had only peered in from the door, nodded and left. Sometimes she would wake and Peter would be slumped in a chair by the window, his eyes closed. When he felt her gaze on him he would open his eyes and the look they exchanged told her not to ask too much. What she'd gleaned was that the bottom half of the land was still inundated by corrosive seawater, while the top section nearest the house was left wrecked by debris and salt. The cowshed had been ripped open by the force of the surge and Peter couldn't save about half – twenty of the herd – from drowning. Many of his beloved Friesians were dead. Some of the hens had been found floating on a haystack. And over by the beach, the pine trees had been battered and the Jubilee Café had been swept away completely. She took all this in, passed on in hurried fragments, as if he was a long way away in another world. Far more urgently, she wanted to ask him about Jack and about Arthur but it was impossible. She hadn't forgotten the morning with Arthur – so long ago now it felt like an age. That day was a maelstrom of contradictions that she couldn't bear to examine.

Sometimes she heard whispers outside her door.

But she couldn't wait any more, stuck in this prison. She heaved herself up and sat on the edge of the bed to get her breath, then pulled herself over to the window. The view was oddly unchanged, looking out beyond the pines to the grey, churning sea. But as her eyes adjusted to the unaccustomed pale wintry light, she saw that the nearest fields were filthy with flecks of dirty white and yellow – the deposits of salt and sand – and the trees were misshapen and haphazard as if someone had taken shears to them and chopped them about in anger. Even worse, further down towards the sea, where the end fields had been, it was like a looking-glass reflection of the grey sky. Above them seagulls screamed and swooped, feasting on dead worms. The cold reality of what it meant seeped into her bones: the farm would be unusable for years. She was enough of her father's daughter to know that. And yet, it was removed from her now. She had plotted her escape route. She had Jack. Her heart quickened. It was treacherous, yes, to abandon the farm when she was most needed (though what could she do? she asked herself, and pushed away the thought that another daughter would do anything) and there was a pang of guilt at leaving Peter with this mess. And Arthur. But another, far stronger emotion was gathering force: the thrill of a real decision, the thought that was rushing up through her. That she would really, actually leave. Give it all up. Oh God, she *would* do it, she would throw it all away, to go and live, to really *do something*.

In a state of trembling excitement, she pulled on some clothes and went downstairs, holding onto the rail as her legs were still wobbly. She couldn't bear the thought of the ruined front rooms. All her mother's furniture, some of it saved from the demolition of Felford – the last fragments of that old world – gone.

Instead, she went straight to the kitchen, where Mrs Timms was whacking some meat with a rolling pin and dropped the pin with a clatter when Verity came in.

'You startled me there, creeping in like a ghost! What are you doing up? You should be in bed.'

But Verity smiled. 'I feel much better. And I'm starving, Mrs Timms. Is there anything I can eat?'

Grumbling about people who miss breakfast, Mrs Timms made Verity a luncheon meat and pickle sandwich. There was a faint smell of damp in the kitchen but it had been masked by the scents of cooked meat and she noticed that the housekeeper had put up sprigs of lavender all around the kitchen.

'Any sign of my father? Or Peter?'

'Oh they're both out all hours, Miss. There's so much to do. All the poor animals and the mending and what not.' She paused and looked doubtfully at Verity.

'How much of the herd is left?'

Mrs Timms paused and pursed her lips. 'I can't rightly say,' she said.

'It's all right,' Verity said, seated at the big wooden table. 'I know how bad it's been. Peter hinted. I'm fine now, really. I just want to know about what's happened in town.' She cast around for a better way of getting information out of the housekeeper. 'Town' was too vague. 'Did the Americans come and help?'

Mrs Timms nodded grimly. 'Oh they were heroes, Miss, real heroes. They lost so much. Say what you like about them and I wasn't keen myself when they first came, I don't mind admitting it, but they were there for us in our time of need.'

'Yes, I'm sure. But what did they lose exactly?'

'Didn't you know? Some of their lodgings, where the families were, was completely destroyed. Like the prefabs. Oh that was terrible, that was. All them homes, smashed like dolls' houses. All them people, still with nowhere to go.'

'Yes. That's awful. What happened – to the Americans?'

'Some of them died in the flood and some lost all their possessions. Same as the people in town. Thank the Lord we was spared.' She raised her eyes to the ceiling at that point, as if God himself were looking down from the drying racks.

'Some of them – died?'

'Whole families. Terrible.' Mrs Timms shook her head,

then turned and whacked the meat with such force that it jumped off the table.

'Where were they though, Mrs Timms? I didn't think the Air Force families were lodged near here.'

'Over in Hunstanton. But some of them came down here to help too. Oh, did you hear about the train?'

Verity picked at her sandwich, chewing slowly, and only half listened to Mrs Timms telling her about the bungalow that had crashed into the train causing it to come off the tracks. 'Went right into the bungalows of the American families,' she said. Families, not single men. Jack bunked at the base. And Hunstanton was too far away. Jack wouldn't have gone there. Instead, she pictured him at the marsh shack, trying to save his camera. The shack would be defiled, like everything else. No, he didn't keep the camera there. He must have helped the Air Force like all the others. He'd have been in Wells, she was certain. He'd been there already, at the dance, and the flood was coming then. He wouldn't have had time to get back to the base. She had a sudden thought: what would have happened if the flood had reached the airbase with its deadly cargo? But it hadn't happened. She would ask Jack about it when she saw him, though. She would ask him straight out. No more evasions. It felt like the flood was a warning.

She fetched a coat, hat and scarf and ventured out into the sodden garden. Dark clouds blew across the sky and the day was bleak. The apple trees were torn and bare, the grass grubby with the same streaking of salt and sand as the fields. She swayed, slightly dizzy. The meat and pickle were sour in her mouth. 'Come,' she said to the empty sky. 'Please come.' In reply, a magpie squawked in a tree. She walked down to the end of the garden, across the stile and onto the first field. There were Gypsy and Heather as if nothing had happened, blithely chewing hay in the paddock. And to think she'd gone out in the middle of a flood for that horse! She stroked Gypsy's mane and nuzzled into him. It didn't matter. The horse was alive. She stayed like that for a long time, feeling the animal's warm flank move beneath her, until she heard the crunch of steps behind her and swung round, heart in her throat, imagining Jack. It was Peter.

'Funny, isn't it? You nearly killing yourself and your horse is absolutely fine the whole time.' He looked ravaged, she could see it now in natural light, his face hollowed out from physical exhaustion and worry. She felt guilty for wishing he was Jack but she still did.

'I know,' she said, 'but I forgive him. It was stupid of me. I was worried about you too, you know.' She looked down. It was more than either of them had said before.

He snorted. 'I told you to stay in the house.' But he didn't sound angry with her, more weary, embarrassed.

'Sorry,' she said. There was a pause while they looked at the horses. She knew it was selfish to ask him but she had to. 'Peter, I don't want to ask but... do you know where Jack is? I thought he might have come to see me – you – us.' She could feel the heat rising up her neck and she continued to stroke Gypsy's coarse, thick mane with an insistent rhythm.

Without answering, Peter came into the paddock and brought some hay to Heather who already had enough. 'I haven't seen him. He's probably at the base but the lines are down. Arthur's been but Mrs Timms keeps turning him away. Bit rotten really. He found you, after all.'

Her hand stopped stroking and gripped onto the horse's

mane as if she needed something to hold onto. She faltered and her vision clouded. The horse whinnied and pushed his head at her. His glassy black eyes came into focus and she leaned her head against his muzzle.

'But why hasn't Jack come too?'

'God, I don't know. There could be lots of reasons, Ver.' He paused and she watched him feed his horse. 'I've been thinking the same thing. But I have enough to worry about burying half of our cattle. And Father is no help. He comes out here every day supposedly to help, but he can't face it. He's back in the study by lunch time, drinking himself into a stupor. The whole herd might have to go, Ver, the Friesians, all of them. The grazing fields are still under water. If it stays submerged for much longer, it'll be worthless, sterile like the other fields, and there'll be nothing for them to graze on in the summer.'

They were silent. There was nothing to say. It would break their father to lose the herd he'd built up since the Thirties, and Peter too. All his plans for expansion had been sunk.

Stupidly, tears pricked at her eyes and fell silently onto Gypsy's mane, trickling into the hair. She could feel Peter tense but she didn't care.

'Don't do that, Ver. Look, he's probably helping with the relief effort. Everyone's flat out with it. Anyway,' he said with a deep breath, 'I don't know what you got yourself mixed up in but it's not worth it.'

'You know absolutely nothing,' she said, and turned her back on him.

'Nor do you!' Peter shouted at her back. But she kept walking, determined not to turn round.

Against her reason, she imagined Jack standing at the rear of the house, casually leaning against the brick wall. She walked slowly back to the house to keep the possibility alive. It had happened so quickly. In the village hall, that night, he had been there, his back to her, his copper hair bright in the electric light, his arm around Peter, and he'd turned and winked at her. That was it. She couldn't even remember the last thing he'd said to her. Why hadn't she gone back? She should have found him and held onto him.

Arriving at the farmhouse, there was a light on in the kitchen and her heart jumped in hope, but of course it was Mrs Timms.

Light-headed with lack of sleep, Arthur surveyed the shop. Everything up to four feet had been covered in a layer of mud and sand, and the marks remained despite his mother's efforts to remove them. There was a musty, rotten smell in the air that pervaded the whole town and made his head reel with nausea. But the smell was so much stronger in here, a sour odour of decay like that of a decomposing animal.

The first day after the flood, he'd limped through the reeking town – wrapped in a blanket someone had given him – to the wreck of the shop and to his mother, who clung to him. His limbs were aching and his right hand was throbbing and sore. All he could think about was Jack in the boat, his face indistinct but brightly lit, singing. Don't let the stars get in your eyes. He couldn't remember how he had got to Verity or the moment when he had lost Jack. He supposed he was in shock, like the men from the war who had hallucinations and facial ticks. But he was so tired, he didn't want to think. In the state of half consciousness before sleep, Jack was singing, his eyes turned to stars. Then welcome oblivion.

In the morning, he had woken with an image of a dark figure slumped against the end of his bed. He blinked and it was gone. It was a dream. In the dream it had been Jack at the end of the boat, collapsed, like a discarded toy.

In a state of disorientation, Arthur had stumbled downstairs to a scene of devastation. Over the days that followed there was little opportunity to do anything apart from trying to clear up the shop. His mother developed a mania for cleaning that verged on the hysterical, so determined was she to get the shop open again. From morning to night she scrubbed and cleaned, wiping the surfaces over and over with vinegar. What supplies they had left had been moved upstairs to the flat and were now stacked in the kitchen so they had to squeeze round them to get a cup of tea. She wouldn't let the goods into the parlour for anything. They didn't talk about the damage or the money lost. There was no insurance, he knew, but when he asked his mother how they would replace the stock she glared at him as if he had blasphemed.

'Not now, Arthur, there's too much to do,' she said, and shooed him away with her cloth.

He persuaded her to make up some emergency packages for the people with nothing and it gave him an excuse to get out of the dank, claustrophobic shop. They, like many other people in the town, had received gift packages from the airbase in Lakenheath – two bedsheets and two pillowcases – and the Canadians had sent food for schoolchildren – sardines, cod liver oil and malt, that kind of thing – but

Arthur knew that the flood relief was going to be slow in arriving and most people had very little. As soon as he left the flat he felt as if he could breathe again. Although a faint odour of decay clung to the whole town, it was nothing compared to the smell in the shop. That stench travelled up the stairs and invaded their rooms: a persistent, overpowering tang of damp and sewage that got into your nostrils and tainted everything. He could barely eat in there any more. Everything tasted rotten. All the food and drink, even the boiled water they'd been told to drink, was infected with the reek of stinking mud and decaying carcasses. Despite his mother's constant scrubbing and polishing, the shop itself felt permanently scarred and fouled. She rubbed and rubbed at it, but she couldn't quite remove the dirty tide mark along the wall.

Out in the town, he delivered the small packages of tins and dried goods, salvaged from the wreckage. A policeman had brought his old bike back and, apart from signs of rust, it still worked fine. He looked at it as an artefact from a different time – a symbol of his demeaning job working for his mother even though it allowed him to get out. But the town was not the balm he hoped for when enveloped in the foul odour of the shop and flat. Cold grey skies pressed down on the broken town, littered with the filth and debris of the flood. There were still people camping out at the village hall, mostly those from the prefabs. He scanned the faces, wondering if any were those he had saved the night of the flood. But when they looked at him he was quick to shift his gaze because what had happened after that was too appalling to contemplate.

Afterwards, he wandered over to the beginning of Beach

Road and the bank, reluctant to return home. From there you could see where the road ended abruptly and a great gash had been torn in the embankment by the raging sea. In all his dreams, he and Jack were in the boat and Jack was unmoving, his red hair hanging down, his face slack.

On the third day, he walked to the village hall again. The sky was low and thick with snow. He pulled his coat tighter around him against the biting wind coming off the North Sea. Lists of the dead were placed on an inside wall. The telephone lines were back up and he thought the base must have been in touch with the police about the numbers of missing or dead. He tried to imagine seeing the name in someone's black scrawl in order to face it, to see it off, but it merely produced a queasy wash of unease.

At first, he couldn't see it. He scanned down the names: Patricia Blackfoot, 72; Maurice Blackfoot, 78. It was all old people. Frederick Gittings, 15 months. He swallowed. Muriel's baby brother, it must be. But then underneath, he saw that someone had tacked up another list with tape. This one listed people from the neighbouring parishes and included the Holkham airbase. Whole families were listed, and the names rolled over his vision like newsreel. The name he was looking for. He couldn't see it. It wasn't there. He felt like laughing but held it in. But what exactly did that mean? Had Jack survived by some miracle and was back at the base? Why, in that case, wasn't he here? He looked at the names again and his eyes snagged on one name on the list from the base: John Henry Doherty, 27. His first thought was Jack had told them he was twenty-two. Why would he lie about that? Then: Missing. For a few seconds he breathed heavily but slowly. Different scenarios crowded his brain. If Jack was still missing, he could be far away from here, perhaps he would never be found, perhaps they would forget, in the turmoil of the flood and its aftermath. They would assume he'd been in Hunstanton. He could tell the police, he could tell them Jack had been with him but then had disappeared, he could tell them... But the thought of speaking to the police made him falter and stagger back from the wall. The names merged and bled.

He half ran, half stumbled out of the hall. Grabbing his bike, he cycled down Staithe Street to the quay and kept going until he reached Beach Road. He had no real idea of what he was doing.

The Army and other volunteers were repairing the breach in the flood wall. Watching them, he couldn't help but remember the journey in the rowing boat out to the farm but it was hard to fully imagine now. The bank seemed so familiar in daylight, the sea choppy but not out of the ordinary, the floodwater almost completely receded. The marks of damage were everywhere and yet to remember himself within the storm felt impossible. It was like trying to capture the feeling of being on a motorbike after you had got off it. And there it was again – the shadow of Jack. He felt a rush of dizziness and leaned his bike against the harbourmaster's house and crouched down next to it. No one had asked him about Jack. No one. Then he wanted someone to ask so he could get it over with, burn the wound, cauterise it. The US Air Force must have noticed he was gone. Yes it had been chaos, but why weren't they even asking about him? He didn't understand. And surely Peter would be in touch. It was as if everything was normal. He almost expected Jack to appear along Freeman Street with his motorbike. But he wouldn't be doing that, would he?

'You aright down there, boy?' A grizzled old man was peering down at him. Arthur recognised him as the man he had seen at this spot on the afternoon of the flood. His face was puckered with deep creases and he was chewing on the end of a pipe.

Arthur blinked up at the old man and tried to smile but his mouth wouldn't do it and he felt the muscles twist into a grimace.

The man nodded as if he understood. The nod turned into a shake. 'Terrible what happened. You lost someone?'

Arthur hesitated then nodded. He had sunk to a crouch on the edge of the bank.

'Right sorry to hear that, boy. We all have one way or another, ent we?'

Arthur stood up straight now, embarrassed to have been caught in a pose of such craven self-pity. The man didn't offer any more information and Arthur didn't ask. The man gestured to the mending of the breach.

'They'll fix it right back up soon enough,' he said, 'but it'll happen again, mark my words. These fields and this marsh was all sea, once upon a time, and the sea'll come again to claim them.'

Arthur thought how bitter these words would sound to anyone who had really lost a loved one in the flood, or their livelihood: their fields, their livestock. He wished the man would go away and leave him alone. He had been wrong to say he had lost someone. He should be more careful. It occurred to him that he should go at once to the farm to see Verity and Peter to find out what they knew. He could no longer avoid it. He stood up and made to fetch his bike.

'I seen you,' said the man, 'the night of the flood.'

'What?'

'You was with another fella. Uniform he had on, carrying a boat you was, the two of you. Past that torpedo what come up on the quay.' He gestured towards the *Terra Nova*, all 160 tons of it, still perched improbably on the quayside, and carried on nodding to himself, chewing his pipe.

Arthur's insides collapsed and he felt unsteady and gripped onto his bike for support. His mouth was thick with saliva. He swallowed painfully. 'Did you? I don't remember.' Then with a flush of relief, he thought – but it was all right! He'd taken the boat past the torpedo when they went to help the prefabs. He was sure of it. And so what if the man had seen him with Jack? Anything could have happened after that. He smiled with giddy relief. 'Oh yes!' he said, far too loudly. 'We took it out to help people.'

The man nodded again. Arthur had begun to think that was his response to anything. 'Right you are,' he said.

Arthur began to gabble. He must get home, help his mother, things to do. The man just nodded and as Arthur got on his bike he again felt like laughing. But the laughter died on his face and caught him with his lips curled up in a sneer. His sanity was slipping away in the mist.

He turned to look back and the man had gone.

Instead of riding home, he rode along the Holkham Road, out of Wells and up Leafy Lane to the farm. But Mrs Timms said Peter was busy with the clean-up and that Verity was recovering from a fever.

'I'll tell her you called,' she said, the door already closing on him.

That night, the flood returned to Arthur. Black and white. Black night, a black sea and a white moon. Arthur is in the boat. Jack is saying something. Jack's mouth is moving. The words hurt his ears. A tornado of rage and humiliation whirls through his head. He has to stop the words. His head hurts. His heart hurts.

'Shut up!' he shouts into Jack's ear. He punches him round the head, white-hot anger surging through his body, mind as pitch black as the sea. He feels the bones of Jack's head under his fists and smashes into them again and again, imagines grinding them to a pulp. Shut up. Shut up. Shut up.

Jack says something. Perhaps he says 'Stop.' Jack's body writhes like a fish, his hands against his head. But Arthur keeps punching and punching. Shutting up the jeering, leering, grinning mouth.

He stops. The writhing and jerking have ceased. Jack has fallen away from him. The cold night air and a chill fear shiver through him.

'Jack?' he says but there's no answer. His hand throbs. There's a groan from the other end of the boat. He breathes out, reaches forward to touch Jack's body. He prods it, half imagining that it might spring up. But it doesn't move. The churn in his gut tells him Jack is dead but it doesn't seem possible. They were just talking.

'Peter?'

It is the voice again, the one they thought was Verity but

now he thinks he has gone mad and there is no voice. His mind feels very slow and heavy. Think. *Think*. He must get away from here. Get the boat to safety. But he's being stupid. The boat is leaking. The body is weighing it down. He realises with a rush of deliverance what he has to do. He heaves Jack's body over the side of the boat and hears the splash as it goes under the water. He waits seconds, minutes, he counts in his head to sixty, one hundred. He tries to move the half-submerged boat with the oar but the motion makes it worse and veers him alarmingly low to the water. If he stays on the boat, he will sink with it.

The water is so cold it stops up his throat. Somewhere he remembers that he has only minutes before his body will seize up. How many? He drags his arms and legs forward, one, two, one, two, counting in his head to keep going, the rhythm of it. He doesn't know if he is swimming towards anything he can hold onto, or back, to the sea and certain death. His hand brushes something hard and he hears a scream. He imagines Jack is pulling him down into the dark. How long can he swim? Salt in his mouth and eyes. The Drowned Man. How long? He will drown and no one will ever know what he has done.

'Who's there?' It's a voice, a human voice. He must be hearing things, because it sounds like Verity. He *is* hearing things. It can't be real.

'Jack?' says the voice and then he knows it is her.

Jack is dead because he has killed him. It is his, Arthur's, fingers which touch hers.

*

ate, everything turned her stomach, even cake. She drank endless cups of tea for warmth, but the cold of the flood had got into her bones and she couldn't get rid of it. She smoked the Camel cigarettes Jack had brought her from the base, rationing them to eke them out, and kept the ruined Zippo in her pocket.

Finally, she took Peter's bike out. There was snow on the ground, but only a thin covering. The roads were just passable. The plan was only half formed in her mind. It was her body that took her along Leafy Lane to the Holkham Road and past where she had been so many times. The journey felt long and slow without Jack's motorbike and her legs ached with the effort. But they kept turning, pain shooting up her calves and thighs to her groin, and she welcomed the pain because it felt like she was at last *doing* something. She existed. The sky was a clear, pale blue and the white-streaked fields sparkled, and although there was a cold wind coming off the sea, that too gave her a sensation of her body as part of nature, that she was alive, as it was.

On the little track that led to the marsh, she pulled the bike through a snowy arbour of trees crackling with old snow hardened to ice. The weak sun lit it up like a glittering ice tunnel. Then onto the marsh. Her walk slowed as if she no longer wanted to get to the endpoint. The door of the shack was frozen shut and she had to get a stick to lever it open. Inside it was so cold she shivered despite the effort of the ride and her layers of woollens. She stopped in the hallway, listened, and heard only the whisper of wind in the old chimney and through the cracks in the windows. It must have been flooded too. There was scum on the walls and the smell of salt was strong as if the sea had reclaimed the space that had once been theirs. Which in a way, it had. Her feet wandered to the kitchen but there was nothing there: just their two enamel mugs on the side by the stove. She thought she heard a scuffle and started, heart lurching. She looked around wildly, but then heard another rustling and she remembered the mice.

In the bedroom, their bed. It was still as it was the last time they had been here, when they had argued. The sheets were crumpled in a ball at the end of the mattress, there were indentations on the thin pillows at the head, and on the floor, a chipped saucer they used for an ashtray with stubs of their cigarettes. Her legs couldn't take the weight of her body and she lay down on the bed, full-length, in her coat, hat and scarf, face pressed against his pillow. The mingled scents of sex and sweat were faint, but still detectable. If she closed her eyes and breathed through her nose, she could suck in his distinctive scent that was just him: the musk of his cologne, the tang of the Brylcreem and the particular sharpness of his sweat. She lay there a long time, crying, but not sobbing, letting tears wet her cheeks and soak into the sheets. It was as if she had no energy for the breakdown she expected. She'd hoped in some part of herself that he would be here, knowing at the same time that he would not be. There was still a chance he would be found, a voice said, and she tried to pin her thoughts on that. She couldn't let herself think he was gone forever, because it would all be gone then – the secrets they'd shared and the promise of escape he meant.

It would soon be dark. Her body felt bloated and tender as if a mere touch would bruise her. She should leave, but she couldn't bear to. It was here they had been together.

She wanted something of it, something to take with her. But what was there? A couple of chipped enamel mugs, her sketches. In the bedroom, there was a dark, heavy wardrobe. The door was stiff and she had to wrench it open. There was nothing in it, just some old wire hangers, and she was going to shut it, but then at the top, on the hat shelf, there was a darker shape. She couldn't quite reach so she got a chair. It was probably something belonging to the old crabber who'd lived here, but her heart was pounding anyway. When she pulled it down, it was a black leather bag, like a briefcase with a metal clasp and a small keyhole. It was locked. She tugged at it; she tried to saw it through with a knife but it wouldn't budge. Exhausted and defeated, puffy with crying, she lay back down on the bed.

With the light ebbing from the sky, she dragged herself over to the window and stared out, not seeing. There was the silver line of the path that led through the marsh to the woods and the sea. Her body was a heavy, swollen sack. She could not imagine moving. As she watched the daylight leave the marsh, something white shifted on the horizon. She realised she was watching people along the line of the pine trees. Mesmerised by the movement, she watched the tiny figures disappear out of sight. She was about to turn away when there was another flicker of movement by the woods, much closer now. People – two men – were in front of the pine trees. Something made her keep looking. She never did know why she didn't just turn away.

In the nightmares, words came out of Jack's mouth.

Playing at spies.

A kid's game.

I should have told you about Vee.

It's complicated, Art.

His own voice cut in.

Shut up. Shut up.

Arthur woke, gasping, his body cold and clammy with sweat.

A rapping at the door. 'What is it, Arthur? You were shouting.' His mother.

'Nothing, it's all right. Just a nightmare.'

In the kitchen, she handed him a cup of tea. He must have slept in. 'I didn't like to wake you. You look so tired.' She reached up to touch his face but he flinched. He couldn't bear to be touched. All skin felt so slimy and cold. 'You were shouting in your sleep,' she said. 'You were shouting – "Shut up!" Raving. I think the cold's got to your nerves.' She talked on and on about the doctor and remedies but he stopped listening.

Then she said, 'I almost forgot to tell you. A policeman came round this morning, while you were asleep. He was asking about that American you were with. He wouldn't tell me why. I said he'd have to wait for you to wake up, but you'd be happy to go down to the station to help them. He seemed like a nice sort of young man.'

A chill rippled through him.

It would be easy to open his mouth and say, *I killed him. I killed him. I don't know how. I don't remember how I did it, but I did. I think I did.* He wondered what she would do. But his mouth stayed shut.

He ought to have told someone straight away, when he and Verity had been rescued from the tree. He ought to have said that a man was out there. And yet the lie had already been told by then. He'd told Ver there was no one in the boat and when dawn came there were people, and there was never a moment to say it, to speak the truth. Now it was too late because everyone would wonder why he hadn't said anything before.

What could he say? *Officer, I have something I need to tell you. The missing American, John Doherty, known as Jack, was with me the night of the flood.* Oh yes, they would say, pencil poised, waiting, curious. *He fell out of the boat, officer. There was nothing I could do.* He disgusted himself with his pathetic humbling act. He could not explain, that was the trouble, he could not explain. *I lost him in the dark, officer. I wanted to tell someone but...* It was a lie. A lie. They would know it was a lie.

'You're not eating properly, Arthur.'

He looked down at the remains of the gloop in his bowl, but couldn't stomach another mouthful. He picked up the bowl and scraped the gluey remains into the bin. 'I'm not hungry,' he said.

'But you have to eat,' his mother said, imploring.

'I'm fine,' he said. He held the spoon in mid-air. What if they just wanted to ask him some questions? He didn't have to tell them the truth. He was with Jack, then he disappeared. Nothing about the boat. *No idea what happened to him, officer.* Although he felt bad at her fallen face as he left, he couldn't do anything about it. He had to go, now, right now, before he lost the nerve.

Inside the station, a police constable was at the desk with a pencil in his mouth, drumming the counter. Arthur recognised him. He was not much older than him, a callow, thin youth with a hint of old acne around his jaw. He hadn't noticed Arthur coming in and he was about to cough when the PC put a finger up, keeping his eyes on the paper in front of him until he had finished with the form he was filling in. His name was Blowers; Arthur remembered him as one of the raggedy kids who used to run around with Muriel – the village children as opposed to those at the grammar or, certainly, the big houses, like Howe Farm. It would have been easier for Arthur if he'd embraced a job like this, a cut above shopkeeping but nothing too startlingly out of his class. But he despised the likes of Blowers, that was his problem. He'd left them behind when he went to the grammar but he'd never belonged with Verity's class either. He was lost.

'Hello, Mr Silver, thanks for coming in. Stay there.' He waved at Arthur to remain where he was and called through the back, 'Doris? Can you cover me?' A neat middle-aged lady with half-moon glasses and a pinched mouth smiled at the policeman and took his seat.

Blowers emerged into the waiting area, still talking, holding out a large warm hand for Arthur to shake. 'How's your mother? Terrible damage to her shop I heard. This way, please.' He put his hand on Arthur's elbow and steered him to a bare, windowless interview room.

'Yes,' he said, trying to keep his voice light. 'She wants to reopen as soon as possible.'

'That's the spirit,' said the policeman. There was a long pause. Arthur could almost see the gears changing in Blowers' brain. 'I wanted to ask you about one of our American friends.' The policeman smiled. He waited patiently for Arthur to say something.

'I was with him on the night of the flood.' Blowers' face remained unperturbed, merely waited for Arthur to carry on. 'We rescued some of the people from the prefabs. Then we went out to the farm. We wanted to help our friend Peter, you see. Only he hasn't been found.'

'Peter? Do you mean Mr Frost's son Peter? He's absolutely fine. Well, as fine as any of us can be at the moment. Over at the farm right now, I should imagine. Terrible what's happened out there though—'

'No!' Arthur almost shouted. It was going wrong and he was afraid he wouldn't be able to get it out unless he did it now. Constable Blowers' bright, beady eyes widened and he pulled back slightly in his seat as if alarmed by Arthur's manner. Arthur lowered his voice. 'Sorry, I know about Peter. I meant Jack, the American. He's missing. He went missing that night. He'd been with me.'

'Yes, there's still a few of them not found. Awful it is. I feel for their families, not knowing. I mean, they do know they'll not turn up, not now, but it's very hard not having a body to bury.' He stopped and peered at Arthur. 'I spoke to your mother, Mrs Silver. Friend of yours then, this Jack?'

'Sort of. The thing I was trying to tell you was that we were out on a boat, and afterwards, he went missing.' He stopped. This was the moment to tell the man the truth; that Jack had been with him on the boat, at the end. He felt faint as if all the blood had drained from his head.

'It were you what found Miss Frost, weren't it, Mr Silver? Reckon you've had a hard time of it yourself.' His voice was gentle but his small eyes were sharp.

'Yes,' he said, then in a rush, 'the boat sank and I swam and found Verity, Miss Frost I mean, but... But I don't know what happened to Jack. I should have said something when they found us. I'm sorry.'

The policeman was looking at him across the counter with an expression of kindly concern. 'That's all perfectly understandable, Mr Silver. Terrible things happened that night and people forgot themselves. You were probably half mad with cold. I know I was. I said to my mother that I could imagine what it must have been like for Oates on one of those Antarctic expeditions, I did.' He went on in the same vein, telling Arthur his dull, pointless tales from the night of the flood. Arthur nodded and murmured interest, but he wasn't listening. His words had flown up and disappeared. The policeman seemed to have no interest in the missing man at all.

But then the flow of reminiscing abruptly stopped. 'You said you didn't see Mr Doherty, Mr Silver?' He said it as if it had only just occurred to him but Arthur's heart banged hard.

'I did, earlier on. Then I lost sight of him.' This was a form of the truth.

'I see. An Air Force officer called in the day after the flood, you see. Let us know there was one of theirs they were keen to locate. This Mr Doherty was the name he mentioned, funnily enough. Didn't tell me why. I presumed he must have been important in some way for them to make a special point of mentioning it.'

Arthur's blood raced. They *had* been looking for him. They just hadn't connected Jack to him.

'Tell you what, how's about this? If it'll ease your mind and mine, what about we do another trawl of the area, see what turns up?'

Arthur could not think of anything more horrifying. But surely, the body might never be found. Then again, he'd have a head start on the Air Force if he found it first. He couldn't think straight. 'Right. Yes, that would be good,' he heard himself say but through a thick membrane of fog.

The policeman beamed at him and took him back to the waiting area. He bustled around behind the desk. Arthur could hear talking round the back but couldn't make out what they were saying. Maybe someone senior would come and talk to him. Why had he come? He had come to confess, hadn't he? He thought that if they came now, someone sympathetic, who could see into his soul and see the rot there, if they came with a cup of tea and a kind word, a hand on the shoulder, he would tell them everything, all of it, just to rid himself of the sickness. But he waited and no one came except thin-faced Constable Blowers. He said that if Jack had gone missing from Wells as Arthur said he had, then the chances were his body would turn up further along the coast. 'Could be anywhere up to Cromer now, but you can never be too sure of these things.' Arthur began to think that the young policeman was more astute than his slow, Norfolk drawl implied. He was conscious of the twitching of his fingers, the involuntary tapping of his foot. He must scream *suspicious*, even to a local plod like Blowers. But he couldn't very well refuse to help find his 'friend'.

As they drove in the police car, Blowers chattered on about the nightmares of the last week as if he and Arthur were old friends. He talked as if he was an old hand at policing although he couldn't have been more than twenty-five.

'My poor aunt lost a littlun,' he said, 'tiny mite of a thing

284

he was, she couldn't hold onto him and he was taken from her arms. Terrible thing,' he said, shaking his head. 'Wave came and swept him away. We found him, though, that's something.'

Arthur muttered a platitude. He thought of Muriel running to her family, the mass of them in those slum-like cottages, exposed, so close to the sea. They drove back through the town to Beach Road.

'Aren't we going on the coast road?' he asked.

'I doubt he's gone far,' replied Blowers, cranking the gears.

'But what about what you said?'

Blowers continued to talk as he parked the black Wolseley next to the harbourmaster's house, right on the quay.

'Truth is, I read a lot of crime novels. Got a bit carried away. They don't float away usually, bodies, they sink.'

Arthur imagined Jack's body at the bottom of the sea, clouded with mud and silt, entangled in seaweed. And then he remembered Mrs Frost's body, like a dead mermaid on the sand. Her body had come back. But it was a fleeting thought because the shop was across the street and he couldn't help but turn in the direction of the dark eyes of the windows. He glanced up and thought that he could make out a shadow behind the net in the parlour window upstairs. They were now walking along Beach Road and he felt as if his mother must be watching them as they walked. He swallowed and regained his voice.

'But if they sink then why are we coming out here on our own? Wouldn't we need to dredge or something?' PC Blowers had some kind of rope with him but nothing mechanical.

'Oh, I reckon he'll have floated up by now. But he'll not have gone far. They usually come in where they drown.'

'How do you know where he drowned?'

'I don't,' said Blowers, glancing at him, 'just a hunch.'

Arthur didn't respond. His heart was hurting, it was beating so fast. The workers mending the breach were having a tea break, brought out to them by the Red Cross, and had mittened hands clamped tightly round steaming mugs, facing away from the North Sea to protect themselves from the cutting north wind. They nodded at the two young men as they passed, noting the PC's helmet and keeping a respectful distance. Blowers waved at them as if he was out on a day trip to the beach. Arthur kept his head down. Ahead of them there seemed only ruin and destruction. They came to the end of the road, the old Pinewoods caravan site down on their left, but where the Jubilee Café had stood there was nothing there.

Blowers handed him a pair of long boots, like anglers' waders, and they spent a few fruitless minutes picking their way through the debris of broken chairs and tables that must have come from the café, or the caravans.

'Thank God the caravan site was closed,' said Blowers. Arthur murmured agreement. He had his eyes trained on the water, imagining at any moment he would see... But he wasn't sure what he would see. If they found Jack, what would he look like? He could hear his own breathing very loudly in his ears and felt as if his body had dislocated itself from his brain because it was moving automatically forward, as if the pull of the water was irresistible and someone was leading him step by step through the churning brown liquid.

'It was near here where your boat sank, weren't it, Mr Silver?'

'I don't know,' he said faintly. 'It might have been near here. It was dark. I got lost.'

He followed the policeman as he waded along the edge of the pine trees. They were exposed, out here, the ruined fields and marsh in front of them. This place of sanctuary, dripping with memories, had been desecrated forever. They moved further away from Pinewoods and Beach Road, past the bottom fields of Howe Farm, whose dark presence he felt rather than saw, as only the tops of the chimneys were visible. He imagined Verity watching him from the house, though there were no windows in sight. They were almost at the end of the pine trees where the trees stopped and there was only open saltmarsh and winding creeks to the sea. He had an uncomfortable feeling of being watched, but there was no one there in this bleak wilderness. They had been looking for a long time now. The meagre light was fading and he thought they would have to turn back. Surely they hadn't come this far in the boat? He began to feel a dangerous hope that they wouldn't find Jack's body, that the policeman was wrong. The body had drifted after all.

'Oh, blimey.' Blowers was somehow ahead of him, close to the trees. For a second Arthur didn't move. He kept staring at the swirl of muddy water below him, eddying around his boots. He heard the tone in Blowers' voice and knew what it was. He thought that if only he could stay staring at the water and not ever look up, he could keep the sight out of his head. But that was impossible and he lifted his gaze to where Blowers was looking. At first, he saw nothing but the constable's black cape and preposterous helmet.

'Stay back, if you don't mind, sir,' said Blowers in a newly officious voice.

Again, he considered how he could turn and flee and never see what Blowers had seen. And again, he moved towards the policeman and then he saw.

It was a strange sight at first: not a branch but an arm dangling down from the tree. In the shadows of the wood, with only a sickly light from the pregnant snow clouds, he could only see the outline of an arm and a hand attached, white against the black of the tree. An arm. A tree. Perhaps it was not Jack after all. Perhaps it was another man. But then he saw the body too, the head drooping down behind the arm, the legs hanging above. The hair was copper red. And on the ghastly, greenish, bloated face a dark, purple mark blooming on the forehead. He had moved past Blowers who tried to stop him and he shook him off – 'Sir!' His legs had taken him towards the body, drawn to it. The policeman shone his torch on the body and something glinted bright.

A twisting in his gut and he bent over, clutching his stomach. The remains of his breakfast splashed onto the puddles in a gush of bile.

'Best get back, sir,' Blowers was saying. But as Arthur uncurled to stand up, he saw what it was that had shone – the metal chains Jack wore were hanging from round his neck – two ID tags, some kind of phial and a key on a chain hanging down behind the appalling, deformed body. In a swift, automatic movement, Arthur reached up and slid the key and chain over the lolling head and put it in his pocket.

Behind him, Blowers was saying something but Arthur couldn't hear him. Then something wrenched the air. A haunting cry like an animal in distress. He looked up to see

Verity, running with her long legs towards them over the marsh. He had no idea why she would be there or where she was running from. She had appeared from nowhere. The skin on her face was so pale it was almost translucent and the shiny dark of her hair and the black of her eyes made her look ghostly. He grabbed hold of her to stop her from seeing the body and she fought like a wild creature against him but he was stronger than she was and he spoke in her ear. 'Don't look.'

In his head a refrain played. *Jack is gone. Jack is gone. Jack is gone.*

5.

It was Saturday afternoon, three weeks after the flood, and Arthur sat in a booth in Askey's milk bar on Staithe Street. The low light made stripes across the black and white checks on the floor and illuminated the kids sipping shakes and coffees at the bar. In front of him was a library copy of *Brighton Rock*. He was not really reading. Rather than the lines of the book he saw the grotesque fish eyes in Jack's swollen body.

He reached into the pocket of his jacket and his fingers touched sharp metal. The key was still there.

Peter told him the US Air Force had taken over the investigation into Jack's death, but so far, no one had come to ask him about the night of the flood. Neither the local police nor the RAF, nor the US Air Force. He didn't know what to make of it. Peter said the local police had tried to keep hold of the case but the Americans had insisted they must have jurisdiction – and given no explanation. It confirmed to Arthur that they were hiding something. If Jack had military secrets, they wouldn't want anyone getting hold of that, would they? And he had to keep reminding himself: no one knew he'd been with Jack in the boat. That spotty youth of a copper had been funny with him but he didn't *know.* No one could know what had really happened. But the very fact of Jack's body being found made him nervous. He wondered if anyone knew about the key. What was it for? He was certain Jack had been involved in something secret. If he could find out what it was, perhaps Verity would come back to him. She had screamed when she'd seen the body. But it was him she had been with the morning of the flood. Him, not Jack. And Jack was gone now. He was gone and he'd been a traitor. Arthur had seen him in Norwich, passing something to that man. Could it be negatives of bomb sites, targets in the Eastern Bloc? If she could only see what he'd seen. But he needed proof. It went round and round in his head with no answers, no resolution.

He hated being at the flat on the quay – the wrecked shop and his mother with her frenzy of restoration and cleaning. It wore her out and sent her, sighing, to her bed. He asked her if she'd seen the doctor again and she said she didn't want to bother him, not at a time like this. But her face was drawn in pain and she lay fully dressed on her bed, clutching her stomach. He knew nothing about cancer and what he should be doing.

In Askey's, he was half eavesdropping on the young kids in the milk bar and their talk of American music. He saw in them the same desire to get away, to hear and feel the world, but they were talking about pubs and jive nights in Norwich – it wouldn't occur to them to see beyond Norfolk – and they possessed a contentment he had never had. He envied them their easy, untainted consciences and their talk of be-bop and jive, as if these were the only things that mattered.

A hand touched his shoulder. Muriel stood in front of

him, wearing a tight-fitting dark green coat and hat, holding a teacup and saucer. The coat emphasised her nipped-in waist. Her complexion was even paler than usual despite the rouge on her cheeks, her eyes red-rimmed and, behind her lipsticked smile, the shadow of loss. The memory of her black-smeared face in the rain came back to him.

He half stood. 'Muriel, I – how are you? I haven't seen you. I heard about…'

She gave a flick of her hair and sat down opposite him. 'It ent just us.' She opened up her handbag and took out her cigarettes. 'I hear your mother's got the shop open again,' she said.

'I should be there now.'

'Why aren't you then?'

'I can't face it any more. Since the flood, it's all… I don't know, everything seems ruined.' He drifted off, then remembered again. Little Freddie Gittings. The policeman, Blowers, had told him that the boy had been pulled out of his mother's arms. 'It's not important. How – how is your family?' He should have said that first.

She took a drag of her cigarette and blew a plume of smoke out of the corner of her mouth. 'Mother's not herself. She's raving. Says all sorts. Keeps saying his name over and over again and there's nothing any of us can do.' Another drag. 'She's on some pills what the doctor brought her. They make her all funny and drowsy and she looks at us, all blank and empty, like a sort of animal that's been stunned. Whole families've been coming round and bringing us scraps of food an that but she hardly notices them.'

Arthur heard the voice of Blowers saying about his aunt. Blowers was Muriel's cousin. Of course. He'd known that.

He had a sudden lurching thought that the policeman might have told Muriel about him finding Jack's body.

She noticed him watching her and flashed him her teeth, then paused, biting her bottom lip. Without meaning to, he'd put his hand on hers. He withdrew it and, to do something, lit up one of his own fags. There was a white triangle of skin beneath her yellow scarf and above the top button of her coat. He imagined putting his lips to the soft, cold flesh, pressing his fingers down into the depths below. The image spread, filling his head, and he allowed it to, strange though it was, because it made his skin tingle and his blood pulse. Nothing had done that to him since the flood.

'I saw you through the window and I thought – I need to say thank you for what you did,' Muriel said.

He shook himself away from his reverie. 'No you don't, I didn't do anything. I wish I had, maybe we could have avoided…'

'Don't talk like that, Arthur, it ent going to change anything. Anyway, I came in to say thank you, so there you are.'

She raised her eyebrows at him and put her little finger into her mouth to bite her nail and there was a kind of challenge in it that made his stomach twist.

'What are we going to do now that's done? No use feeling sorry for ourselves, is there? There's worse off than us.' She had finished her tea and was stubbing out the cigarette in the ashtray, looking at him so directly he could see himself reflected in the pools of her stare. He blinked and tried to take a sip from his now empty cup, then put it down again. He closed his eyes and saw himself kissing her red mouth. He swallowed, amazed at the thought of it. With Blowers and her being cousins, he ought to keep clear. But then everyone was related in this tight-knit, suffocating place. And he'd had enough of being alone in his head and here she was, an offering.

'You want to go somewhere?' Her voice came from a long way away.

He looked up and realised what she was saying. 'I – I—'

She was a blur of green. He could hardly think. He saw Verity's ghost-like face when she'd seen Jack's body and he wanted to get it out of his head.

'Where?' he said, as if that was important.

She laughed and shrugged. 'You'll work it out.'

'Fine,' he said, and if it sounded as flippant as he thought, she didn't seem to mind. She smiled with conspiracy and he noticed the way her lipstick bled at the corners of her mouth.

How they got to the shop he couldn't say; it was as if he was propelled there by something other than his own legs. She put her hand into his and it was small and burning hot. What if someone saw them? His body was a foreign thing, a jumble of nerve-endings only. He felt her pulse throbbing against his too-big hands and imagined tracing a line up her arm to the breasts beneath her coat.

At the door he couldn't look at her. He held his finger to his lips. Upstairs there was silence. Through the grey shadows of the ruins of the shop he led her through to the storeroom and, with the key he kept in his pocket, locked the door.

Dark and cocooned in the windowless room, he could barely see her, just a dim glow from her hair and, close up, the whites of her eyes. There, alone, with her facing him, he realised how tiny she was – she only came up to his chin – and he felt as if he could scoop her up and into himself. There was a moment when he saw himself standing in his stockroom with Muriel. A fisherman's daughter! He wished he was half-cut, but then her soft little fingers felt along his jaw and he emitted a small groan. His own rough skin found the triangle of smoothness and he felt, as gently as he could, along her collar-bone. Her body juddered and shivered and reached up to him.

Muriel's mouth was warm and alive; her tongue flicked his as he drew the tip of it along the edges of her teeth and he bit, gently, her lips and her neck.

She helped him take off his shirt and he pulled at her blouse. Her coat and hat were already in a heap on the floor. Their fingers were a flurry of buttons and braces and clasps, of cold metal on skin, and then sudden warmth when all at once there was nothing else left; they were stuck together. He wished for a second he could see her clearly but then it didn't matter because he could feel her and that was enough, too much.

Her body was soft and hard at the same time and he couldn't believe he was touching this perfection, the curve of her back, the smoothness of her shoulder. He didn't trust himself to touch her chest, he felt them, her improbable breasts, pushed against him and he fell into her, still holding her body tight to his. And then he was almost bent over double, she precarious, as he tried to lower her down to the floor. She started to laugh. 'Stop,' he said but he was laughing too. She nibbled the finger he had put to her mouth and her hand reached down and there was no way he could stop himself. His knees buckled and they collapsed onto the floor and he pushed her down with an urgent need to capture and possess the salty, smoky, living flesh of this girl who was giving herself to him. He no longer knew who or what he cared about and it didn't matter that he was on top of Muriel on the dusty, cold floor of the storeroom. The only thing that mattered was the violent need to push and push until he could be released. He gave himself up. He was here and yet not here, somewhere else entirely where neither Verity nor Jack nor his dying mother existed.

'Oh God,' he said. 'Oh fucking God.'

He murmured into her hair, his hand stroked the line of her hip and across to her rounded little stomach. His legs were sticky and his upper body exposed and cold. He wished he had a blanket to cover the two of them, but with her lithe, warm body still against his, for the moment, he couldn't move, didn't want to.

'I always liked you, Arthur,' she said, into his chest.

There was silence at the kitchen table. Father had taken his breakfast early and was out already. The vet was due to make a visit to see about the disposal of the carcasses of the dead livestock. They'd buried all the drowned chickens but there were cattle they hadn't yet found. Verity watched Peter drinking his tea. His face was drawn and she saw the shadow of her father in his features. Her toast lay picked at on her plate. Every time she tried to eat she saw Jack's greenish-grey head, hanging down from the tree, and the purple bruise on his temple, and she felt sick. They said he knocked his head on the boat.

An image of the window in the cabin swam into her vision. She would never have seen his body if she hadn't been at the cabin. She had picked up the binoculars that Jack had brought from the base, and put them to her eyes. At first she could see only the marsh. Then she raised them too high and it was only sky. Adjusting down, she came to the pine trees and turned the knob to focus. There was a policeman, quite clearly, framed in the circles. His face was animated, pink as if scrubbed raw. He was saying something. She swung the binoculars to the left and there, impossibly, was Arthur. He was kneeling on the ground and above him was a sack hanging from the tree. No. It was a dead fox. And in the same moment she thought it was a fox, the binoculars fell from her hands, her arms dropping as if someone had taken away all the life in her body, and she knew.

Death was a constant on a farm – a cow haemorrhaging after a breech birth; their old dog, Baxter, slowly dying of liver cancer; their mother's horse, mercifully shot when she broke her leg. And her own mother. She thought about what Arthur had said about her mother being found in her nightdress. Goosebumps rippled over her skin. That's why she'd insisted on looking at Jack's body. This time she wouldn't be denied the truth.

But she could never have foreseen the horror of it, the grotesque dangling of his beautiful body hung like a stuck pig. Her fingers tapped incessantly on the table.

Peter coughed, clattered his teacup on the saucer. 'What

I don't understand,' he said, 'is how he ended up there, if he was helping people in the town.'

The orange marmalade glistened on the toast. She could taste bile in her throat and she thought she was going to be sick.

Peter spoke again. 'What did Arthur say about where he left Jack?'

'You keep saying the same thing. I have no idea,' she said.

'I can't get over how we saw him at the dance—' Peter stopped and looked down at his hands. 'Ver, listen, I know you and he had… were…'

Tears fell onto her plate, soaked into the marmalade. She was not just crying for him but for all he meant. No one would ever know that they had loved each other. And the dreams he'd spun and that she'd almost believed had vanished. No one would ever know that they had ever even existed.

She heard Peter's chair scrape and she tensed, sniffed, waiting for the unwanted contact. Peter was standing awkwardly at the table. 'He was your friend as well,' she said. He sat down again as if all the air had come out of him.

He coughed. 'I suppose the Air Force will find out what happened,' he said, and opened the newspaper, rustling it loudly. 'Our new queen is coming to Norfolk,' he read. Then he added, 'Eisenhower's turned down the Rosenbergs' appeal against the death penalty. Nasty business.'

Verity didn't answer. She thought about the briefcase she'd found in the marsh shack, the pill in the ampoule, Jack's frequent disappearance. All the evasions and shadows.

They both looked up when the front doorbell rang

through the hallway and Mrs Timms came clattering out of the kitchen, puffing, 'I'm coming. Hold your horses,' as the bell rang again.

'It'll be Arthur,' Peter said, 'I asked him to come. He's bound to want to talk it over.' Something wary and hesitant passed between them wordlessly.

The room changed when he came in. They were stiff, bristling. He stood half illuminated in the pale light of the east window and he seemed defiant, uncomfortable, as if he didn't want to be there. She hadn't really looked at him the day they found Jack, and now she saw that his eyes were sunken in his head, with grey smudges in the hollows. But then he smiled at her and, although it was an awkward smile, there were plenty of reasons for that and she tried to return it.

'How've you been, old boy?' Peter asked, standing up and ushering Arthur into the room. He called for more tea and toast for Arthur, and Mrs Timms went off to get it, grumbling. 'Have the police spoken to you about Jack?'

'No,' said Arthur, 'why would they?'

'Because you helped them find the body and you told them you'd seen him!' Verity blurted out.

'Leave him alone, Ver,' said Peter, but Mrs Timms came bustling in with the tea and toast and there was an awkward pause while Verity poured tea. Arthur buttered the toast and spread marmalade and thanked Mrs Timms and them all.

'Hasn't anyone told you, though, old boy?' asked Peter finally. 'Because I've heard they're going to do a post-mortem.'

'How do you know that?' Verity asked, and at the same time, Arthur spat, 'What?'

'One of the nobs at the police told Father, who let it slip,' said Peter hotly, as if how he knew a thing was none of their business. 'The Air Force have been nosing around since the body was found. But funnily enough, it's the junior chap at Wells who's asked for an autopsy.'

Verity tried to block it out but the image of Jack's sodden, misshapen body hanging down from the tree rose in her mind again. She saw his body on a marble slab being cut. The pale, freckled skin she had touched and kissed, sliced open with a blade like paring the rubbery skin of a fig to reveal the soft pulp inside. A sound came from her and she felt herself the object of both Peter's and Arthur's gaze.

'Why do they need to do a post-mortem if he drowned?' she said, seeing the purple bloom on his forehead.

'Yes, it is rather fishy,' said Peter. 'I did have half a thought that he might have been up to something somewhat *clandestine*. That might explain it. He was always disappearing to God-knows-where. Maybe they suspect murder.'

A knife jabbed behind her eye sockets. Arthur cleared his throat. 'Speaking of which, do either of you know anything about a box or a trunk that Jack had? Something with a small lock. He said something about a locked box the night of the flood and he made it sound quite important. I wondered if he'd mentioned anything like that to you, just in case you had any idea where it might be. We could help the Air Force if they're after it. That is, if it's important.'

Verity's heart was beating hard. The pain in her head intensified. Was there a box? And again, she thought of the briefcase and its secret contents. Of their shack on the marsh and what it had meant to her. She'd thought it had meant the same for him. Their place, just theirs. *What were you hiding, Jack?*

'No clue whatsoever,' said Peter, 'though you might want to mention it to one of the military types. I heard they'd been in touch with the local plod, you know. Ver – are you all right?'

Her vision blurred and her stomach was retching. 'Sorry,' she choked and, clutching her mouth before she was sick on the kitchen floor, she ran to the bathroom and vomited the pathetic amount of tea, toast and marmalade she had managed to keep down, into the sink.

After she cleaned herself up she told them not to worry, it was probably just a bug. But she excused herself and went to bed. At some point that day, she no longer remembered exactly when, she stared at her reflection in her mother's dressing room mirror and felt the force of the truth. For she had truly got herself in a mess. The sickness, the tenderness of her breasts, her revulsion at the smells and taste of food, her jags of crying; the undeniable fact that her cycle had stopped. She had known all this but it had been easy to explain away. She had been ill; she was sick with grief. *Go and see a doctor*, she imagined someone saying. Someone who cared about her, someone who noticed the changes in her. But there was no one to do that. And she couldn't go to a doctor – the family doctor was a bald, jowly man who'd reluctantly gone over to the National Health Service – but the thought of him and his fat fingers examining her – no. The shame of it. She couldn't face it. *Oh Mother*, she prayed, *tell me what to do*. But the looking-glass only reflected her own bloated, blotched face swimming in a blurry film. She felt as if she was underwater, trapped, with no access to air. Is this what drowning felt like, Mother? You meant to do it, didn't you? *She*, Verity, should have drowned in the flood, along with Jack. Silly girl, she chided. But that was it: she would drown the thing inside her, make it go away, flush it out. She had a dim memory of a girl at school talking about gin and hot baths. Downstairs was quiet. It wasn't tea yet and the men were out. Mrs Timms was in town shopping for supper. She could do it right now.

She crept downstairs and turned the immersion heater on for the hot water and went to the drinks cabinet in the parlour. There was a half-empty bottle of gin. She held it in a shaking hand. Maybe it had to be hot too. She warmed a big glassful in a pan on the stove, praying that no one would come in. Then she scrubbed the pan, refilled the bottle with water to the level it had been, returned it to the cabinet and went upstairs with the hot glass wrapped in a tea towel.

In the bathroom she turned on the taps and waited for the water to heat up and slowly fill the bath. It was such an incredible luxury to be having a bath in the middle of the day she almost laughed. What would Mrs Timms say? Oh how horrified she would be! The housekeeper referred to it as 'your mother's bathroom,' with an implicit disapproval of such louche, unnecessary home comforts. When Verity stripped to her underwear she put her hands on her stomach and felt its egg shape. In the glass she peered at her stomach. Standing sideways it appeared to stick out, distended and ugly, but she breathed in and it flattened. It was hard to tell if there was anything there. She wondered whether if she punched herself she could destroy the thing inside, but that was grotesque. She couldn't bring herself to do it. Instead, she took a gulp of the hot liquid and gagged and spluttered, spitting much of it out onto the linoleum floor. It was like drinking turps, and a distant image of herself painting in the school art room blinked in her brain. A lifetime gone since then. The bathroom mirror was steamed up and she could no longer see her reflection and that was a good thing. She wanted to efface herself, to float away from the horror of the present. Tightening her throat, she took another gulp of the vile gin and entered the bath. It was scaldingly hot but that was good too. She felt that the heat inside and around her would clean her out, strip off her layers of filth and muck, cleanse her of the fluids sloshing about inside her, the growth sucking the life out of her. She took the glass, only warm to the touch now, wet with steam from the misty room, drained the remaining gin and sank deep into the bath. Her skin prickled and burned hot pink in the scalding water, her head lolled as if loose from her neck and her mind felt as cloudy as the hot, dripping room.

It was easy to close her eyes and sink under the water, to let the water take her in. It was like sleeping. It wouldn't be so awful if it ended this way.

A knocking in her head. She opened her eyes. Everything was white in the steam of the bathroom, just the taps glinting metal through the mist. She wished her head would stop the banging. Then she realised someone was shouting her name.

'Ver! What are you doing? How long have you been in there?'

It was Peter. She hadn't died. And she was ashamed for thinking that she might. Remembering, she felt the slight curve of her belly with a detached horror. At the pit of her stomach was a deep ache. Perhaps the thing, the growth, had gone, drowned in the bath, its new, flickering life choked off.

A banging on the door. 'Ver, for God's sake, open up! What's wrong?'

'All right,' she said, her voice cracking with lack of use. As she raised herself out of the bath, her back scythed with pain and the ache in her abdomen cut into her and she groaned. She looked down between her legs into the still warm water but there didn't seem to be anything floating in it, no pink, bloody swirls; she wasn't even sure what she was looking for.

With a towel around her, she opened the door.

'Bloody hell,' said Peter, 'it's like a Turkish bath in here. You look ghastly,' he added, squinting at her.

'Thanks,' she said, and sat on the edge of the bath, her legs soft and jelly-like. Her fingers were shrivelled and her skin was covered in goosebumps.

'Peter,' she said, fixing her eyes on the taps at the end of the bath, 'was Mother wearing clothes when she was found?'

Peter coughed and shuffled his feet.

So it was true. It had been there in the whispers and the air of scandal surrounding her death but Verity had never wanted to believe it. She began to cry. Peter's discomfort and impatience rippled through the fetid air of the bathroom. The only sound was the dropping of her tears into the bath water.

6.

All along the coast, men patrolled for the second high spring tide. The streets were sandbagged, sailors had battened down their boats and the police kept vigil. The Snow Moon shone full.

That was the thing about tides. They came back. Muriel's grandmother had told her about 1930 and countless storms before. Her own grandfather had drowned at sea. Muriel always wondered what it would be like to drown. Opening your mouth in shock, taking in the seawater. You wouldn't believe it was happening but the water would already be in your lungs. You couldn't shout because your throat would be seized up and the cold would have shut down your body. Her grandmother always said it was a silent death. And so it had been for her little brother, disappearing without a murmur into the dark wave.

But it wasn't drowning Muriel was worried about, or even the spring tide. She was keeping a mental vigil over Arthur.

7.

'Arthur, I don't think it'll be safe out there today on the bicycle, you'll have to go on foot. It looks like snow.'

His mother was peering out of the kitchen window at the lowering yellow sky. It was just after lunch and she was about to reopen the shop for the afternoon custom and he was supposed to do the deliveries.

'I'll be fine,' he said. He was desperate to be outside, to be doing something. He had to move, to breathe. Thoughts of the dead man and the whispers of the Frosts were like thick smoke clogging his throat. He wondered again about Jack's key. It looked like a safety deposit box key, or for a safe, perhaps. Or possibly a padlock, but for what? The key was small and quite delicate: about half the length of his little finger. His thumb felt along the ridges of the shaft and he imagined it turning in a lock. It was the only thing he could think of that might save him. He would take the bike out and it would give him the chance to think.

Out on the quayside, he looked towards Beach Road and the marsh and remembered finding Jack's body and Verity running at him like a crazed dog. Is that where she had been with Jack? It must be. It was obvious now. They'd been meeting out there, making a fool of him all this time.

And how would she have seen them finding the body if she hadn't been on the marsh itself? There was no way she could have seen him and Blowers from the house. So she must have come from somewhere out on the marsh, somewhere hidden. And he knew what he was going to do.

He didn't bother with the delivery basket and mounted his bike, but as he was about to push off, he noticed at the other end of the quay two figures whom he recognised at once. One was small and obviously female with a green hat and coat and was talking to a tall, thin man in a police uniform. It was Muriel and the young policeman, Blowers. Cold ran through his limbs. Their heads were close up and for a second he thought with incredulity that they were kissing, but he knew somehow, by the tilt of their heads, by some stiffness in their bearings, that they were not. As he watched them, Blowers nodded his comically high, helmeted head and patted Muriel on the shoulder and left her. Then, almost as if she knew he was watching them, Muriel turned in his direction. Behind her, the policeman stopped and also turned. Muriel's hand went to her mouth and then she raised it in a tentative wave. Arthur waved back, but as quickly as he could, without drawing attention to his actions, he pedalled off hard in the opposite direction, down the Holkham Road towards Leafy Lane and the farm.

Muriel saw the figure coming out of the shop at the other end of the quay and she felt a sense of déjà vu. She stood, stuck in indecision, her fingers turning purple in the sharp air.

'Muriel?' A hand touched her shoulder and she jumped.

It was cousin Rod. 'What's wrong?' he said. 'I saw you just standing here and I thought you looked a bit lost, if you don't mind me saying.'

She laughed. 'Don't be a lummox, Rod, I'm fine.'

'Best get inside,' he said. 'Weather's turning.'

'I know that,' she said.

Rod said nothing. Then he indicated the Holkham Road where Arthur's figure was getting on his bike. 'He's a friend of yours, isn't he? Arthur Silver.' She opened her mouth to say something but he continued, 'It's none of my business, it's just—' He stopped.

'Spit it out,' she said.

'It was him what found the body of the American you was asking about, did you know that? Actually, it was me, but he led us there. I thought it was a bit odd at the time. It was almost like he wanted to tell me something.'

He had her attention now. She looked at his slightly pinched, acne-scarred face. He was Gert's son, her mother's sister, the sister who'd done good, married a railwayman, son a policeman of all things. Lived out of the town in clean new houses with no damp and an inside toilet. They had airs, that side of the family, and her mother was resentful of her snooty sister. But Rodney Blowers was no fool. Muriel remembered Arthur's body on top of her and she thought perhaps it was she who was a fool. Next to her, Rod was fiddling with his gloves.

'There's something else, ent there?'

'I don't know if I ought to tell you,' he said. His face was pink.

'What?' she said, sharply. 'You got to tell me now.'

'Well, I suppose you are family. It's only, when the body

of the American was found, an old man came to tell us he'd seen him the night of the flood. He'd seen the two of them together. The American and Arthur Silver. And not when Arthur said neither. Later. Past midnight. The Air Force want to talk to him, you know.'

'What you going to do about it?' she asked him.

'Can't really say,' he said in his policeman's voice. But then he added, 'It might be nothing.'

She nodded, running her teeth across her bottom lip.

'Best be off now,' he said.

She turned to see if Arthur had gone but he was still standing next to his bike as if he'd been watching her the whole time she was talking to Rod. She waved. He raised his hand then finally got on his bike and rode away.

Muriel still didn't go home. There was work to be done, her mother to check on. But there was also Arthur cycling off into the early dark, his bike light a tiny dot now. She wanted to warn him, to help him somehow, but she didn't know how.

8.

By the time Arthur reached the driveway to the farm, light flakes were falling and the sky had darkened to a sickly yellow-grey. Already it was hard to see far ahead on the bike. He pedalled without thinking, stopping only when he came in sight of the farmhouse.

He didn't really know why he was here. He had only felt the urgent need to get away from Blowers. He looked up at the house, which was half obscured by the snow falling, heavier now. It was soaking into the driveway but had started to settle on the ornamental trees. The house stared down at him. He had been happy here, but it felt like long ago now. The windows were blank. He wanted Verity to open the door, to tell him he was forgiven.

While he stood holding onto his bike, someone came crunching around the side of the house. Instinctively, Arthur shrank back against the trees. It was Peter, hunched against the cold, in his flat cap and tweeds. In his right hand, he was carrying a rifle. Arthur silently watched as Peter opened the door to the gun store, returned the rifle and shut it again. Arthur's breath curled up and vanished into the freezing, whitening air. He could call out to his old friend, ask him for help. But in what words, he couldn't think. And he imagined Peter's and Verity's faces when they found out the truth – the horror, the disgust, the revulsion. He wanted to cry, then, to know that this was no longer a place of safety for him. He felt a sense of vertigo – as if the earth had cracked open and he was teetering on the edge of a void. He swayed against his bike, his hands clenched white around the handlebars and his body tensed as if for a fight. Peter disappeared around the dark side of the house.

The car. He could take Mr Frost's car: the old Jag in the garage. He could drive along the Holkham Road and see what was out there, what Jack had hidden.

In the house, lights flickered on in the upstairs rooms. Peter would be in there. If he found out what he'd done he would hate him. But at this moment, Peter was all he had. He leaned the bike against a tree and crossed the drive quickly to ring the bell.

Peter had left Verity in her room with a book and a tray of tea and bread and butter that Mrs Timms had brought up for her. His sister was deathly pale and distracted. There was definitely something wrong; she might be sick, but he had no idea what to do about it. He felt the pang of loss of their mother, who would have stroked her hand at the very least. Verity always protested that Mother had been distant but it wasn't how he remembered her. To him, their mother had been a barrier between him and his father. He wished... but it was pointless wishing.

Downstairs, he was pouring himself a second large glass of whisky when the doorbell rang. Mrs Timms had gone home. She said the snow was coming and she'd better go now or she'd get stuck. He had a funny image of the shapeless, furry brown hat like a small dog that she wore in the winter, sticking out of a snowdrift. Father was out cold on the sofa next to the fire. They'd spent the day repairing fences and had found the carcass of a rabbit stuck in the wire. Peter couldn't think who on earth would be calling at this time but he took his drink and cracked open the front door.

'Peter.' Arthur was shivering in the doorway, shifting from one foot to the other in his greatcoat.

'Hello, old boy. What are you doing here? Come in and warm up with a drink!'

'No, I – I can't come in. Listen, I wondered if there was any chance I could borrow your car?'

Peter frowned, bewildered. This was such an unexpected question. Arthur was talking hurriedly, as if desperate to get the words out. 'Got some tricky deliveries, awful weather, but I don't want to let them down, you see. The old dears.' He trailed off. He was lying, Peter knew it. He fixed his eyes on Arthur. The lie hurt, but it made him alert. Arthur had been acting strangely ever since the flood. Something must have happened between him and Jack that night.

'Yes, I see, right. Thing is, Arty, there's absolutely bugger all petrol. Just used it up getting supplies for what's left of the cattle, you see. Awfully sorry.' Peter's conscience was hammering on his skull. There was the emergency petrol store. He could give it to Arthur.

Arthur nodded slowly and rubbed his hands in the cold. 'Right,' he said at last. A gust of icy wind blew a few flakes into the hall. 'Yes, I understand. I better get back then, can't keep them waiting.'

'You sure you don't want a nip of whisky or nice juicy port to keep you going?'

Peter waited as Arthur looked longingly towards Peter's glass and the faint glow of warmth emanating from the drawing room. If Arthur came inside, he'd lend him the car, he'd say he made a mistake. But Arthur looked up behind Peter to the banisters and first floor landing, and frowned as if he'd seen something. 'Love to. I really would. I can't, though, Peter. Sorry.' Immediately, he turned on his heel and disappeared into the dark of the drive.

Peter shut the door but didn't move. He almost opened it back up and shouted to his friend to please come in for a drink, to force him. To say, *Listen, old boy, I just remembered. There's a secret stash of petrol. Take it!* But the seconds ticked by and he was still at the door, listening. There was no sound. Arthur must have gone. As Peter's shoulders relaxed, he thought he heard a noise outside. It was probably an animal searching for food. Again he heard the sound of something creaking. Gently, he turned the catch on the front door and inched it open. At first, he couldn't see anything. Then he realised the door to the gun store was open. He was about to step out and shut it, when someone came out.

For a fraction of a second he thought it was a burglar. It was a figure in a greatcoat and he'd taken one of the shotguns and was now mounting a pushbike. But the way the figure moved was familiar and Peter knew it was Arthur before the man glanced back and his face was half lit by the light of the hall.

He opened his mouth. 'Arthur?' then, 'Wait,' a bit louder, but Arthur just seemed to shake his head. Then he rode off down the lane and disappeared into the darkness.

Peter stood still on the stone step with his drink in his hand in the yellow glow of the hallway as faint, wet snow fell around him. He was sick with indecision. Arthur was his old friend. But Peter had loved Jack, no matter what he had done. He suddenly remembered Skitmore telling him that Arthur's gun had gone off on the partridge shoot last autumn and it had nearly got someone killed. He'd felt uneasy about it but it sounded too preposterous. But what if Arthur had wanted to scare Jack? Had hated him all this time? He'd taken a gun, he was acting distinctly rum. It was all coming together with a horrible inevitability. And if Arthur had really hurt Jack – it was unforgivable. He downed the whisky and breathed through his nose. Then he went back inside and picked up the telephone in the hallway and called the police station.

At the other end of the line, it crackled. He had a nasty feeling the lines hadn't been fixed since the flood but he was flustered because, of course, he knew they were. Finally, a man's voice came through on the other end.

'Can I speak to PC Blowers, please?'

'Blowers, you say?' said the voice on the other end and a guffaw. 'Don't see why not. Who's speaking, can I ask?'

He told the man. Then he heard a muffled exchange. 'Wants you,' said the older man, evidently amused, and Peter remembered that Blowers was the junior man at the station. But he didn't care. There was no one else he could tell.

'Mr Frost, how can I help you, sir?'

Peter hesitated. Arthur was his oldest friend. 'We – that is – I – thought you ought to know that a friend of ours

– a close friend of mine actually – has been acting, uh – strangely. I'm terribly worried about him.'

The policeman would be sure to dismiss him outright, and rightly so, he thought. And that would be that. But Blowers just said, 'In what way, sir? Would you mind telling me where you last saw the gentleman?'

When he put the receiver down Peter went upstairs. He needed to talk, to tell Verity, to be reassured somehow that he'd done the right thing. He had only said he was worried about Arthur. It was all he'd done, surely. He couldn't bear it for anything bad to happen to Arthur. He leaned his head on Verity's door before opening it. But she wasn't in her room and although he called and looked all over the house, she was nowhere to be found. Outside, the snow was falling more thickly but through it he could have sworn that he heard the sound of a horse's hooves.

Arthur breathed out, a ragged, shuddering breath. It had been a mistake to come here. They had a petrol stash, he knew it. Which meant Peter had lied to him. But at his back, in the town, was Muriel and her cousin, Blowers. That callow, lanky boy was on his tail, he knew it.

He could leave Wells. A clean break. He could go to London. But the train station was still closed after the flood, and how far could he get on his old pushbike? And in snow? *Think*. He could still find Jack and Verity's hideout. But there was no way he could get out there on the bike now anyway. He had hardly any time. He imagined Blowers on the telephone to the base; the Air Force, the officer he'd seen Jack talking to a million years ago at the Midsummer dance coming for him. There would be lights tracking him, sirens...

He flung the bike down and set off across the marsh with the gun.

9.

Into the narrow beam of her torch, the snow fell in thick flakes into the darkness. Although Verity knew the route to the cabin as if it was imprinted on her hand, the night and the snow made it foreign and strange, and she was thankful she had remembered the torch. But beyond that, she wasn't at all sure she knew what she was doing. She'd taken Gypsy and ridden the usual way along the Holkham Road, past the entrance to Harborough Hall and towards the little path that led to the cabin. She left the poor, cold horse at the same place she used to leave him, by the clump of deformed hawthorns. He had whinnied and stamped in agitation, and she patted his muzzle, telling him she'd be back soon.

The door was iced shut again but it wasn't hard to prise it open. It was old and rotten with the damp from sea spray. It was no warmer inside the cabin than outside except there was some protection from the wind coming off the sea and a sudden quiet. Although it was tempting to light a candle or the little stove, she knew she could not. She switched off the torch and used her mittened hands to feel her way down the passage. She had heard Arthur talking to Peter. She would know Arthur's voice anywhere and the very fact of his turning up unannounced on a snowy, winter night was odd. And then asking for the car – the Arthur she knew was too proud to do that. She'd watched from her bedroom window as he'd left on his bike, then, in increasing confusion, watched as he'd dumped the bike and set out on foot across the front fields towards the marsh. She remembered what he'd said about the key he had and she'd felt an urgent panic to get the briefcase, because wasn't that what he was after? He hated Jack and wanted to destroy the memory of him. There was no point following him across the marsh. It was faster as the crow flies but she had Gyps.

Now in the cabin, she imagined Arthur here before her, but he had no idea where it was. There was no sound but the scurrying of mice. All of this was tumbling through her mind but hardly consciously as she fumbled through the dark passage to the bedroom. In the wardrobe, the black briefcase was where she had left it. She took off her mittens and her hands felt its smooth, cool leather as she pulled it down from the top shelf. It wasn't heavy and she wondered if she'd got it wrong, that there was nothing in it after all. But why would anyone lock an empty briefcase?

She turned on the torch and the metal clasp shone up at her. Oh Jack, what were you doing? She laid the briefcase on the little table in the kitchen and scanned the room with her torch for something she could use to open it. Leather could be cut. There must be something. She got down on her knees and reached through the little curtain under the dirty old sink. There was nothing. In the kitchen drawer, old knives, but nothing sharp enough. Then she had an idea. She remembered that there'd been a cupboard with crabbing equipment, rusty traps and buckets. In one of the buckets was a small knife. It had probably been used for slitting open crabs. She ran her finger along the blade. Sharp enough. She hacked and hacked at the leather and at first it hardly made a mark. It was like slicing through tough, old skin. She tried not to think about how Jack had been sliced open. Soon, the briefcase had a deep, jagged line carved into it, below the lock. She pushed her hand down inside the slit she had made and felt shiny paper. Ripping the slashed leather further apart, she pulled out the handful of papers inside, spread them out on the table and shone the torch on them.

Photographs. A4 size, printed onto high-quality photographic paper, black and white and artistically arranged, as if they were paintings. Not Top Secret or Classified documents. All of women, lying or sitting, most of them on a bed, looking away from the camera. Half naked. Their white thighs, bare shoulders, exposed flesh shone out in the gloom of the cabin. Most of them she didn't know. They were strangers. Prostitutes she guessed, with dark make-up around their eyes and dimpled skin, a breast lolling into an armpit. With a shock, she recognised one of the women, clothed this time, taken outside. With fumbling, urgent hands, she flicked through them and dropped them on the table. She was nauseated. He was a voyeur and a pervert. This wasn't it. This couldn't be it.

She reached in again and pulled out more sheaves of paper: landscape shots he had taken from this cabin across the marsh to the sea; pictures of unidentified, old English streets she didn't know. Then in among the larger shots, one small snapshot of him in front of a plane, with the rest of the crew. Her hand shook. The plane was RAF, she thought:

the target roundel was just visible. The men were lined up in front of the nose of the plane. On the nose someone had painted a huge, bloodshot eye, the veins like tentacles clearly visible across the cornea. Jack was at the end of the row, his shoulders slouched and slightly leaning to the side in a relaxed pose. It didn't seem to make any sense that he would have flown with the RAF. At the bottom she saw Jack's handwriting, curled and expressive, the words – *Holkham, January 1952*. January? He'd arrived in May, with the jet bombers. She thought back to when she'd met him, in the lower field. He *had* said he'd just arrived. But it wasn't true.

This was the only shot that had anything to do with the military. The rest were innocuous: more landscapes, more streets. There was a self-portrait he must have taken with a timer, squinting into the sun, a white shirt open at the neck, tents behind him. She couldn't look at it. Then one of a boy. A bright-haired boy in a polo shirt grinning at the camera on a lawn somewhere. Behind him a blurred figure, female. She brought the picture up close. The camera seemed to gaze at the boy lovingly, focusing on him rather than the woman behind, the light of the sun shining on him like a halo. She wondered who the boy was. But she couldn't linger. It wasn't what she was looking for. Trance-like, trembling, she sifted through the rest of them, faster and faster under the torchlight until, finally, she came to what she had been dreading. Photographs of her.

Snow fell onto the sea and the ground and blew sideways into Arthur's face. He imagined it melting into the damp marsh and the black sea. The snowclouds obscured the moon and there was no other light. He could barely breathe through the wet flurries and his chest was tight with panic. What if someone came after him? But no one knew where he was. He saw Peter's boyish, worried face at the door. He might go out looking for him, he might find the bike, dumped on the lane, but it seemed unlikely. Peter would do nothing.

Arthur's boots were filled with icy water and it reminded him of the night of the flood, but he had to block that out. He had to keep going. He had to find the place where Jack had hidden his secrets. Negatives, details of contacts – there had to be something. Ahead of him was a small ball of light, burning yellow-white against the pale flakes of snow. He tried to speed up but he stumbled into mud, silt and sand, tripping on tufts of grass. His boots were wet and his trouser cuffs soaked through. The light was still flickering. Perhaps he was imagining it. The closer he got to it the brighter it seemed to burn. Then to the left of the eerie light, another appeared, a tiny moving prick of fire. Unsure which to follow, he stopped and watched. The warm, flickering light hovered in the air. He thought it must be a will-o'-the-wisp, come to guide him and he must resist it. He moved towards the other light but as he did, it extinguished like a candle flame and he was suddenly disoriented, snow in his mouth and hair. He could not get lost out here. He waited. The light came on again. He hurried towards it, the bitter wind from the sea pushing him on. The tiny yellow dot was coming from a building of some sort, a rickety old barn or something. And though he couldn't know it, he felt that the box he was looking for must be here. There was nowhere else. Someone had beaten him to it. But he still had the key. And the gun.

With cold, stiff fingers, Verity gathered up all the photographs and stuffed them back inside the briefcase. She couldn't let anyone find them – the shame of it. There was one in which she was asleep on the bed, the blanket across her thighs, the curve of her spine like the skeleton of a fish, her hair black against white skin, and under her left arm, the shadow of her breast. He must have taken it while she was asleep and the thought of him watching her sent a wave of goosebumps over her skin.

The sounds of the night were muffled in the snow. Through the bedroom window there was a peculiar silvery glow. No vision and no sound. There could be anything out there and she wouldn't know. She wanted to be home, warm and safe; she shouldn't have come here. She switched off the torch and stumbled back down the passage with the torn-open briefcase and was outside, running now, the snow against her face. She found her way along the path, tripping, almost going down but righting herself again. A bramble scratched her face but she pushed it away.

'Gyps,' she called softly, and heard the familiar whine of her horse through the thickening flakes. Falling onto him, she clung onto his neck. She felt the warmth of his animal-blood pumping through the veins in his neck on her cold cheek. 'It's all right, it's only me. What is it, boy? Just the ghosts out at night. It's all right. Let's go home now.'

Something moved.

'Who's there?' Verity said, trying to sound brave.

A figure stepped towards her and, although she couldn't be certain who it was, the shock made her gasp and grip tighter to Gyps. The figure came closer and she cried out. It was Arthur. The particular line of his hair and jaw was clear to her dark-adjusted eyes. Despite everything, she wanted to cry. He was so familiar and this was so unfamiliar, so plainly ridiculous: the two of them out there by a decrepit shack in the middle of the marsh, with her horse stamping his hooves and the snow softly falling on everything. It was like a Second World War spy film. She half expected someone to shout, 'Cut!' A noise came out of her mouth, halfway between a cry and a laugh.

'What's funny?' he said, and something in his voice, the urgency of it, made her relief wither and fear take its place.

'Nothing. Just you and me, here. It made me think of a nativity scene, like you'd see in a church. Gyps is like the donkey. We just – we just – need a star…' She was babbling nervously and he wasn't responding. She scrabbled in her pockets, grabbed the torch, shone it at him and he put his hand up to shield his eyes.

'I… I heard you talking to Peter,' she said, desperate now to get away. 'Did you get your deliveries done then?'

But he didn't answer her. 'Is that it?' he said, looking down at the briefcase.

'What do you mean?' she said. It was far too late to keep up this charade but she didn't know what else to do. She shrunk back and drew the briefcase closer to her body.

'We can still work this out, Ver. It's not too late for me. For us. If you let me have the briefcase, I'll show you the truth. I've got the key. Why don't you let me open it and we can see what's inside.'

She almost laughed. There was no need for a bloody key, but in the dark, with the torn leather crushed against her body, he couldn't have seen that.

'I don't want to,' she said. It sounded pathetic.

'Come on, Verity. He's gone. It's all over.'

'No,' she said. It came out like a sob.

'You don't owe him anything, Verity. Jack was a liar and a bloody traitor. The police should see what's in there. Give it to me and we can take it to them.' He was snarling now, the anger barely suppressed.

'The police?' she said, with a mad laugh. 'The police are on their way, Arthur. They know you're here. They know... they know what you did.' It was a wild stab.

'Don't be stupid, Ver, no one knows either of us are here,' he said, but his voice had a tear in it that let in doubt.

Peter – she thought – Peter does. But Peter had never been here.

'What did you do to him?'

Silence apart from the sound of the wind in the reeds. Then he spoke. 'It was an accident. I didn't mean to. We had an argument. I don't remember—' She was aware of a humming sound in her head getting stronger. Then he said, 'Listen, Ver, don't get the wrong idea but look, I've got a gun.'

The humming sound burst. A kind of strangled noise came from her mouth. This wasn't her Arthur.

'I'm not going to use it, of course I'm not, but I'm telling you because you need to give me the briefcase. Give it to me. Please, Verity. It's only right that the public finds out what he's been doing.'

'I can't.'

'Why not? He's dead.'

'Because it's not what you think it is. There's nothing important in here. Only to me.'

'You're lying,' he said. 'This is in the public interest. They've been spying on Russia without anyone knowing; they've been carrying atomic bombs and endangering us all. What if there was an accident at the base? What then? It affects all of us. We can't just let them all get away with it.' He sounded excited, as if he'd forgotten she was there.

'I'm not lying,' she said, bewildered.

'Ver – enough. Stop protecting him. I've not even told you the worst of it. I saw him handing something over – when we were in Norwich – he was a spy, Ver. A dirty, bloody spy.'

An exhalation came from her mouth, but nothing articulate. It couldn't be true.

He carried on. 'He gave a metal box to a man in Norwich. I think – I think he was selling something to them.'

She breathed out. It would have been the film pack of negatives from his camera. It would have been the naked photographs. She wanted to say, *He wasn't a spy, Arthur, he was just a…* But she couldn't say what he was.

'You've got it all wrong, Arthur,' she said, but he wasn't listening.

'Give the briefcase to me, Ver. Now.' She could hear the threat and the cajoling in his voice. He moved a step closer to her. She cast about wildly for something to do, to say, to stop him.

'Don't,' she said, 'I'm pregnant.'

He laughed and at first she thought that it hadn't worked. She swallowed hard but she heard him let out a deep breath and saw the mist of it curling in the air.

'Is it mine?'

'Yes,' she said, firmly now. 'Yes it is. Please calm down, though, Arthur. Please.'

He reached forward and for a moment she thought he was going to try to touch her but in his hand he was holding a shotgun with the barrel facing towards her. She screamed and jerked back. For a moment, he was disconcerted by her reaction and she pushed him hard. The force of it knocked the gun out of his hand. A shot rang out across the marsh. She thought she heard it thud softly behind him into the reeds. In the tussle the briefcase had fallen on the ground.

Photographs spilled out of the mangled leather and drifted down to the damp earth where they lay scattered like leaves. Arthur, on his knees, stared at them. The pictures quickly became mottled and distorted by the snow and the wet. A few of them were lifted up by the wind and flew into the snowy darkness, flapping like paper birds.

Without waiting to see what he would do, she began snatching up the wet, floppy sheets with bare, shaking hands, shoving them back in the briefcase. She caught sight of the one of Jack and his crew with the RAF plane. It was half covered in mud and ice but she grabbed it and crumpled it into the pocket of her coat.

On the wet ground, Arthur was mesmerised, like a figure turned to stone. He clasped a photograph in his fingers and he was looking at it with a face distorted in pain. In her hand she still had the torch and the pool of yellow light made him look sick and unearthly. She snatched the photo out of his hand and he grabbed her wrist. 'No!' she shouted and heard Gyps whinny to her. In a surge of desperation, she wrenched her hand away from Arthur and threw herself on her horse. She grasped Gypsy's neck and kicked his side. The horse reared up. At the edge of her sight, she saw Arthur clambering to his feet. He was shouting. He grabbed her foot. She thrashed out at him, but the horse was already at a canter and she clung to him and didn't turn back.

'Verity!' he shouted. 'Stop!' But she'd shaken off his grip and he was thrust backwards, panting, slipping on the ice-crusted ground. The photograph he'd seen was of a woman's face in profile, dark-haired, her upper body in shadow but naked. It was dark: how could he be sure? In his bones, he felt the chill of her deceit. She had lied to him. He'd known it, in his heart. He'd known the truth. With a groan of rage and misery, he whipped round to look for the gun. Without her torch, the night was suddenly thick and smothering.

Crouching, his hands scrabbled on the ground and the ends of his fingers touched the wood of the butt. The gun was on the edge of the marsh, damp but not submerged. He grabbed it and ran down the path, chasing the sound of the horse's hooves thudding on the ground. Blood thumped in his ears. He couldn't see anything apart from wet, white flakes whirling in front of him. The path was narrow and overgrown with brambles and she couldn't go very fast. He thought the shadow of the horse's rear appeared, a grey mass, and he raised the gun.

He was a good shot. If he'd wanted to kill Jack back in the autumn he could have done. He pulled the barrel up, but wavered, his finger hovering on the trigger. If he fired, even if he fired in the air, Gyps would throw her. His hand shook and slackened. He couldn't do it. He removed his finger from the trigger. Far away, coming from where the road must be, there were lights and the sound of car engines. Sirens. Peter must have called the police. Maybe it was the Air Force too. He felt the fact of it sink into his stomach. The horse neighed in the distance. Trembling, he flung the gun down.

'I didn't want this,' he said hopelessly, but the wind and snow took the sound. He could sink now into the quaggy marsh. He could merge with the water and the mud and wait for what would come. At this moment, he could think of nothing else. But if they found him he would be humiliated. He would be hanged. Shouts rose from the distant road. She must have found them. He couldn't be caught like a rat in a trap. He ran, away from his pursuers, further into the dense reeds behind the shack, towards the dunes and the sea.

Running into the snow, he could see nothing but the flakes stinging his eyes. His feet felt narrow paths below. The paths ended in thick reeds or worse, a tidal creek. He kept on, towards where he thought the sea was, away from the shack. The reeds got thicker. Seawater, laced with stinging shards of ice, sloshed over his shoes. The tide must be coming in. He kept on running. No choice now. He could no longer see the lights on the road so he must be going the right way. Think: he would run down to the woods and hide there, circle back through the fields to the ruined lowland where the prefabs had been and into the town. And then?

Tired, with aching legs, he stumbled on a clump of some marsh plant. He splashed and pitched forward into the sharp, silty saltwater. He went under briefly and surfaced, choking and spitting. Grabbing the reeds at the side of the creek, he hauled himself up and lay face down on the boggy ground. His coat was dripping and thick with mud. It was heavy and dragging him down, but without it he would die of hypothermia. His body shuddered. Something fell out of his pocket and dropped into the creek. He struck his hand in his pocket, but his fingers were too numb to feel anything. But he already knew the key was gone. What did it matter anyway? The briefcase had nothing but filthy photographs of nude women. Verity.

Snow whipped around him and stifled the sound apart from the thin whine of the seawind, and the purring call of geese and then an owl. The waves were a faint murmur. He had no idea where he was but surely he must have outrun his pursuers. He felt as if he had been out here for hours.

From behind, a thin light swept over him. It illuminated in a brief flash the silver fingers of tidal creeks. They were surrounded by pitch blackness except for the specks of white falling into the dark. He was badly exposed. He breathed out. Slow down. He had to think. They must be on foot – you couldn't bring a boat into this maze. But if he stood up and ran again, he had no light, he couldn't see – he'd be running blind. He could fall again – they would find him. Fear rose sharply in his chest and he remembered the hunting and killing of the fox. He didn't want to die like that. Ahead of him was the remorseless sea, behind him – he didn't know who they were. Police? Blowers? The Air Force? Spooks? It made no difference now. He had no proof. And they wouldn't believe him if he said it had been an accident.

Hauling his body up, he forced himself on, following the thin vapour of his own breath. The woods couldn't be far now. He would go so deep into the marsh they wouldn't be able to follow him. But quickly, the reeds became too thick and he fell splashing into a creek and had to wade. It was in his shoes, around his waist, up to his armpits. A faint miasma of rotten egg rose from the water. The wind cut into his skin and he barely seemed to make a step. Blind and deaf. His hair was crusted with ice slivers; his eyes stung with salt tears. His ears ached in pain: he wished he could cut them off. He was close to the end now.

A torch swung past him, carving an arc of light through the darkness. Arthur was back in the boat with Jack again. Forever, rowing in the boat. He thought he heard a breath, someone panting. How could that be true? In time with the breath, there was a rhythmic shushing of water. Someone else's breathing. He didn't know if he was imagining it, out of his mind from the cold. He waited, shaking, trying to judge how near or how far they were, but without the light from the moon it was hard to tell where they were.

His eyes strained but he couldn't see anyone – there was nothing but a circle of white in the dark and, again, the slosh slosh of something lapping at the marshy water.

'Mr Silver,' said a disembodied voice he didn't recognise. He had no idea from what direction it was coming apart from the light, weakly shining through the veil of snowflakes. Maybe it was in his head. Maybe Verity was there.

'There's no need for this, Mr Silver, we're here—'

He heard nothing more as his foot caught on something in the creek – a dead animal – an old rotten piece of wood – and he was sent off balance. Foundering, clutching, he fell forward with his hands outstretched into the muddy creek, grasping at nothing. As he fell, he tried to shout her name but no sound came out. Down he sank under the cold mud and salt. He tried to take a breath but swallowed the silted saltwater. Fell again. The weight of the freezing creek and the reeds bore down on him, pushing him down to the seabed. Blind under the water, he thrashed his lead-heavy limbs but couldn't move. His lungs were crushed with lack of oxygen. He saw Jack sinking. He sank with him. Mrs Frost, drowning in the sea. No breath. He couldn't get the air into his lungs. His throat tightened and tightened to nothing. A sudden vision of a man, face looming above. His father, he as a boy in the bath. Father. 'Arthur,' says his father. 'Get out of the bath, son.'

A buzzing in his ears. Then hands around him and pure air, beautiful air, in his lungs. The cold night embraced him. Snow on his tongue. He inhaled the air in gulps, coughing, choking and spluttering. Someone heaved him into a boat. Mud-blind. A light shone in his eyes and a woman was saying, 'It's all right, Arthur, it's all right.'

'Ver?'

But the effort of speaking made him gag and he doubled over, disgorging the dirty seawater onto the bottom of the boat.

10.

In the shack on the edge of the marsh, Verity sat on a wooden chair with a blanket round her shoulders that had once lain on the bed she had shared with Jack. It smelled of dust and age and salt but nothing more and she thought how quickly a person fades. The sharp light from the bare bulb in the kitchen made her head ache and her red, watery eyes sting. A young constable had taken her back here after they'd found Arthur – for warmth, he said – but she'd only wanted to bury her face into Gypsy's pulsing flank. Peter was standing in the doorway, with another policeman she didn't know and someone tall and severe in the navy-blue uniform of the US Air Force and another man in the brown uniform of the RAF. They were talking in hushed voices. Blowers, the constable, had already taken Arthur, and Muriel had gone with them. Muriel's arm was around Arthur's shoulders and Verity remembered how she'd tended to Jack when he had crashed the motorbike back in the summer, a different world.

It was Muriel who had found Arthur, her brother said. Muriel had used an old crabbing boat of her father's, hauling it out here in a police truck, although how she knew to do this, and where Arthur would be, Verity had no idea. Peter himself had driven in the old Jag. He'd called the police station and taken the car to look for her. When he arrived at the point in the road where the path led down to the marsh shack, the US Air Force were already parked there in one of their jeeps.

Out on the Holkham Road, Arthur had turned to look at Verity in the headlights of the police car. Someone had put a green coat on his shoulders but he was shaking, soaked in mud and seawater, and his dark hair was gleaming wet, so he resembled one of the marsh creatures in stories she'd read as a child. He looked at her with such despair that she had felt impaled by it. He had killed Jack, but she could summon no anger towards him. She was so tired. Her body was aching and she couldn't get her fingers and teeth to stop their incessant quivering, as if they were palpitating in guilt.

The American officer patted the older policeman on the shoulder and left. The RAF one had already gone. He had barely glanced at her. He probably thought the whole affair rather sordid. The Americans were relieved, it seemed to her. They had thought Jack had stashed something secret, some hint of the flights he'd been on, and they couldn't let that get out. They weren't interested in the photographs. They would have been if they'd known when Jack was alive. He'd have been a blackmail risk. The local policeman had the remains of the black briefcase in his hand. Verity had left the photographs of the prostitutes and the landscapes of the marsh. The rest of them – the ones of her, of Muriel and, inexplicably, of the unknown boy – she had stuffed underneath her and was sitting on. She put her hand in her right pocket and felt along the crumbling, damp edge of the photograph of Jack.

'You've been very brave, miss, and you've done the right thing, giving us this,' the policeman said, nodding at her. But it was Arthur he was talking about. Leading them to Arthur.

Under the blanket, her arms cradled her stomach. Oh, what had she done? She thought of him with his hungry face and sticking-up hair as a child. Her right thumb traced the tiny scar on the back of her left hand from when they had crouched in the woods, all those years ago, and rubbed their blood together.

11.

Muriel smoked, tapping her feet to the song on the juke box. She was in Askey's with her cousin, Rodney. There was a faint smell of rot in the air. The flood had washed away lives but it had stripped back the layers too, revealing the bones beneath. Barely concealing his frustration, Rodney spilled out that they'd been forced to pass the case to the Americans and that they'd decided Arthur was going to be released. Could you believe it? The Americans had thought someone had killed Jack for spying, but it hadn't been that at all. He'd been selling erotic photographs. It turned out he had a wife and child back in America too.

It all made sense to Muriel. He'd been that kind of man. She could write to them – the wife and the son. She had the address after all. But what would she say? She felt no malice towards Jack – he was dead – or towards poor Verity. Muriel had other priorities.

The flotsam and jetsam from the tide, the debris left on the wrackline were there for the taking. She peered out of the steamed-up window of the milk bar. The music drowned out Rodney's chatter. At the end of the street, she could just see the hulk of the torpedo boat, which was still resting on the quay. This strange, wild place, neither land nor sea, was in a state of constant flux. They could reclaim the marsh for grazing, they could plant pine trees to stabilise the dunes, but the sea would always come. The tide would rise and fall and rise and fall over and over again. The shore would be reformed after every storm, as they were. That was how it should be. And she was only one tiny part of that ancient, relentless wave.

She lit another fag. No use hurrying home.

15th May 1953

Howe Farm

Dear Ver,

You know how much I hate writing letters but I thought I should give you some news from home. It is a pretty bleak picture I have to paint but at least you are nowhere near. You are better off where you are.

Father stays inside and drinks. I make any excuse to go out on the land but as there are hardly any cattle left there's little to do. A small portion of the grazing land is usable so the cows are out on that but most of the arable land is ruined by the flood. And we haven't had enough rain this spring to wash away the devilish salt. I can't see how we'll be able to grow anything on it for years. Some of the compensation has come through but it's a pittance. Desperate times and all that. My little plan is to run bigger public shoots in the autumn. It's that or the farm goes.

There was a ceremony for Jack. They've given him the George Cross. Apparently he'd already been awarded the Air Force Cross. It was all very proper. There was an American flag and a General read out something about his bravery. He'd been in Korea. Did you know that? They didn't say anything about how he was found or anything like that. Or why he'd received the Air Force

Cross. But another airman told me that they give that to men who've flown secret reconnaissance missions. 'Ferret flights' they call them. Whatever secrets Jack had, they died with him and that's all that matters to the Yanks. Rodney Blowers told me that the Air Force chaps – Strategic Air Command – took the briefcase you'd found but never discussed a jot about it since. He seemed a bit miffed, though I can't see why he thought those types would share their secrets with a Norfolk policeman.

I've actually bumped into Blowers a few times in the Shipwright's and he bought me a pint recently, which was decent of him. He said we didn't need to worry about 'our friend' because the Air Force weren't interested in him at all, though he gave me a look which I rather interpreted as that Blowers himself <u>was</u> interested in what really happened. But I don't think we'll ever know for sure.

I suppose Blowers has got his tabs on Arthur anyway, because Muriel is looking after him. Since Arthur came back from hospital, she's hardly left his side. She's moved into the flat with his wretched mother and helps her out with the shop. It's hard to say who's more hard done by out of this arrangement but I rather fancy Muriel's chances in a spat with Mrs S. I've quite come round to Muriel by the way. She was at the ceremony for Jack, too. Do you remember how we used to pick cockles with her when we were children? I have a horrid feeling we were awful to her.

One more thing – I hesitate to write this but feel I must – they mentioned Jack's family he'd left back in

America. It was a surprise to me too. Muriel's told me all she knows. It can wait until you come home if you're up to it.

Father has no idea I have written. He is the same. He asks about you. I know you must hate him after all that was said, but he has no idea how to live after Mother, and, frankly, I don't think any of us do. You do know that he always loved you far more than me. I'm too dull-headed. Don't bother arguing, you know it's true. It's because he had such high hopes for you as the boffin of the family that he's so dashed by your predicament. I think, by the way, that he's sorry about Oxford. He seems to think it's somehow his fault. The other day he said, 'She could have gone,' and I had to tell him that you'd just had some rough luck but he looked at me as if I was mad. So, you can see, he's feeling awful for not supporting you more. God knows why you wanted to go to bloody university anyway.

It will get better, it has to.

Perhaps you and I can sell the farm and for the pittance we'll get for it we can run away somewhere warm. What do you say? I rather fancy Greece. I think Mother would approve.

Tell me what it's like? Is it awful? Are you painting? Are you going to watch the Coronation? Mrs T is cock-a-hoop about it.

Must dash now, I'm famished and it's Mrs T's day off so I'll have to forage in the pantry and force Father to eat something.

Peter

P.S. Mrs T insisted I include some woollen items, hence the vast package.

18th May 1953

St Mary's of Woolnock
Herts.

Dear Peter,

Thank you, thank you, thank you for writing. I do believe it is the longest letter you have ever written! Any news is oxygen.

I, of course, have no news. I expand like swelling fruit. You would find it quite a shock if you could see me. I look like a fat old matron with a voluminous cardigan (it is always cold and draughty, even worse than home) and my hair is shapeless as no one's cut it for weeks. All I do is knit and take walks around the grounds. No painting, not yet. Just sketches. And sometimes I take photographs, but I have to hide Mother's camera as we're not allowed them. Another of the many rules.

I'm glad you went to the ceremony. It sounds as if it was interesting.

Yes to Greece! Now I am completely unmarriageable, that's one consolation at least.

Please say hello to Father and give Mrs Timms a kiss to say thank you for the things she sent.

All love, V

P.S. Please put some flowers on Mother's grave for me.

18th May 1953

Dear Arthur,

I have written many times and destroyed the letters because I can't find the right words. I was too angry for a long time. I have heard that you are now with Muriel and hope you will be happy. I mean it sincerely; she is a good person. I have been punished for what I did, I think. I wonder if you know where I am? It feels like a purgatory. I can't tell Peter how dire it is because he needs me to be strong.

~~I was going to write that I forgive you but I don't know if that's true but I want to because~~

I remain your friend,

Verity

Multiple versions, unsent.

1954
A year after the flood

It is spring again.

In the May after the birth of her baby, Verity takes the train to London from Norwich. The line from Wells has still not been fixed. Peter waves her off, a tall, lonely figure out of place in the bustling station in his country boots and jacket.

'Look after yourself,' he says. She thinks she'll cry but it doesn't come.

'Does he know about the—?' She cannot say *the baby. Jack's baby*.

He shakes his head. She knows he rarely sees Arthur any more. Since his mother died, Arthur runs the shop with Muriel.

'It was the best thing to do,' he says, as if she had asked.

She nods, although she has no idea if this is true. People keep saying it but she wonders how they're so certain. Now she knows Jack lied to her so thoroughly, this is how she should feel. All traces of him gone.

'Have you seen this?' says Peter.

The headline on the newspaper he hands her reads:

FIRST DETAILS OF ATOM-BOMB BASE

'Take it,' he says. 'Something to read on the train. Arthur was right all along.'

Not about everything.

In March, the Americans detonated a bomb in the Pacific. The newspapers said it was one thousand times as powerful as the bombs they dropped on Hiroshima or Nagasaki. No one seems to be awfully worried about it. She's read that scientists in the US have created something called the Doomsday Clock and they've set the time as two minutes to midnight. Midnight is the apocalypse. Meanwhile, their own little corner of the world carries on regardless. Peter says the base at Holkham is having an open day and visitors will see the jet planes that carry the atom bombs. Atomic warfare as tourism. But still the public doesn't know about the secret missions Jack ran over the Baltic States in Russia. Each time he went, unarmed and vulnerable, Jack could have been shot down and there would have been no recovery and no return. Neither the British nor the Americans would have been able to rescue him. She remembers the ampoule from around his neck – the pill inside it must have been cyanide. They would have expected him to have killed himself rather than be captured. And she wonders what Jack found over there, over the mountains and steppe, what it was he saw. What has he left behind? There must be other photographs of missile bases and hidden weapons, developed in a laboratory somewhere, rather than the half-naked pictures of women and the bleak Norfolk marshes that she'd found.

And his fatherless child who has a brother he'll never know. How unbelievably pointless all that risk was when the real danger was waiting for him in the flood.

She takes the paper, knowing she won't read it. 'You'll visit?' she says and is embarrassed to feel a catch in her throat.

Peter laughs. 'What would *I* do in London?' And it *is* funny, the idea of him lumbering around the crowded city streets in his tweeds.

She smiles and squeezes his arm. 'Come anyway. Please.' She can't bear the idea of him stuck at the farm with their father. It doesn't seem fair. It had been his idea to apply to the college; he who visited her in the awful place in Hertfordshire; he who fetched her when the baby had been taken away and she was left, broken and empty; he who broke the news about the baby to their father and stopped him from raging. He bought her the train ticket to London. She thinks now that he hadn't been joking about Greece.

On the train she can't read the paper even if she wanted to: her vision is blurred from the pooling, undropped tears and none of the words go in. Out of the window she looks at the flat fields ticking by; each farm building on its own in an empty field reminds her of the cabin. A light drizzle streaks the windows but ahead, a break in the clouds, a thin sliver of light.

On the overhead rack she has put her mother's old trench coat, and her case. In the handbag beside her on the seat is a letter of recommendation from Miss Cecily Gardiner, schoolmistress. In a large, flat black case next to it is her portfolio: all the paintings and sketches she's done recently, most of them just from the last lonely months, and in a separate section some of the pictures she's taken with her mother's old camera, the one Jack loved. In among the shots of the grounds of the home and the farm, there are some of the girls and their babies. The college probably won't be interested in those but she's brought them anyway. It's a record. In her suitcase, the tiny camera in a case and at the bottom, tucked into the underwear compartment, the broken Zippo lighter, the postcard Jack gave her, and three photographs she will show no one. One is the only photograph of herself she has kept. Many times over the last year she's taken out the picture and inspected it, trying to find in the gaze of the camera a love that was not there in the pictures of the other women. It was there in the photograph he took of his son. The second is his self-portrait. The wet and the mud have distorted his face but it's still him. The last of these fragments, these pieces of memory, is a blurry photograph she took of James, the baby she gave away, just a dark smudge of a thing in the awful woollens she knitted.

The train is quiet and in the empty carriage her thoughts are too loud. She applies lipstick as the rows of London terraces come into view.

Her interview is the following day and tonight she'll stay in digs. The train arrives at four o'clock. Time to wander, to window shop in the streets between Liverpool Street and Soho. But when she emerges into the road above Liverpool Street station, the flutter and cacophony make her change her mind and she drags her case and folio back down the stairs and down again to the tube station and takes the underground to Pimlico. The Thames glimmers in the distance as she walks towards it.

In the gallery, she seeks out Turner's *Snow Storm*

– *Steam-boat off a Harbour's Mouth*. It's smaller than she'd expected. It's just a painting. Deflated, she slumps down on the bench in front of it and tears finally fall, streaking down her face. The painting begins to bleed and swim in her tired, bleary eyes and the dark brush strokes detach themselves from the two-dimensional surface and envelop her. She remembers what Jack had said about it. It was *wild*. She doesn't know what or who he was but he has given her this.

Back on the Embankment, the sun is low in the sky. Without a watch, she has no idea how long she has sat in front of the painting. The Thames is darkening and she peers down it, listening to the chug of a boat somewhere beyond her sight. She feels the great machinery of the city carrying on beyond her and without her and she wants to stay there on the banks of the Thames forever, and never venture back into the bowels of the throbbing beast of the city. Somehow, she has broken free of her moorings and is now untethered and a feeling of lightness comes over her as she leans on the bank. Across the river, lights come on in a squat building and are reflected in droplets of gold in the eddying water.

This last year has been a series of humiliations and catastrophes one after the other as if her life had been ripped from its moorings and flung out into a storm-wild sea to be bashed senseless on the rocks. Everything has been taken away from her. Perhaps it is her fault they have gone – her mother, Jack, the baby; she did not love enough; she has been careless. She was gazing so hard at her own image that she did not see what she had done to Arthur. On the banks of the Thames, she is so light with grief she could float away, disappear underneath the dancing lights.

Acknowledgements

The *Night of the Flood* is a work of fiction but it was inspired by real-life events. The following books were useful in my research:

The Great Tide by Hilda Grieve

1953 Essex Flood Disaster by Patricia Rennoldson Smith

Flood Alert! Norfolk 1953 by Neil R.Storey

Sculthorpe Secrecy and Stealth by Peter B.Gunn

This novel was begun on the Bath Spa MA and was given a much-needed boost by the insightful critiques and encouragement of Tessa Hadley, Nathan Filer and Kylie Fitzpatrick, to whom I am very grateful. I would also like to thank my lovely, patient supervisor, Beatrice Hitchman.

It took a long time after the MA to draft and re-draft and in that process I owe much to my friends and fellow writers from the course. Thanks go to Deb McCormick and, in particular, to Anna-Marie Crowhurst for being such an inspiration and cheerleader. I would also like to say a huge thank you to one of my greatest supporters and early readers, Harriet Bosnell. Finally, thanks go to Lily Dunn, whose post-MA course in Bristol gave me the final push

I needed to complete the novel, and to the brilliant Beryl Readers who all encouraged me in my writing and continue to do so.

Most sincere thanks to my wonderful agent, Laetitia Rutherford, for believing in this novel and making me a much better writer. I am also incredibly grateful to my editor, Madeleine O'Shea, for her unswerving enthusiasm and expert editing, and to Tamsin Shelton for her brilliant copy-editing.

I must also thank family, especially my dad, James 'Bert' Bremner, for a book-filled childhood, and my sister, Sophie for driving me around Norfolk for research, and my amazing grandmother, Bessie, for all her love. A special mention must also go to my parents-in-law, Sue and Gordon Somerville, without whom I would never have gone to Bath Spa in the first place.

Finally, my greatest and most heartfelt thanks must go to Will, who as well as being my most critical reader, is also an endlessly supportive husband, and to Alex and Jessie, who remind me there are other things in life than books.

About the author

Zoë Somerville is a writer and English teacher.
Having lived all over the world – Japan, France,
Washington – she now lives in Bath with her family.
After completing a creative writing MA at Bath
Spa, Zoë started writing her debut novel, which
is inspired by her home county, Norfolk, and the
devastating North Sea flood of the 1950s.